SHRINK THYSELF

"Philip Roth may be putting down his pen, but I think Bill Scheft has picked it up."

—**Elinor Lipman**, author of *The Inn at Lake Devine*

"There's rank irony in the whimsical idea that a guy would drop psychotherapy in order to find himself, but adding an inept defrocked shrink to the fellow's journey rigs the boat for full-on satire. With his sly social observations of this postmillennial world, a talent for nurturing his emotionally hemmed-in protagonist, a soupçon of Jewish angst, and a gift for word play— 'my rate would jump Shylockingly'—Scheft offers laugh-out-loud commentary on life, love, and loneliness."

—*ForeWord Reviews*

Bill Scheft

A Vireo Book · Rare Bird Books
Los Angeles, Calif.

THIS IS A GENUINE VIREO BOOK

A Vireo Book | Rare Bird Books
453 South Spring Street, Suite 531
Los Angeles, CA 90013
rarebirdbooks.com

Set in Goudy Old Style
Printed in the United States
Distributed in the U.S. by Publishers Group West

Cover photographs by Alice Marsh-Elmer
Cover artwork by Bruce McCall

10 9 8 7 6 5 4 3 2 1

Publisher's Cataloging-in-Publication data
Scheft, Bill, 1957-
    Shrink thyself : a novel / by Bill Scheft.
    p. cm.
    ISBN 978-1-940207-11-7

1. Psychotherapy—Fiction. 2. Neuroses—Fiction. 3. Boston (Mass.)—Fiction. 4. Dysfunctional families—Fiction. 5. Anxiety—Fiction. I. Title.

PS3619.C345 S57 2014
813.6—dc23

To Adrianne, all my dedications. And all my devotion.

Also by Bill Scheft

The Ringer
The Best of the Show
Time Won't Let Me
Everything Hurts

"Psychotherapists may become the new spiritual leaders of mankind. A disaster. Goethe was afraid the modern world might turn into a hospital."

—Charlie Citrine, Humboldt's Gift

"This me who is me being me and none other."

—Neil Tarnopol, My Life As a Man

Shrink Thyself

a novel

I

H E CLEANED HIS GLASSES on his sweater, a move that never works.

"So, this is it?" he asked.

"Ideally, yes."

"You know, Charlie, it's customary when you end therapy to give some notice, like a month, so we can wind things down. It's not a hard and fast rule."

"I understand."

"It just is."

"I figured as much. And I've given this a lot of thought," I said. "And if you don't mind, I would just as soon give you a check for four sessions. Or four sessions plus this one. Five."

"That's certainly a possibility."

"Or we could spend the next two sessions talking about whether the check should be for four or five sessions, or why it even needs to be a check. Whatever is comfortable."

Travis Waldman–Travis Waldman, PhD, MSW, NYU–gave me an off-the-clock laugh. There was nothing to parse here. When a patient, okay this patient, okay me, says, "Whatever is comfortable," it is not another stroll down the Boulevard of People Pleasing. It is *Our time is up*. Or rather *My time is up*.

That, and the coat in my lap. I kept my coat in my lap. Unlike the glasses rubbed against a sweater, it is a move that works. And it is never a rehearsal.

I had readjusted my coat-covered lap and turned the chair directly to face Dr. Waldman, my therapist for the last twenty months. "You know what?" I had begun, "I think we did good. I feel like we're done."

"Done with therapy," Dr. Waldman had said more than asked.

"Yeah," I said. "Now you're caught up."

"So, ideally, this would be our last session."

"Yes."

"Well, Charlie," he smiled. "It's 'ideally...'"

The coat came off my lap. The better to write a five-session check on one's knee. Seven seventy-five and no cents.

"Thank you, Dr. Waldman."

"Please, it's Travis. And if you don't mind, I'd love to just run to the men's room before we finish up here."

"Uh, fine." *Travis runs to the men's room.* It really was over.

He returned, smoothing his moustache with his right hand. In his left, he pinched his glasses between some spare toilet paper. He asked me if I was okay. I said I was real good. So good I elaborated.

"I feel as if we've taken care of everything I came here for, and more. I understand my behavior. Well, maybe not fully understand, but I recognize it and can, in your words, *integrate* the feelings as they arise, *unbidden*. And I'd love to think of myself as a complicated man, but I am not. Especially these last couple of months, when it seemed that the conversational part of the session, the beginning and the end, was getting longer."

"Oh."

Dr. Waldman was still standing. He began to go to work on his glasses with the toilet paper.

I told him I liked him. And I do like him. And I appreciated that he had been in this with me. It made things safe, and sped them along. "I'm grateful," I said. "And before I started coming here, gratitude was what I felt when I got away with something."

"That's good. Is that yours?"

I wasn't sure that line was mine, but I told him he could have it anyway. Then I stood up. I never realized Dr. Waldman— "Please, it's Travis"—and I were the same height. I knew he was four years younger from lingering over a date on a diploma during an early session. But the height? Surprising. Six foot and no cents. Never underestimate the possibility of a hunch.

"So, you're going to try to live the life between sessions?" he asked.

"Life between sessions. Can I have that?"

"That ain't mine," he owned up. "Let me know how it goes out there."

"I will."

"In fact, take me with you."

Funny thing for a shrink to say. We laughed like classmates. And if I hadn't snooped at a diploma, I might have thought we were.

Dr. Wal—Travis—finished cleaning his glasses and tossed the wad of toilet paper on his desk, next to the check. He cleared his throat, which even the non-therapized know means there's a speech a-coming.

"I can tell you now, Charlie. I've been waiting for you to reach this conclusion for a couple of weeks. You came here a year and a half ago, maybe a little more, because even though you were happily divorced six years, you couldn't understand how your marriage had ended. Not why. How. That took a lot of courage. I get dozens of people who come in afraid. Very few who come in unafraid."

"Thanks."

"And the ones that do don't stay very long. They don't have to."

Did we have to do this part of it? The part about courage and fear? I put my coat on quickly, as if I was trying to bolt before the other shrinks on the floor burst through the door with a cake and canned champagne. And I went for a combination of real and imitation self-deprecation.

"Watch me calling you inside of a month, blubbering over the phone," I said.

He patted my upper arm, then leaned over his desk.

"Here's my home phone number. I'm your friend now. Feel free to blubber into my machine. Drives my wife nuts."

"Hah!" Now, that was funny. "Now, that was funny."

"Tell you what," he said. "I'll call you in a month. If you're okay, we'll have dinner."

"That would be great." I meant it.

"If you're really okay, we'll hit a bucket of balls at Chelsea Piers."

"That would be better." I meant that more.

č

"I'M GONNA GUESS YOU'VE never played before."

"You'd be wrong."

"I've just never seen a right-handed player wear a glove on their right hand."

"But I'm right-handed."

"Dr. Wal—Travis, I know that. I can tell by the way you signed your credit card. And the right-handed clubs you rented. But it's customary to wear the glove on the left hand. The top hand. The brake hand."

"Maybe you do," Travis said. "Never felt right to me. Not when I was thirteen. Not now."

"So, the last time you swung a club was thirteen?"

Travis Waldman stopped trying to peer into all the space-age elements that composed the electronic card/automated ball delivery system in Booth 39. He straightened up and instead peered back at his former patient. "Thirteen...that could very well be."

Travis had called me two weeks later, not a month. I teased him about how he should have played hard to get and he came back with, "Hey, Gladys, you want to hit balls or not?" I liked the familiarity of the remark. I missed that. That's one of the things about being married they never mention in the pamphlet. The familiarity of discourse. I really miss that. Sometimes you get a little too familiar with each other, you say things that land a little too hard and it's more mark than remark. But mostly, it's "*Hey, Genius...*," "*Hey, Romeo...*" Or the catch-all, "*Uh, honey...*" My ex-wife Jennifer was very gifted at all that. "*Excuse me, Mr. President...*" Funny. Haven't thought about that, and I'm not going to. I'm cured. I'm living in the moment, remember? But once Travis called me Gladys, I laughed and never thought twice about meeting up earlier than planned. He was probably as eager as I was to play hooky. Maybe he was a golfer. Maybe he was a good golfer. Maybe I could get a lesson.

Before I saw the glove on the incorrect hand, his outfit convicted him. Other than covering one's privates, the Golf Center at Chelsea Piers had no dress code. It was nothing to see Wall Street guys beating back the day by launching one hundred balls in a puddled suit and tie atop a pair of $300 Johnston Murphys. Sanitation workers and sort-of off-duty police came by in various stages of uniform. Women, skirted and hosed in from day care or boss care, kicked off their heels and put their bags where they were in eyeshot of every backswing. Restaurant and bar shifters undid black vests to free up their clubhead takeaway before heading off to tipping points North, East, and South. Sure, you had more than your share of chaps who were dressed as if their only goal was to be mistaken for a touring pro, teaching pro, or someone who should be photographed as such. Sure. But the beauty of the Golf Center at Chelsea Piers was its Ellis Islandic quality of nonjudgmental inclusion. You can say that about any public driving range, but when you drop a three-tiered minimum security G-pop hacking cage on the Hudson, it is a decidedly Manhattan snare. Get in. Get out. Do your business. Move on. Show's over.

And—as is the cornerstone of any good golf swing—keep your head down. Unless—and this is critical—there's a man in a mirrored bicycle helmet, down vest, and leg warmers in Booth 39.

You heard me. Bicycle helmet, mirrors, down vest, leg warmers.

I had made one light foray into the field of costume changing when we were first setting up in the booth. "You know, Travis," I had said, "it's safe to take the helmet off."

Travis stopped holding his driver cross-handed. "I know that. But it looks sporty. It looks too sporty to take off."

So, bring on the stares.

And keep them coming once the swing commenced. The golf swing, as conceived by Travis Waldman, was actually two unrelated physical statements, as if his body needed to hastily write a correction box. Things actually started quite benignly. Travis addressed the teed-up ball fairly convincingly, with the assurance of someone who had paid attention at a 1983 screening of *Caddyshack*. Then, suddenly, the left foot would reconfigure into Fourth Position and the club would be jerked Magnetic North and both hands would quiver above his head before he yanked the driver or 7 iron or it really doesn't matter straight down, like he was pulling a rope in a belfry. The head of the club clanged the booth's all-weather carpeted metal floor, that startling report of loud clumsiness, which was immediately followed by the non-sporty exclamation of "CUNT!" At no time was the ball in danger of being struck.

The second movement, the one-handed polo-style swat, sent the ball scurrying fifteen yards dead right. Just encouraging enough to renew the entire process. *Caddyshack*, Fourth Position, jerk up, quiver, belfry down, *clang*, "CUNT!," polo swat.

"You know what you might want to try?" I began to delicately toss over from Booth 40 as Travis teed-up another regret.

"Charlie, please. As my friend, I hope I can tell you that I did not come here for a lesson."

"Absolutely," I said too loud. And then, louder, "Aw, shit. This machine's broken. I gotta move down." I grabbed the three clubs I had brought and headed for Booths 46, 48, 51, before settling on #63, where *clang*-"CUNT!" was five yards out of earshot. Can I tell you something? I hit ninety-nine balls with a consistency hitherto out of my element. Each shot leaped out of the booth and hissed over the Hudson before the farthest netting prevented it from becoming a resident of Jersey City. My swing was steady, true, organic, bordering on meditative. Free. The freedom of a man who never paused during those ninety-nine blows to ask himself, "What the fuck is it with Travis?"

ع

TRAVIS WALDMAN WAS RECOMMENDED to me by a guy at my gym. Bill Myers. Not just any guy at my gym. Bill Myers was the guy who had the appointment after me with the personal trainer. Nice guy, Myers. A little older than me, a little more in need of a personal trainer. He ran his own successful headhunting firm, so he never stopped trying to find the right fit for anyone who was interested. Or wasn't interested. I had a job, so that meant he kept trying to fix me up with women. In adjoining cubicles, in various stages of undress, he would pitch me the latest possibilities on the market. Each time, I would politely decline, even throw in a "She sounds great," then explain again that I had only been divorced five years and wasn't really looking. Bill Myers tried five or six times, then on the way out to his training session, threw back the curtain to my cubicle and shoved a business card with Travis Waldman's number into my damp hand. "He's a therapist," he said. "I'd call him. Or don't. But someone your age who looks like you doesn't wait five years after they're divorced."

Don't get excited, ladies. What I'm sure he meant when he said "someone who looks like you" is that I was neither overweight nor menacing. I am notoriously nondescript. Many people are shocked when they find out I'm Jewish. Average height and build. Younger-looking than I am. A plurality of brown hair, still-brown eyes. Always, and I don't know why except I just don't pay attention, a little unkempt. Hair unconsciously hand-raked, pant leg hiked, shoe untied, a less than thorough shave, maybe a nick under the nose. If I lived near a police station, I could make some nice side money as a line-up filler for any crime involving white males forty/forty-nine. I'm fifty-two.

It took me five months to call Dr. Waldman, because I am a man of action. I might have been nervous. In the first ten seconds of the phone call, I hurriedly mentioned Bill Myers' name three times, and it came out like I was trying to get into an after-hours club and Travis was the bouncer looking at me through the door slot. All he said was, "Did Bill tell you I don't take insurance?" I probably know how to answer a question put that way now, but two years ago it seemed like code. It seemed like a hooker asking you if you're undercover vice. So, I blurted out words to the effect of "Look, I'm divorced five years, I don't date, a guy gives me a number..." Got a little laugh, an exhale, and a "How's Wednesday morning at ten?"

I could go through my checkbook for the last two years, or the invoices I sent my insurance carrier to get back seventy percent of forty percent of my visits, but I probably saw him seventy-five times. And other than some of the stories he told me (which I lovingly called True Tales from the Degenerate Files), the only session I really remember was the first. I remember because I walked in thinking it would take me six months to catch him up, and forty-eight minutes later, I was recounting that morning's breakfast of poached eggs in a cup, bacon, and no toast.

That's when Travis Waldman spoke for the first time. He hiked his pant leg to show a swath of vertically striped yellow and black sock. He smoothed the corners of his moustache and showed he was a much better shaver than me. He smiled and said, "Charlie, you're in the right place. And for someone who's never been to therapy—do I have that right? Yes?—you show tremendous respect for the process. You've laid out everything quite admirably. The only question I have is how long have you been living with your parents?"

I'm laughing now. I laugh every time I think about that question. Even that day. "Dr. Waldman," I said, "I haven't lived with my parents since I graduated from school in 1975."

Travis uncupped his chin, a gesture I would come to know. "But you said," looking at no notes yet reciting for the record, "The last couple of times I've been home, my mom has said things like '*How about the way your ex-wife Jennifer has moved on so well...*'"

"Uh huh."

"You said 'home.'"

"Yeah."

He brushed the front of his sweater. "I just find it interesting that you would refer to a place you haven't lived in almost thirty years as 'home.'"

I put up my hands and said, "Hey, yah got me..." And our time was up. A month later, Jennifer called me about some paperwork and I told her that last exchange of the first session. "I like this guy," she said. "He's good."

ع

"I NOTICED YOU'RE NOT wearing your wedding ring," I mentioned over lunch.

"What are you, a cop?"

"No, but when you haven't seen someone in a couple of weeks who you've spent two years sitting three feet across from, you look for the familiar."

"Wow, someone is doing very well without me."

"I try not to think about that," I said, even though I thought a lot about how well I was doing without him. "I'm sure you took it off because we went to the driving range."

Believe me, I would have preferred not to notice anything at lunch. Like the way Travis annoyed the waitress by poking his entrée, salad, and dessert with his left index finger as each course was being lowered in front of him. I haven't met any extraterrestrials, but I am pretty sure this is how they sample the food of my planet.

Travis scooped up the last half-spoonful of sorbet. "Did I ever tell you about when I had to work in the ER at Lenox Hill?"

"No."

"That's odd... Well, you have to. It's part of our training. One night, a man comes into the emergency room, carrying a bloody handkerchief. The admitting nurse says, 'What's in the handkerchief?' He says, 'My testicles.' Well, sure enough, he opens the handkerchief and there they were. 'What happened?' she says as we start to gather around. 'I cut them off,' the man says. 'Why did you cut off your testicles?' she asks. And, just before he passes out, the man says, 'Because I'm conflicted sexually.'"

"Uh-huh."

"Man," said Travis. "I could go for another espresso."

Look, I know "uh-huh" is not exactly glib, but "Man, I could go for another espresso?" Besides, I had already put my card in the check caddy. I was late, and even if I wasn't, I did not wish to add another two ounces of liquid, let alone ten minutes, to this outing.

"Be my guest," I said. "But I need to go. I have a realtor showing the apartment."

"Did you say anything about that?"

"What are you, a cop?" I tried laughing at the callback. Nothing from Travis. "You're right, Travis. I didn't say anything about the realtor, probably because I hadn't anticipated we'd be eating for almost two hours."

"So now it's my fault?" he said.

I would not try laughing again. Instead, I fished for a bluff. "Good one."

Travis winked and pointed. "Almost got you."

"*One point is an accident. Two points is a line,* huh?"

"That sounds familiar. Who said that?"

The waiter handed me the check. With my head down, I muttered, "I can't remember. Either Khalil Gibran, or you."

And then Travis Waldman shrieked like he was on vacation from his regular laugh. *KHALILGIBRANORYOU-OHMYGODDD!!!!!!!!* came trilling out, followed with a series of *heeheehee, heeheehees* at an octave lifted clean off a mid-80s Michael

Jackson album. Mercifully, the outburst occurred in the restaurant wasteland of late afternoon. Only a handful of customers and staff had to pretend they hadn't heard it. I threw an extra ten into the leather check caddy. Too-late-to-hush money.

"I never got to talk to you about something," Travis said outside.

"Really?"

"Yes, really. We could talk about it in the cab. Nah, that would be awkward."

I was dying to remark on the word "awkward" coming up this late in the day. But instead I said, "I gotta take the subway. Quicker."

"Okay, then. Next time."

I waved my three golf clubs over my head as he crossed Ninth Avenue. "Next time," I remembered to say too late. Or not late enough.

Ƈ

THIS IS THE LAST time his name will come up, but Freud once said, "New York is a place where neurosis passes for energy." Spoken like a man who never sat in an uptown subway car while this guy walked through:

"I need to see Mayor Giuliani. I am fully aware he is no longer the mayor, but I hear he is planning to run for President. I need to see him and tell him, 'Hey, Rudy. Julie. I know how you can win. I'll tell you, but there's one catch. You have to put me on the ticket.' I would appreciate any help in this matter. I will accept a phone number, address, electronic mail, fax, telex, or a sandwich. My name is Dawson Denson and I am a global regulator. And you are all aboard the Double-D train to success..."

What I, Charlie Traub, pocketed from the presentation by Dawson Denson, Global Regulator was this: *I am going in the right* direction. I am on the Double-D train to success, but more important, I am moving away from Travis Waldman. And that is what was now separating me from Freud.

What if I'm not crazy? Is that what living a life between sessions was? I had sought help for the silly yet profound chain of events that had ended my marriage, owned up, had the behavior in my adjusted sights. And now, here was an opportunity to lead a non-psychological life. Not unexamined. Just examined in real time. To proceed as if there was nothing wrong. What a relief. To live, not dwell.

What if I'm not crazy? Is it crazy to even entertain that thought? Non-alcoholics do not take the "Are you an alcoholic?" quiz in Reader's Digest. Isn't this the same thing? You think, What if I'm not crazy? only if you are?

"Stop it!" I hissed out loud to myself, but loud enough for the other passengers to think it might be meant for them. I coughed and waved them off. Okay. Let's try for the non-psychological life rather than try to chase What if I'm not crazy? We won't need Justice Potter Stewart to tell us; we'll know it when we see it. Until then, on the way, on this right direction, I would just shoot for showing up, mind and body, all at the same time. And on time.

I made it back to the apartment just ahead of the lobby buzzer. The real estate agent was downstairs with acuteyoungmarriedcouplewhocannotwaittoseetheplace. When wasn't it that?

A red-faced, tie-askew, glad-hander named Gary Brentemen panted the couple into my two-bed/two-bath with a balcony. Turns out they were cute. But they were no match for the Boston Terrier who jailbroke in ahead of them. If you don't know, and why should you, I have limited tolerance for humans and unlimited tolerance for dogs. I can't give you a concrete reason why, other than the fact that a dog never screwed anyone on a business deal. And yet I've never owned a dog. This is an ingrained and original truth with me. So, limited tolerance for humans, unlimited tolerance for dogs. It has nothing to do with living the non-psychological life, and everything to do with the fact that it might be possible.

I just wanted to get to the dog, who had a name like Pepper or Merlot, but who needs names when you want to get right to the behavior? And the dog clearly wanted to get to me. But first, I showed the couple in and said, "Go ahead, look around. You won't find a better place in the neighborhood. I'm an idiot for even thinking about selling, but that's my shortcoming and your profit."

Gary Brenteman thought he had a partner. "Charlie, tell the Ruprechts what you were telling me about the building staff..." But I was done. I had dealt with enough creatures on two legs. I dropped to my knees in the last resort way a fifty-two-year-old man does when looking for his keys and got face-to-face with Cocoa or Kahlua or Kringle or whatever handle this putt-putting, tail-parrying, lick-the-air-it's-close-enough, mask-and-grins creature was going by.

"Make me an offer... Make me an offer..." I gasped out of my now-drenched face. The realtor tried to distract me his way and renew the sales meeting. Good luck to you, sir.

"You know," said Gary Brenteman, "you wouldn't know it to look at her, but she's going to have twins in July."

I stopped, but did not look up. Instead, I stared at the Terrier and squealed, "Are you gonna have twins in July? Are you? You don't look pregnant! Who's a pregnant girl? Who's a pregnant girl? Who's a preg—"

"No!" the realtor said. "Her."

I began to rise, nodded. "Oh." Cute young Mrs. Ruprecht bravely smiled and scooped up her dog.

Hey, I had showed up, on time, and was truthful. Maybe the non-psychological life might be possible.

Well then, let's test it out.

II

"WHERE ARE YOU STAYING, dear?"
"Where? I thought I'd sleep in Dad's bedroom, like I always do."

Gwen Traub, my mom, dropped her shoulders and fake bowed her head, as if she was about to disappoint her eldest child for the first time.

"That room is our office now."

Our office? Office? Our? Fucking who OUR? But instead, I said, "Mom, this is an apartment at an assisted living—"

"Independent," she interrupted.

"Congratulations on your independence. Seriously, unless you're leasing space to a coroner, there is no need for an office here."

"I'll show you," she said. "Before Sy gets back."

"Sy? Is that his name, or the extent of what he can do?" That comment is a little nastier than usual for me.

"Shush. He's brilliant. I'm just glad I finally have some help around here."

Before I could ask, "What kind of help?" we had walked through the small kitchen, across the notion of a hallway, into what had been my father Charles Traub, Sr.'s bedroom for the last half-dozen docile years of his life. He'd been dead just about two years, and the room had been maintained by my mom as if he was gone for yet another two-day congestive-heart-failure stay in the hospital. In less than a night, I had gotten over the initial creepiness of sleeping in my old man's bed, but I always told mom it was a waste if the room was only used quarterly. "Nonsense. It's your room now, dear," she would say. Even before I thought about seeing a therapist, this concept, *It's your room now, dear,* was preshrunk.

Okay, so she finally made a move. So, I'd have to spring for a hotel. It happens. Rooms change. Don't be a disappointed fifty-two-year-old only son. Don't be a cliché.

I wouldn't. I wouldn't.

"What the fuck, Ma?" came out of me.

"Excuse me?"

"Seriously. What the fuck?"

"You need to watch your language."

"You're right." I took another look inside the room. "*Perdóneme?*" Two women were sitting quietly in folding chairs reading magazines. They giggled and waved at me. A bridge table with a Canon personal copier that was a must-have item in 1982 took up whatever space there had been between the girls and the bed, now crushed length-wise against the back wall and covered in cartons of what was surely reams of writings that had gone unread since a quarter-past Eldridge Cleaver. The French doors of the closet had been yanked away at the *J'accuse...!* point of a Phillips screwdriver to create a walk-in supply bin and manifesto annex. The only article of clothing was draped over a box of Canon toner. A bathrobe. Eighty percent cotton. A hundred percent not my dad's.

I waved again at the women—*What else was I gonna do?*—and walked Mom into the kitchen.

"Do they work here, or is this where they're being hidden?"

"Don't be silly," she said. "Of course they work here. We are organizing the dining room staff."

"What?"

Gwen Traub replanted her feet. Here she goes. "If one of us has an accident in the dining room, the waitresses and busboys have have to clean it up. That is health care. That is not part of their duties. That should be the job of the nurses' aides or caregivers. But the caregivers never move. We want to set up a fund where they get paid to clean up. All it would take is for everyone here to pay an additional two dollars a month in rent. The other residents are fine with this. Okay, not Rowena, but she's a Neocon pill. Management refuses to go along with our demands."

"But management does not work for you. And management hired them."

"We'll see."

"What do you mean we'll see?"

Mom looked around, as if her kitchen appliances might be eavesdropping. Her voice lowered. "Are you familiar with screw mousing?"

This took me about a second and a half to decode. She was referring to the Nixonian Era term for dirty tricks. "Rat fucking?"

"Exactly."

And it would have been so great if we could have continued on this line of delusion. But we were interrupted. Not interrupted. Whatever word is a more jarring version of "interrupt." I'll think of it later, when I am not jarred. It came from just inside the front door. Loud. "I KNEW I HAD A FEW OF THESE LEFT OVER FROM LOVE CANAL!!"

"Sy, I'd like you to—"

"I'll jolly him later, dear. The girls are due back on the line."

This half-a-question-mark of a man in an ill-fitting gray cardigan shuffled into the office, his office, accompanied by the clacking plastic of four or five cheap whistles on lanyard gimp. Wow.

He began to speak to the workers. Listen to this, because I cannot.

"Desiree, Enid," he says, "*Vamanos esos* around your necks. Necks. *Aquí. Sí. Sí.* Give these to the other *camareras. Sí.* Don't blow them. *Como se dice* TWEET! No tweet. No tweet. *Solamente* wear them. If anyone asks, *doña de residente. La doña de Señor Siegel. Dice no mas.*"

Enid blew her whistle and pretended like she was directing traffic. Desiree giggled.

"*Amiga.* No tweet! *No mas. Gracias.*"

"So, we'll see you at dinner, Mr. Siegel?" Enid said in the most unbroken of English.

"*Sí. Mucho gusto. De nada. Solamente* the beginning."

"Goodbye, Mrs. Traub."

"Goodbye, girls," my mom said. "We're going to make this happen. Cheer up." They giggled their way out.

"Do you want the door closed?" one of them turned back to ask.

"Yes, ple—"

"—*No gracias, Desiree!*" came screaming from the room they had left. And then he thudded out in a Rockport Comfortech gait to make sure. I kept my head down, because the girls had done enough giggling.

"Sy, why couldn't you take five seconds to meet my son?"

"Because I'm not an aristocrat like you, Mrs. Gwendolyn Traub."

Mom laughed. Thank God. "Yes, I know. And that's why the front door has to be left open. Sy, please say hello to Charlie."

The gray cardigan moved in a little too close, as if for a sniff. A hand emerged from somewhere under a fold.

"Sy Siegel. Hello, Traub scion."

"Hello, first person in the last fifty years to use the word 'scion.'" I had to say it. Again, I'm usually not nasty, but come on.

Sy Siegel straightened up as much as life would let him. For a moment, he was less than half a question mark. Aligning just enough to almost make a point. He grabbed my elbow and smiled at my mother. "I like this one. Can't talk to him. Wish he was useful." He let go and his spine was summoned due south. He began to shuffle back into the, uh, office.

"So," I asked, "they wear the whistles, but don't blow them, and this statement somehow plays with management's head enough to be threatening?"

Sy Siegel chuckled or coughed, and hummed the first few bars of a classical piece I would never be able to identify, let alone identify with, before closing the door behind him.

I waited until we had walked back into the living room. "Mom, I hope he's got one giant cock on him." Again, I had to.

"Charles Traub, Jr.!"

"Mom, I like him. Hell, I'd like to have him in my building."

"He's brilliant."

"No question. And I'm happy you found someone."

"I haven't found anything."

"Which is my next point. I know I just got here, so I don't want to draw the wrong conclusion, but how much time do you spend together, and how much time do you spend in proximity to one another?"

"What do you mean?"

"I mean what is the set-up between meals? You out here watching Book TV and him in dad's bedroom drafting a proposal to replace the Board of Windgate Point with the night shift at the Mobil station?"

"Don't be petulant." One of her favorite words, but usually reserved to describe those outside of the family. She continued pitching. "He's a far-thinker. He's someone who believes there are more important issues at this facility than getting them to show a porno movie in Function Room A on Thursdays."

Did I want to say, So, I'm wrong about the giant cock?

"So, I'm wrong about the giant cock?"

"Shhhh!"

"Mom, are you shushing me because I'm wrong, because I'm right, because you're embarrassed or because somewhere in this building a porno movie is about to start?"

"I was just giving an example."

"Gwen Traub, you're seventy-nine. That example expired for you fourteen and a half years ago." I got up and pressed the back of my hand against her cheek. My mother smiled at first, then became Gwen Traub and furrowed suspiciously.

"What's with that?" she said, nodding at my hand.

"New move of mine. I try to let people know everything is okay."

"People?"

"Okay, you."

"Well then," she said. "I like it." I got up and walked back toward the kitchen, "Where are you going?"

"I'm going to pee, then make some coffee."

"I usually put the pot up, then go to the john," she said.

I did not stop. Instead, I said, "Hey, another new move to try." Which made no sense.

On my way back from the bathroom, I noticed a book leaning against the door of my dad's former bedroom. The title: *America's Revolutionary Heritage: Marxist Essays Edited with an Introduction by George Novack*. Okay, the title's a grabber. Sure. Without question.

A folded sheet of looseleaf paper poked out inside the paperback cover, the top tattooed with the multiple ballpoint-traced inscription: **CHARLES TRAUB, BACKYARD ANARCHIST.**

Oh, how I wanted to read the note. But the handwriting was much too small for the unlit hallway. And I knew the contents were meant to be read aloud to Mom after I finished what I'd come to discuss. And after we had some coffee in us.

$$\varepsilon$$

"So," I SUMMARIZED, CUP clinking saucer. "I'll be a little farther away. Five hours, with all the ferries, as opposed to three and a half now. But I'll come up just as much. Maybe more, now with the time I'll have."

"Uh-huh."

"You don't want to talk about this?"

"Sure I do. I just want to hear what's in Sy's note."

"Yeah, I know you do. So do I. But I've just told you that I'm taking six months off from work and plan to live out on the end of Long Island."

"Yes, you did."

"Yes, I did."

"So you said."

"So I said?"

"Uh-huh."

Whatever comes before nowhere, that's where this conversation was going. I pulled the note out of the *America's Revolutionary Heritage: Marxist Essays Edited with an Introduction by George Novack* while the Widow Traub pantomimed applause. I started to read, making sure to emphasize the occasional ballpoint bold-faced words or phrases:

Charles Traub—

*Your mother, such that she is, tried to impress me (or impress **upon** me. I cannot remember if there was force.) that although you carry the burden of a Harvard undergraduate education, you spent some formative years producing a subversive television program in Washington. At my age, I do not have the lung capacity to disabuse her of the coupling of **"subversive"** and **"Washington."** I'm sure you can understand. And if you cannot, I'm afraid the Traub double helices are impenetrable.*

But I will try.

*George Novack was the foremost writer and lecturer on Marxist philosophy this country has yet to produce. He was also Harvard class of 1926, which, as Marx might say, made him a **communist specter haunting** alumni reunions. I can just see him, the Trotskyite chatting amiably among the bourgeoise Cantabridgians, both sides knowing the next social upheaval would find them shooting at each other behind barricades hastily thrown up in The Yard. (Athough, **traditionally**, Harvard men do **not** do the actual shooting. Too vulgar. They use **proxy armies** for that sort of thing.)*

*Novack was one of **18** socialist labor party members jailed during World War II under the Smith Act. I'm sure you were once held against your will (or **George Will**) at a K Street cocktail party.*

*So, get reading. You are encouraged **not** to return this book. When Cheney's myrmidons come hooded into the building to search out sedition, I prefer this work be found in **your library**, not mine.*

Cordially,
S. Siegel

We buried our faces in sofa pillows, laughing. "I know, I know," was all she could say.

Finally, my mother composed herself and resumed the niggling process of appearing drawn into her son's life.

"Why would you sell that apartment?"

"Two reasons. It's worth two and a half times what I paid for it. And..." I never got to the second reason, which was, "I've decided not to be a New York neurotic anymore." Which was a break, because she jumped all over the real estate section.

"Two and a half times what you paid for it?" she said. "Is that even a number?"

"It's a lovely number."

"You really are your father's son." Gwen Traub leaned into the line with the full shoulder of eight decades in Boston. *You really ahhh yah fahhhhthahhhz sun.*

I laughed at her pronunciation. Another new move I was trying out. I knew exactly the story she was referring to. Seven years ago, my parents had decided to move out of their condo in nearby Concord to this assisted—Christ, okay—*independent* living facility, Windgate Point. They had been living in Israel Putnam Village for twenty-five years, during which time the modest two-bedroom, two-story attached cottage they had plopped down $70,000 for had cartwheeled to seven times its worth. The equity leap was a combination of two factors: the discontinued "Redwinged Blackbird" floor plan (an envy-engineered layout that included a spacious basement), and the spontaneous combustible demand created among non-Colonial History-educated Jews who assumed the "Israel" in Israel Putnam was not a reference to the young patriot who yelled "Don't fire 'till you see the whites of their eyes!" but code for *"Condo living for our kind."*

When my father told me what the place was worth and how the onsite realtor was salivating all over the discontinued floor plan, I said to him, very slowly, "Dad, you are in the unique position of not needing the money from the sale of your house to pay for the next place you live. Sure, the condo may be worth $490,000 today. But sit back, relax and watch people fight over it. And watch the price go up. Your realtor will just have to wait on her rising commission."

That advice had been uttered on a Friday. Sunday morning, Ducky Traub had called his boy. (Yeah, yeah, I know. Charles Traub, Sr., but Ducky to you. That's the name he preferred. The only good thing about it was when my mom yelled "Charlie!" we both didn't yell back, "Wha?" But other than that, yeesh...)

"Well, we sold the house," said Ducky.

I was stunned. "What? What happened to sitting back and watching the price go up?'

"You know," he answered, "I'm sure I could have gotten another fifty grand for the place. But that's the kind of thing my brother Teddy would have done."

On that day, I waited just long enough for my mind to assemble a response of due-diligent logic.

"Yeah, Teddy," I had said. "What a putz."

"Exactly."

Now, seven years later, and with that remark, *You really ahhh yah fahhhhthahhhz sun*, I saw no need to pursue any further the conversation I had come to have. I would shut up, let my mother approve, disapprove, or not give a shit. I would kiss her on the forehead and expect nothing. I would be my father's son.

"I'll come back when I get settled."

"Charlie, if you're looking for something to do, Sy and I could always use help here."

"I'll hang onto some bail money in case they reinstitute the Smith Act."

And then, from behind a closed door. "You don't even know what the Smith Act was!"

I stood up to the door and did not knock. "Federal statute passed in 1940, signed into law by Roosevelt, making it a criminal offense to knowingly advocate, abet, devise or teach the duty or desirability of overthrowing the government of the United States or any state. The Supreme Court overturned many convictions under the Smith Act as unconstitutional in 1957, but the statute remains on the books."

The door opened, "Collect your apology from the Politburo," said Sy.

The guy was funny. I gave mom a hug and did the hand on cheek thing again. "Maybe I'll be back sooner."

On my way to my car, I thought of the time near the end of my job in Washington. I had to fire one of the segment producers at the nightly show I was running, *Beltway Today*, for stealing *Beltway Today* sweatshirts and cups from the stockroom and selling them on eBay. The culprit, Bobby Something, broke down in his office and said, "I had a horrible childhood."

I had squeezed his shoulder, smiled and said, "Good news, Bobby. It's over."

Now, when I got into the car and looked in the side view mirror, I noticed. Same smile.

$$\mathcal{E}$$

YOU'LL NEVER GUESS WHAT I did next. I took the two vacation weeks I had left at the network (where I freelance produce the weekend morning news show that people are always meaning to watch) and drove to Scranton, Pennsylvania, and spent eight hours a day making campaign-debt fundraising calls for Bob Casey, who had defeated Rick Santorum for Senator. Santorum, the third-ranking Republican in the Senate, had suffered the worst defeat for an incumbent in over a century. The midterm election thumping of this particular pro-Iraq, pro-torture, pro-life, anti-gay marriage stalwart reverberated "uh-oh" back to the Bush-Cheney-Holy Ghost trinity with such topspin, I'm sure it startled the victorious Casey camp. My point is anybody can rah-rah it up to Election Day and then pat himself on the head until the domestic champagne hangover is chased. It takes a special kind of ego evacuation to have zero to do with a result, and then read from a script like you're auditioning for the role of the committed but apologetic loan shark (*Your call for change has been rewarded, but before the real work for change can begin, we need to responsibly take care of some bookkeeping...*).

That was Week One. Week Two, I drove 301 miles to Santorum headquarters in Penn Hills, just outside of Pittsburgh, and did the same thing. Santorum stood and stands for everything I'm against, including famously equating gay sex with "man-on-dog," but my feelings ended with being happy he had lost. Now, it was about seeing if I could dispassionately reach out to his supporters and have them cough up the deductible for this wreck that wasn't their fault. Maybe the first call was inside-joke weird, but after that, it was assembly-line familiar. The script was virtually the same, just a different name, and the phrase "Your call for change has been rewarded" was replaced with "Your voice in Washington still hears you." (Wow. I just realized that is some hearing. Like a dog's.)

So, two weeks, eight hours a day making phone calls that I was gloriously detached from. It's as tedious as it sounds, and ultimately, a silly experiment in just showing up and doing a day's work without identity which proved nothing except I don't want to make phone calls and I don't want to live in

Pennsylvania. Hardly a bombshell. Here were the two things that were surprising. Surprise One: The losing Republican campaign with the bigger debt paid for lunch every day. The winning Democrats had a six-foot hero stretched across an unoccupied desk on Monday and Friday. Tuesday through Thursday, we were on our own, like methadone addicts who weren't told the clinic hours had changed.

Surprise Two: I got laid by a fellow Rick Santorum volunteer. She stood against everything I'm for, other than my cock. (Although over the last eight years, my cock and I have agreed less and less.) Believe me, I had not planned any of this, and it is barely worth recounting, but you're here. I offered to give her a lift home after our phone bank shift ended at 6:00 P.M. and I overheard her complaining to another volunteer that her car had failed inspection and she didn't want to call her ex-husband. She had a name like Louisa, Lisa, or Alicia. I'm sure I tried all three on her, but she never corrected me, as I assume polite, slightly round, late-thirties Rust Belt divorcees are taught. Originally, she wanted me to take her to the Second Presbyterian Church because her two boys had choir practice till 7:00 P.M. and she wanted to see the last forty-five minutes. On the way there, I told her I was leaving the next day after the shift and had spent the previous week making calls at Casey Headquarters. I may have mentioned the six-foot hero. For some reason, and living a less-examined life allows me not to examine why, Louisa, Lisa, or Alicia found all of this inescapably naughty. She looked at the clock on her BlackBerry and said, "Well then, Charlie, I think we need to go to your motel."

"What about choir practice?"

"I'm not in the choir. And you're not gay. There's a Wa-Wa Market at the next light."

The Wa-Wa Market is Pennsylvania's provincial reconfiguring of 7-Eleven. Beef jerky, motor oil, Tas-T-Kake, lottery tickets, and condoms.

I'm stalling.

The sex brushed up against regret. Brushed up, but regret would have been too strong a feeling on both sides. It was more like we had both mistakenly enrolled in a nonrefundable continuing-education symposium at the Y but knew we could leave during the smoke break. The only thing remotely resembling dirty talk was when I asked, "Are you okay?" more than twice. Louisa, Lisa, or Alicia never asked the same of me, even though I was the one clearly winded. She made some noise, but was no louder than Lou Dobbs shrieking about Nancy Pelosi. Afterward, just as I started the engine in my rented Impala, we giggled a little and shook our heads as we looked out our side windows. Made it to choir practice before the two-hymn warning.

And that's how I found out I'm not gay. So, I guess it was worth recounting.

This last porn-free excursion is more than I talked about sex in all the time I was seeing Travis. It's not that I was reticent to talk about it, it's that I was reticent to talk about it after Dr. Waldman weighed in with one of his True Tales from the Degenerate Files. Here's one, and stop me if you've heard it: A twelve-year-old girl is continually being felt up by her father. She finally finds the courage to tell her mother. The mother's response? "Most little girls would love that kind of attention from their daddy." I believe the example Dr. Waldman had been going for there was either "You want to hear denial?" or "This is a safe place. You can talk about anything. I've probably heard it already." I did talk about anything, until I ran out. And I'm grateful I ran out before I got to the Wa-Wa Market.

ʅ

OKAY, OKAY. IF YOU guessed that I have not had an overwhelming number of sexual partners, at first I would be insulted, then tell you you're right. Counting the woman I just dropped off at choir practice, my career total is, uh, five. All right, four. If you guessed that this might figure into why someone single, fifty-two, straight and healthy is not just alone, but aggressively alone, well then, bravo, we really don't need to go on. You have figured it out twenty therapy months faster than I did.

I am alone because it is better this way. This is not self-pity. This is the height of self-awareness. (*You must be this tall to be self-aware.*) It is not complicated. I am about harmony and loyalty. Me unmarried, me alone, is my most harmonious state. The state where feelings are most clear. This is the only way for me to be engaged in others. So, at my loyal-est.

"You know what you are?" Travis said in what turned out to be our second-to-last session. "You're a bachelor. You're a fucking bachelor. And everyone needs to grow up and accept that."

You may hear some things. A former president's name may come up. The fact is I married the first girl I thought was too good for me and waited patiently for her to come to that same realization. Sixteen years. Kept waiting for her to tell me she wanted a family or someone else. Jennifer Bright. How can you have a name like Jennifer Bright (which she never changed when she was with me) and not see that you've settled? Not settled down. Settled.

But this is not about her. She has her own history. She didn't leave until she had to and I never saw it coming. Never saw it coming, because I was too busy unconsciously setting it up for a decade and a half.

What is this, this rehash? Is this my idea of the non-psychological life? I'm not supposed to be thinking this way.

What happened to being present in the now? "Charlie," Dr. Waldman would interrupt. "I don't mean to interrupt, but look at where your feet are." I have just looked at my feet. They are firmly in November, 2006, but my head is hovering between the mid-eighties and late-nineties.

Here's the short version, and I hope the abruptness jolts me back into today. I also hear Jennifer's voice, saying, "So, get on with it." She was, is, and will always be the most capable person I know. Never saw her misspell a word. She is five-foot-three with a coed's figure and an eternal pair of rolled-up sleeves. She puts a pen in her mouth and her long chestnut hair up in a clip and walks toward the next real or imagined situation and you know everything's going to turn out all right. If you're me, and I was, what a relief to be with someone like that. The search is over. And if you're her and know it's okay to lead rather than seek approval, you can relax. We both got married to take ourselves out of the game.

That's Travis' expression, not mine. I met Jennifer Bright when I was twenty-one. I pulled a Smith College T-shirt over her head to see that non-coed body and I was done. Until then, I had previously had sex with two other women and was not longing to become a field project of affection. Okay, one other woman, my unfortunate first. The second girl was a softball teammate of mine, a sympathetic lesbian who gave me a one-time-only demonstration of the control panel "before I send you back out there."

So, up went the T-shirt and bang went the bodies and ding ding ding went the souls and I was done. Search engine removed. Took myself out of the game.

Maybe Jennifer would disagree with that analysis. Though if she had, I'd have heard it. She was not shy about disagreeing.

If I referred to some number-crunching station manager as my friend she would say, "You need to go look up the word 'friend' or you'll continue to misuse it." Not shy. And meticulous. She read everything three times (or when pressed for time, *said* she did), and that served as her preamble for any decision or opinion. *I read the polling breakdown three times, and we need to get out of Framingham...* You cannot be shy or unthorough if your life's work is getting calls in the middle of the night to pack a bag and come fix a broken candidate or re-prop a teetering referendum. She was always packing a bag and thanking me for being so understanding. Well, of course I was understanding. I got to watch a periodic rehearsal of her leaving me.

We both worked in politics, but in the parallel ecosystems of on-the-ground and on-the-air. We succeeded mightily at keeping our careers separate from the world and each other. When we were together, it was all about being relentlessly supportive and treating the rest of the world as if it was a lap behind. When we were apart, we knew whoever was getting home first had to bring half-and-half.

Two-thirds of the way into our sixteen-year marriage, and this is the story I tell to illustrate what we had, Jennifer and I were eating at a burger joint on Connecticut Avenue. We had our heads together and we were catching up on the day, and laughing much more than the other diners. We had a sweet waitress, trying to pay her way through an unpaid Congressional internship. As she handed us our check, she said, "I have to ask you, have you not seen each other in a long time?"

"Not since this morning," said Jennifer.

"Are you going out?"

"We're married," I said.

"Wow," head down, clearing the plates, "because you seem like best friends."

Sounds great, doesn't it? Of course. Sounds enviable. It was. Sounds like you couldn't ask for anything more. And I didn't. And then she didn't. So, more bags packed. Later nights for me at the station. Both bringing home half-and-half. Neither of us noticing that when our orbits did coincide, how self-protective we had become. Sleeping on living room couches or guest beds rather than disturb whoever had dropped off first, and being equally appreciative the next morning. Having sex just enough, as if to prevent a gym membership from lapsing, and being equally appreciative the next morning. How respectful. How, how loyal. All that, and with no precocious child around to play one against the other and carom us into some kind of necessary conflict, some bold revision of the fear-bound handbook we had gone by, unaltered since Disco.

And we might have been able to continue if...nah. Forget what happened. Forget Bonnie Dressler, who you don't know. And forget Bill Clinton, who you do. Get a physicist to explain what part of inertia is fueled by staid, unexamined comfort. The marriage ended because, to her credit, Jennifer looked at the clock and saw the game we had both taken ourselves out of had time left. And the one we had been playing was long over.

You don't have to believe me when I say I am alone because it is better this way. But, golf swing aside, you can trust Travis Waldman. I'm a f~ing bachelor and everyone needs to accept that.

ℰ

THE RUPRECHTS DID NOT bite on the apartment, but someone will. Until then, you can find me in Montauk, staying at my friend Tuck's house. That's the outgoing message on my answering machine. I haven't left the city yet. I'm just trying to put off the next meal with Travis Waldman.

I can't speak for my mom's knight-in-shining-Guevara, Sy Siegel, but this is the last time Harvard will be mentioned by me. I know I just made the same promise about Freud, and I meant it. And I mean it now. You'll like how this turns out because it makes Harvard look bad.

Of all the things Harvard prepares you for, the one thing it does not is the world's bile-fueled disdain for Harvard once you leave. Can't blame the world. If only they knew that some of the dumbest people I ever met dithered in the austerity of Cambridge for four years, then strode out on 2.1 GPA cleats as if the earth was theirs to be devoured.

"You know what?" my roommate said to me with three months to go in our senior year. "I'm really good on the phone. I think I'll be a businessman."

"You're good on the phone," I said as I held an inhale off a mid-afternoon joint. "What have you ever said on the phone except, 'Heyyyyyyy, whaz shakin'?'"

"That's it. I'm going to be a businessman." Four months later, he bought a Shell station two miles from Foxwoods casino, and the path since then has been strewn with concert promotion, cable television, the Internet, ticket brokering and whoever else needs someone good on the phone. That businessman's name? Tuck Davenport. The same Tuck to whose Montauk house I am heading.

If you are one of those people who decided what they wanted to be on the basis of a whim and a joint, and then became that, well, God bless. How'd you do that? And don't say, "Charlie, I just did it," like Tuck says. I need to know. Because that's what I'm trying to do now. I'm trying to become what I want to be. And I'm trying not to examine it, in that non-psychological way I've already talked about too much. And I figure I need to go to the end of the earth to do it. They tell me Montauk is as close as you can get. So, *"Hello, Tuck?"*/ *"Heyyy, whaz shakin'?"* / *"Can I use your place?"* / *"It's yours till Memorial Day."*

I want to be John Feinstein.

I don't want to be him, but I want to be that guy. I want to be the guy who writes a sports book every eighteen months that's a literary and journalistic event. John Feinstein began to reinvent sportswriting in 1987 when he published *A Season on the Brink*, which chronicled a year in the life of Indiana University basketball and its unfiltered coach, Bob Knight.

If the United States of America was just the United State of Indiana, *A Season on the Brink* would still have been a mega-bestseller. His access to the storied program and the superego-less Knight was unprecedented and shed light on a swath of sports culture that sent small-town shades clattering skyward. The book was carried under the arm of every other Hoosier like some Gideon offspring and mere word of mouth spread its provincial marketing seed in the pre-Web era from barn to Barnes & Noble.

Since then, Feinstein has widened his sights to write books about minor league basketball, professional golf, and baseball. He has become his own cottage industry, and the thoroughness with which he explores his subject effectively ends the subject as a subject. You planning to write a book about Tiger Woods' undergraduate days at Stanford? Wait...you heard John Feinstein is thinking about writing a book about Tiger and rented a car at the San Francisco Airport? Lie down and come up with another idea.

John Feinstein is not a biographer. All he wants, and gets, are a couple of intricate personal answers to "Why?" from sports monoliths we thought we knew enough about, and others just off to the side about whom we never thought we'd care. John Feinstein is that good. But he cannot be everywhere.

"So, go be John Feinstein," I can hear my ex-wife Jennifer say. And I would ignore her, because it wasn't practical. And if I wasn't going to be practical, I might as well go nuts and want to be David Maraniss. David Maraniss is a more literary, less limelighty version of John Feinstein. David Maraniss is John Feinstein with a Pulitzer. But, and this is crucial, before he started writing about sports, David Maraniss wrote a book about Bill Clinton. And Bill Clinton helped end my marriage. So, I'm back to wanting to be John Feinstein.

This is the next thing for me to do. This is six months. All you need to be John Feinstein is a subject, a ten-page proposal and a giant advance check. I've given myself six months. Six months longer than I ever gave myself.

I am dying to call Jennifer and tell her. Why? How satisfying could that exchange possibly be?

We get along fine. Always have, but better since she remarried. Morris. Squash player/lobbyist. Something like that. She even asked me to give her away, but we agreed it was a little too "*Lifetime: Television for Women...*" Her uncle gave her away. I gave a great toast at the reception in the ballroom at the Shoreham. That was two years ago, way before I started seeing Dr. Waldman. Okay, six months before. But six months is a long time to me. I only remember one line of my toast. I told the story of how we met on the Luther campaign and I did a couple of impressions of Jennifer that had all her coworkers at the DonorsChoose office screaming. Then I ended with this line: "Morris, I know nothing about you. But I know your best quality."

How can a man who has the presence to say something like that at his ex-wife's wedding reception need a shrink? How can he not?

I think we're up to Bill Clinton.

III

B UT BEFORE THAT, DON'T marry anyone you meet and work with on a political campaign. Just don't. If you work in a politician's office and that's how you meet, and he's already in, that's fine. Just don't meet during the election process. Just don't. Okay, meet, but don't do the other thing. You can even meet, do the other thing, break up and meet again years later, but don't meet, do the other thing, move in, stay together, and eventually get married to no one's surprise.

Because why? Because that which was hatched during a campaign will end. It has to. The passion and urgency is finite. Even if you win, election night is the end of the cause, that fervid fetch that gnawed your heart's ass.

Hmm. It just occurred to me that I may have underscored this point already with the Santorum volunteer. Just now occurred to me. Just now. How about that? Look at me processing in the moment.

Marriage is not a cause. Two months after Stuart Luther lost the 1976 Democratic primary for Essex County District Attorney, I asked Jennifer Bright if she wanted to get married. "Not. Right. Now." She said. Just. Like. That. She might have said something after that, but I didn't hear. I said, "Okay," put my head back and fell asleep for three hours. When I woke up, nothing had changed. Nothing that I knew of. A week later, the phone rang in our apartment. They were looking for volunteers to help with a runoff in Vermont. Jennifer left the next morning. I stayed and learned how to make coffee at a UHF station in Brighton.

We were married six years later. Nothing had really changed, except I had gotten very good at making coffee. Ask anyone in Brighton. Or Schenectady. Or New Haven. All of the stations I worked at before Jennifer and I moved to Washington in 1995. If you can make coffee, good coffee, you can become a television producer. There are other qualifications that are important, and they'll come to me. Six years ago, October, 2000, I was involved with this giant fundraiser/birthday party Hillary Clinton threw for herself at Roseland Ballroom. When I say "involved," I mean I hired the teleprompter operator and handled the script changes for the celebrity performers/presenters backstage. That's all. A favor. And you know it was a favor because Hillary was there with Bill Clinton. And Bill Clinton helped end my marriage.

This giant event, two weeks before Election Day (when Hillary jogged for Senate against Rick Lazio, the hanging curveball New York Republicans threw up), was organized by two heavy-hitting Lower Manhattan-based film people. One kept screaming, the other kept walking up to celebrities and softly asking, "Do you have enough to eat? Do you know where the food is?" My point: One is a narcissistic bully, the other is a producer.

This is not to simplify. Okay, it is not to demean. I wouldn't demean what I do. If I did, I wouldn't be done with Dr. Waldman. Being a producer does not define me, although it writes my bio. It can be a noble profession, if you stay out of the way of the business. I am staying out of the way for the next six months, so I can tell you, with nothing to gain, that I am a damn good producer.

Here's what I'm damn good at: wrangling guests, cajoling talent, giving credit, taking blame, getting credit for taking blame, standing up to and sucking up to management and taking less than ten percent of all of it personally. And I know how to use a stopwatch. And, of course, the coffee. Except for the wrangling, none of this makes a John Feinstein so. So, we're going to give this six months.

Occasionally, I have been innovative. You know the chaotic talking-head political show? I started it. I didn't start it, but I brought it to local television. I mean I brought it to local television nightly. Which, in a derivative way, is innovative.

When I arrived at WDCN as an inexpensive breath of fresh air, *Beltway Today* was a vermouth-free half-hour summary of the day's events in Washington, focusing on the legislative branch. The perfect show for people who wanted to be bored by C-SPAN, but just didn't have the time.

Beltway Today came on at 5:30 and many nights featured dress rehearsal segments for the 6:00 local news. With the same guys standing in front of the Capitol broadstroking for a minute-thirty and invariably closing with something like, "The Senator's comment? No comment. More at the top of the hour with the Action News team. Rod?"

Rod was Rod Richmond, *Beltway Today*'s underachieving host. He was much too good-looking to be as smart as he was. Rod Richmond comes at you with the teeth and the hair, and guys like me wait for a next utterance on the order of "Charlie, I bet you'd be pretty handy at getting us some beer." But instead, the smile becomes a straight line, and you hear, "Am I wrong to imagine what it would be like to uncover a Democrat who doesn't try to be all things to all people?"

I showed up in November, 1995, when every news producer was out looking for the next O. J. Simpson story line. O. J.: the original reality programming. The second night, while Jennifer was at an ERA phone bank, Rod Richmond came to our apartment for dinner and asked me how long it would take me to make him look forward to going into work in the morning. I told him he hadn't had my coffee yet. He, the talent, was briefly cajoled.

And then I got him.

"The show's name stays the same, but we have a new star."

"Who?" he huffed.

"The President," I said. "*Beltway Today* is now 'This Day in Clinton.'"

Little did we know what would wind up in Clinton.

We started with the government shutdown and then revisited all the first-term White House scandals that were just Republicans trap-shooting whatever Richard Mellon Scaife or Lee Atwater might throw into the sky and onto the air. Remember them? Whitewater? Travelgate? Brother-in-law gate? Scandals that were scandals in the same way karaoke is art. But more than coverable. And then it was primary season. Clinton out on the campaign trail, treating the country like he was Chuck Woolery asking the *Love Connection* audience if they wanted a second date. And his opposition? The pasty survivors of the Gingrich Revolution. Let me look them up and get back to you. Right. Pat Buchanan, Steve "Flat Tax" Forbes, Lamar Somebody. And there may have been a black guy. If you remember, Bob Dole emerged. At *Beltway Today*, we were never able to squeeze the natural wit out of Dole on camera that flowed easily while he was getting retouched in the makeup room. Otherwise, who knows? We might all have had to stay up past 8:30 P.M. on Election Night.

Rod Richmond quickly evolved into the best kind of traffic cop. The kind that can pull you over with a smile and a wagging finger. He kept his questions brief enough to be the next town over from probing and could segue between topics with a bridge as flimsy as "this is too enticing for the time we have, but let's try..." And we (see how I spread the credit around?) arranged a lively cast of regular contributors. Reporters, comics, spokespeople, aides, strategists, and actual politicians, but only on the condition that they be willing to shout like a soccer dad on occasion and that they understood there was no greater threat to the country than pontificating through a hard commercial break.

By the time I was finishing up my second year, *Beltway Today* had reached that enviable mezzanine where guests wanted to stop by and station executives didn't. It wasn't *The McLaughlin Group*, but it wasn't "Conservative Piñata of the Week" either. President Clinton was the nexus and the filter. All topics went through him. Rod and the contributors spoke of him as if he were alternately Lincoln, Carter, Fagin, Young Elvis, Fat Elvis, and Renée Zellweger.

I got Rod to look forward to coming to work. And even more crucial, to look forward to going out after work. Nothing moves management out of the way like having a star show up at a hot hors d'oeuvres charity or some youth T-ball league award night. "You do the trained monkey thing six times a year, you train them not to ask for more," I explained. "And 359 nights are yours."

Our ratings had climbed modestly, then immodestly, and the other local stations attempted shameless derivations of the format, complete with see-through titles like *Beltway Beat* and *DC Comments*. Thanks to a sagely selected font, I got the Chyron people to superimpose "with Rod Richmond" on the screen under *Beltway Today* and the battle for viewers never materialized. It couldn't. Those other shows didn't have Rod. They didn't have the access to key sources in the White House and on the Hill. They didn't have booze in the green room. And after January, 1998, they didn't have Bonnie Dressler.

We had met over the phone the day after the day after the scandal broke. A week after Linda Tripp had been wired like an IAB rat. Two days after Lucianne Goldberg started chain-smoking self-promotion and just before William Ginsburg got the knot on his bowtie just right, and nothing else.

Do you still remember all these people? If you do, feel free to be ashamed. I would, but I have so much more to be ashamed of.

It started in our daily 9:30 A.M. production meeting, one of those fifteen-minute *be careful out there* rote runs where nothing gets accomplished unless someone shows up with bagels. I said, as if no one was listening, "We need a smart, good-looking woman to come on and say, 'What's the big deal? The President got a blow job.'" One of the new researchers, Danielle, said, "How about my ex-sister-in-law, Bonnie Dressler?" She said it between bites of a bagel, which was why something got accomplished.

Bonnie Dressler taught an undergraduate course on constitutional law at Simmons College in Boston, just three David Ortiz home runs down the street from Fenway Park. (Though when we met, in 1998, they were still Mo Vaughn home runs.) She had just spent the last six years turning down lucrative consulting jobs from various campaigns because she would never take the candidates as seriously as they took themselves, or worse, who they thought they were. The job offers had come pouring in for 1992 after she appeared on a locally televised legal roundtable and made some Alan Dershowitz wannabe cry on camera when she crackled, "You're making no sense, Carl. Take a break. Come back when your mind is clear. Go out. Get laid."

She never regretted the line, only the acclaim that came with it. She would not be the "Get Laid" Lady, some nineties soundbite-sized version of that old broad in the Wendy's ads who said, "Where's the Beef?" and unwittingly gave Mondale his best line of the 1984 presidential campaign. Mondale. What a whistle-stop train wreck that was. What was Dennis Miller's line about Mondale? "When I went to bed on Election Night, he had three electoral votes. Three. I didn't even run, and I almost tied him." Mondale. Now there's a guy who could have used a blow job.

So, Bonnie Dressler had retired her great-looking mouth and all that danced feistily from it from the airwaves for six years. She was more than content being the most popular professor at Simmons College. That was until January, 1998, when Bonnie Dressler added a second title, most popular divorced woman at Simmons College.

It wasn't until the custody hearing, when she took the stand and referred to her husband, Dave, as "Putzo" 564 times, getting a laugh every time, that Bonnie realized she missed being on TV. Great, but where to go? The world had long forgotten the "Get Laid" Lady. Everyone except Danielle, her former sister-in-law, who had just started at *Beltway Today*, and was the only other person who referred to Dave as "Putzo."

"I'll need a photo and a phone number," I said to Danielle, which got a laugh from the bagel-eaters. That night, after our show, I made the first call, and heard this alarmingly bright woman say "It's a blow job, so what?" while a Bruins-Penguins game blared in the background. That was it. A lot gets by me, but that night I realized that while I had a story out of the White

House that might go away, I had a woman I didn't want going anywhere. One phone call, one "It's a blow job, so what?" and I FedExed Bonnie Dressler an exclusive contract and a check for $6520.00, AFTRA scale for her first ten satellite appearances. Guaranteed money just in case this silly story, a twenty-two-year-old intern giving Oval Office hummers, proved nothing more than Internet whimsy, Penthouse Cyber-Forum.

From mid-January to September, 1998, eight months, Bonnie Dressler appeared on *Beltway Today* fifty-four times. And every time, at some point, she would lean her formidably striking face into the satellite screen and utter some combinations of the words "blow," "job," "so," and "what."

I'm not going to uncork an ode to her beauty. You've seen her. Flame-throwing from her flamed head and high cheekbones and clothed in a hurriedly thrown-on smart-girl sweater. Perfect lipstick because she's no dummy, and if she ever heard me so much as use the word "dummy," she would have turned the lipstick holder into a shiv and, well, you know. After she stopped working for us, she would still pop up on shows from time to time, but the playing field changed so irrevocably. Genuine manpower like Bonnie Dressler didn't get outsourced as much as out-circused.

But in the middle of her run, when she was *Beltway Today*'s exclusive bearer of frank and sense, unfiltered as a Lucky Strike, anyone who happened to catch just one segment of Bonnie Dressler live via satellite would, upon commercial break, blink at the screen and think, *What was that and when does it continue?* She was a bipartisan blushmaker. Who knew the notion of *The President got a blow job. So what?* would be as damaging in its tone of dismissal as in its incessant repetition? Like anyone who purposefully traffics in dirty words, the mere iteration saps the words of their power to shock. But not of their power to impugn. "I can't believe we're still discussing this," she would start. Or, "Would it move things along and save taxpayers money if Ken Starr called me and I talked dirty for $5.95 a minute?" Bonnie Dressler reduced it all to first-degree naughtiness, hardly a high crime, maybe a misdemeanor. And the fact that her language was just as naughty was an irony on the level of the pot calling the kettle self-serving. If it was possible, both Democrats and Republicans wanted her to shut up and keep talking.

I wanted her to keep talking, just not to other networks. And she didn't. Guys from CBS, CNN, Fox, and MSNBC when it wasn't even MSNBC would call me and say, "What kind of hold do you have on her that she won't return a phone call?" And I would say, "What can I tell you?" or something equally faux-pompous. Or fompous.

We had one discussion about it early on. I said, "Bonnie, do you have any idea how many people are ready to throw a show at you?" And she said, "Yeah. I'm embarrassed. For them. Why would they think I would want to do anything like that?"

"Well, there's nobody like you on TV."

"For now," she said. "Don't worry. This will die down, and then they'll find some broad who, instead of 'Is that right?' will say, 'Fuck me' and I'll be irrelevant."

"Hardly."

"I'll tell you what. You come up with a show for us, and I'll consider."

I remember saying something like, "I can't get you in the studio live, what chance do I have coming up with a show?" No, it wasn't that coherent. It was more like, "What? You mean here?"

Now I'll be coherent. The fact was, Bonnie Dressler liked the gig she had and didn't want to work any harder. And she liked that she didn't have to come to Washington to do what she could do in the privacy of the local Boston affiliate. When you're a satellite talking head, you only have to be appealing from the neck up for ten–twenty minutes. And it was impossible to believe there could be ten minutes in a year when Bonnie Dressler wasn't appealing.

Two months into her formidable run, I asked Bonnie to appear live on *Beltway Today*. I wanted her to come on in mid-March, the night after Clinton's most attractive accuser, Kathleen Willey, appeared on *60 Minutes* and Ed Bradley ("Was he aroused?") turned the thing into a Colt 45 commercial. That was Bonnie Dressler's line in our pre-interview: "I tuned in to watch '60 Minutes' and what I got was Ed Bradley doing Billy Dee Williams in a Colt 45 commercial." She was all set to oblige, just this once, but at the last minute, as she was leaving for Logan, there had been some passive-aggressive calisthenics from Putzo and she had to stay in Boston with her eight-year-old son, Boggs. She got to deliver the Colt 45 line three days later, via satellite, when its freshness had softened in the unrefrigerated air of time. She felt bad enough to apologize to me and offered restitution in one sentence. "I owe you a dinner, but you've got to get me down there to collect."

Nothing, right? Just the end of an exchange, right? As characteristically playful as any other remark by her to me in our thrice-weekly phone conversations. And that's what I thought at first. And if I had been living the non-psychological life that I am trying to live now, I would have moved on and stayed moved on. But Freud (who I know I said I wouldn't mention anymore, so dock me) said the unconscious knows only what it is told by the conscious. And if it's told *blow job, so what?...blow job, so what?...blow job, so what?...blow job, so what?...* well then, that's a beat you can dance to.

I would ask myself, more than a little, "Am I wrong? Am I flat wrong?" But I would be shushed by the chemistry of her accessibility over the phone. The self-conscious-free smile as she took her earpiece out while the satellite picture stayed up, just after I said, "Flawless as always, Bonnie." And The Beat b*low job, so what?...blow job, so what?...blow job, so what?...blow job, so what?...*

Five and a half months later, Bonnie Dressler finally came down to pay me the dinner I was owed. She left me a message saying she'd be in by four o'clock and in a perfect world wanted to be done with dinner and on the 10:00 P.M. shuttle back to Boston. In an imperfect world, she wanted a room at the Willard. By then, we must have said "blow job" to each other—*let's see, fifty-four appearances, at least two phones calls before each appearance, at least two minutes per phone call*—216 times. I said it to her, she to me. It meant nothing. You know the Zen-ish tenet, *If nothing changes, nothing changes?* Well, if a blow job is no big deal, any blow job is no big deal. 216 times. My point, and this is not the guy I am now, it's the guy I was then: How tough could the subject be to broach around reference number 220? And over a dinner she herself *owed me?* On *my* turf? Sure, I was married. So was the leader of the free world. But Bonnie Dressler, professor of constitutional law, knew a precedent when she saw one. Why wouldn't she want to see another one? Would the witness please answer the question?

Bonnie pulled into WDCN, our little station, which became little when she arrived because it was clearly not a big enough stage to hold her. There was a line of my bosses waiting to meet her in the parking lot, where her Town Car from the airport was greeted with a seven-breath-spray salute. The rule is you are supposed to look better on camera. That's the rule. Ask anyone. I didn't make it up. You can look as good off camera. That's rare.

Cameron Diaz rare. You are not allowed to look better. Again, ask anyone. She wore a crisp tan sheath of a dress that she had to have bought that morning and royal blue heels from her pre-Putzo days. Watching her emerge from just inside the lobby, as the breath sprayers breathlessly encircled her, I heard her say, "Settle down, fellas. I'm Bonnie Dressler. The girls from the service are in the Town Car behind me. I'm here to see Traub."

Was I wrong?

I might have lingered over the post-cheek kiss handshake before she went into the makeup room to get God Knows What touched up. Maybe half a second. *One thousand-one, one thousand...* and then I let go. Not awkward. In fact, as I walked away, she yelled from the makeup chair that she wanted to eat at the Red Sage. Around the corner from the Willard. Around the corner, ladies and gentlemen of the jury. Was I wrong? Was I flat wrong?

I am not a lawyer. If I was, I would know never to ask a question I didn't know the answer to.

> *"Welcome to Beltway Today, I'm Rod Richmond. This is a treat. In the studio this evening, one of our favorite regular contributors, the outspoken constitutional law professor Bonnie Dressler. Bonnie, thanks so much for making the trip down to Washington to join us."*
>
> *"My pleasure, Rod. How come your chair is two inches taller than mine?"*
>
> *"Hah! Aha—uh how did they finally persuade you to come down here?"*
>
> *"Job interview."*
>
> *"Really?"*
>
> *"Yeah. I'm having dinner with your producer, Charlie Traub. If I give him a blow job, you're looking at 'Beltway Today with Rod Richmond and Bonnie Dressler.'"*

"*Now Bonnie, come on. That's not true.*"
"*Not entirely.*"
"*I thought so.*"
"*I have to pay for dinner as well.*"

SHE CHOSE THE RED Sage because she liked the calf's liver there. She paid for dinner to settle up, and to thank me and give me her two weeks' notice. She'd had enough and was bored. If a blow job didn't matter, she was a hypocrite to keep bringing it up. She wanted a room at the Willard because she liked their breakfast menu, and she had a breakfast meeting with some Armaniac from CNN who insisted on being turned down in person. I was home by 8:15, and Jennifer looked up from reading *The God of Small Things* and said, "I thought you and Bonnie were having dinner."

I'll let this all sit for a second.

IV

To SAY NOTHING HAPPENED that night between Bonnie Dressler and me would be flat wrong. Wrong because it would be grandiose of me to even use the phrase "nothing happened." And I'd been grandiose enough, just not enough to be a guy who deserved to dig up the Rosetta Cliché "nothing happened."

But I did.

Not right away. You need to know a few additional things about Jennifer. She did not like professional athletes because they never showed up on time to political events she helped organize, and when they did, they asked if the candidate could make parking tickets go away. She did not like children's car seats because it meant a child was not far away, and thus, the end of adult conversation. She was appreciative that I did the laundry and even more appreciative I did it well. She liked having phone sex with me from a Comfort Inn at the end of a long day fronting a State House steps demonstration against redistricting. She believed men like Bill Clinton had to be allowed to let their penises roam free in order to govern properly. And to that point, she loved Bonnie Dressler and thought my hiring of her bordered on visionary. Regretfully, it was the border of Visionary and Shameless.

In one of my first sessions with Travis Waldman, I said, "Jen and I used to tell each other everything." And his eyes arched. "Everything?"

"Well," I redistricted, "eighty percent of everything."

He exhaled. "Good. Because you know only a fucking idiot tells the spouse everything everything."

You remember the waitress at the burger joint telling Jennifer and me we seemed like best friends? The problem was I always loved that incident more than Jennifer. And always believed it. Which was why I hated even the thought of waiting two weeks until after Bonnie did her last show to tell Jennifer what a quadraphonic stereotype I had been. And gleefully tell her. Who else could appreciate this cast-iron pot of delusional stew, bouillabaisse-less, that I had cooked up? What woman does not relish another example of their man's inner jackass? What best friend doesn't want to giggle and say, "I do the same thing!" So, I didn't wait the two weeks. I told her that night. Right after she said, "I thought you and Bonnie were having dinner." I laughed and began, "We did. It's fine. She's leaving. And you're going to get a kick out of this..." Flat wrong.

And I told it well. Like the veteran journalist I was, I began with the salient "4-Ws" lead ("*Tonight, Bonnie Dressler said on the air that she was in town to give me a blow job and pay for dinner...*") then went in reverse chronological order ("*The funny thing was, up until she made fun of it, I thought that was what would happen... Because if a blow job is no big deal, a blow job is no big deal... Playful phone conversations... 216 times... Like a drum beat...*") and saved my analysis for the end ("*When your work is all about Clinton, you start to think like the guy... Can you imagine?... You think you're nuts... The whole thing in my head... You married a real whacko...*") epitaphing it with the cliché (*Of course, nothing happened...*)

If I had bothered to look at her in real time, rather than beseeching some future version of her face for a laugh, I would have known instantly the hurt I was heretofore incapable of inflicting. Jennifer was not a crier. It takes too long. She stares. She shakes. She gulps. And then she lets herself, and whoever else is in the room, know exactly what she is feeling, what she feels like doing and what she will wind up doing.

"Still think it's funny, you heartless prick? You think nothing of yourself for telling that story, and less of me. You are responsible for your dick. I'd throw you out now, but I don't want to watch you pack and wonder where you'll go. So, I'll go. You have two days. And you don't have a wife anymore."

So, Bill Clinton helped end my marriage.

I used to say "Bill Clinton ruined my marriage." It was catchy, in a *News of the World* "Bigfoot Stole My Wife!" way. And it ended further discussion, which was the point. I used the line for about six years, and then decided I needed to have the discussion. Which was when I started seeing Dr. Waldman. It took us about a session and a half to give Bill Clinton his proper role. He didn't "ruin" the marriage, he "helped end" it. Those semantics were easy to recalibrate. Some, like *"you are responsible for your dick,"* took longer. So, I stayed another twenty months with Dr. Waldman to untangle all the extension cordage strewn on the floor before the plug got tripped.

You know what I just realized? For someone trying to live a non-psychological life, I am spending an inordinate amount of time on my past. And I'm indulging my future. If I'm going to be John Feinstein, let me start at my kitchen table. Or the desk in my tiny office. Or the giant chest I use for a coffee table. I have a pen, paper, a phone, and a computer. It's all here now, which is the point. Now. I don't need to move out to Montauk for six months like I'm some half-baked premise in a mid-season replacement sitcom (*It's about a divorced guy who moves from the city to a seaside village to be a writer.* / *What's it called?/* "*Fish Outta Water*"). I'm going to observe my life as it happens. I spent time outside with my ex-shrink. Too nuts. That's what I observed. Didn't work out. So, move on. I put my apartment up for sale and the Ruprechts passed on it. Didn't work out. Move on. I'm going to stay here and try to be John Feinstein in my spare time. In my apartment. I don't have to go anywhere. I don't even have to stop working. And I don't have to limit myself to six months. Not now. I just have to start. So, that's where I am. Now. And that's the point. Take it in as it happens. Live the life between sessions. As if I am not crazy. Recognize my issues as they arise. Harmony. Loyalty. Approval. Integrity. Love, I guess.

Okay, here we go...

That must be the realtor calling. I'll hang on to this place. I am not crazy. My mother is right. And I am not crazy for admitting that.

"Hello?"

"Charlie!!!!!"

"Oh, hey... Travis. A week from Wednesday? Uh, no. No plans."

ℰ

WE MET AT THE Polish restaurant downtown on 2nd Avenue. Veselka. The only place in lower Manhattan still where it should be because the owner bought the entire block during the fire-sale 1970s. I hadn't been there since I was producing a field piece on STOMP for the New Haven station. I had kielbasa and egg noodles and a pierogi that night at around midnight before we headed back and thought, "If I ever move to New York, I'll eat here every week." That was 1994. Maybe I'll come back sooner, now that I'm not moving to Montauk. Sit in a back corner table drinking coffee, half-eating a congealing blintz and scratching out my ten-page John Feinstein-type book proposal.

Maybe I'll come back here with Travis, who must have taken a couple thousand milligrams of Let'sNotScarePeople since our last get-together at Chelsea Piers. He was dressed like the Travis I had seen professionally, monochromatically crisp except for a shock of sock color, in tonight's case, electric lime embossed with the face of the ankle-less comic strip star Nancy. And get this, during this meal, all exploratory poking of food was withheld until after the waitress placed the dish in front of him, and done by utensil, not index finger.

And he was conversationally calm, in an almost custom blend of therapist probe-listening and the third interview orchestrated glibness of a job candidate. Which was apt, because, as it turns out, I still had an opening for a friend.

Of all the self-correcting ratchets Travis Waldman had hung from my belt before I sent myself out into the world six weeks ago, the most helpful had been this notion that we always worry about the wrong thing. If I needed more proof that was true, that we always worry about the wrong thing, here we were, shoveling cold cucumber soup and lentil salad, after I had spent the last nine days petrified I was walking myself back into a maw of neediness.

Wrong again. I told him about my mother and Sy Siegel, which he loved. Said I should follow Mr. Siegel around with a camera, which was better by a mile than any John Feinsteinish notion I had gurgled up. I told him about not selling my apartment, not taking time off, not moving to Montauk, but staying in town and trying to write a book proposal. He called that "developing a signature skill" and looked mildly chagrined when I asked him to explain.

He gave the lentil salad a last bite. "Wow, that dressing is good. Developing a signature skill outside of your career. Something you can get lost in. I've mentioned this a few times to you. This is one of my seven points to avoid depression. You know, in addition to medication and therapy."

"Completely forgot," I said. Travis held up the monk dish of dressing and I shook him off. He dipped a piece of bread in it. "Wait. Now, I'm vaguely remembering. What are the other six? Sleep, right? Exercise?"

He pointed and dipped the bread again. "Healthy eating," he added, "altruistic behavior (which thanks to the bread came out "alchewisssic nehabyore") a support group outside therapy and some kind of spirituality,"

I had to ask, "All seven?"

"You want the Dr. Waldman answer or the Travis answer?"

"Seeing that we're splitting lunch, I'll take the Travis answer."

He pushed plates away like there may be a problem if he didn't. "Look, it's just something to keep in mind. There's always going to be shit that works for somebody else and not for you. And shit that works for you and not others. Just find it. You have no idea how many of the seven you're already doing. Some will say that ending therapy is a spiritual move. A leap of faith."

Now I grabbed the bread. "Uh-huh."

"Spiritual, not religious. Something bigger. I told you about the Orthodox Jew who came to see me, horrific lower back pain?"

"No."

"After six months, he bounds into my office. I say, 'How you doing, Yankel?' He says, 'Great. For the last two weeks, I've been seeing a dominatrix. She puts a dog collar around me, then makes me change into a diaper and a leather harness and then I get down on all fours and eat her out. For half an hour. All fours on a hardwood floor. I get up. No pain."

"And let me guess," I said, "He sees her on Friday night?"

"Yes! That's my point. Leap of faith."

"I think I just got the Dr. Waldman answer."

Travis might have laughed more, but the waitress came over and he needed to become the CEO of our table. "Is it possible to get a container of that salad dressing to go? I'll pay. You won't get in trouble. And we'll take a slice of banana cream pie, two forks, two coffees and the check. Thanks a lot."

"I don't know why you would know this," I said after the waitress finished clearing, "but I hate banana cream pie."

"That works out well for me. You never struck me as much of a sweets guy."

"I have my moments."

"A few years ago, I had a patient. You know him. High-profile billionaire. At the time, he's married to a movie star. I'll just say '*Sea of Love*' and we'll leave it at that. He tells me, 'My wife and I made a bet, no dessert for a year.' He's a billionaire. She clearly has been good with her money. The bet is no dessert for a year. I figure the bet has to be at least $50,000, $100,000, maybe a million. I ask him, 'How much is the bet?' He says proudly, 'Hundred bucks.' I say, 'Ron, have a piece of fucking cake.'"

I didn't bother to stop laughing when the waitress came back with the check, pie, coffee, and salad dressing in a to-go cup. Forget Sy Siegel, this is the guy I should be following around with a camera. I stop seeing him professionally and he becomes this confidentiality pureeing raconteur. And I can take it in without my ego putting on track shoes. I can stay. He cannot possibly be the only one like him. Cannot.

This is the John Feinstein idea. This is the proposal. It doesn't have to be about sports. I interview shrinks. They tell me their best-of stories. It's funny, it's horrifying, it's Chassid-eating-out-a-Dom funny and horrifying. This is why I don't need to go to Montauk. It's all here. Now. And I just came up with a title: *Patients and Tolerance*.

"Travis, I just came up with the most incredible—"

He put cash in the check caddy and held up his hand. "I really want to hear it, but I have some great news and I've been meaning to tell you the whole meal. Hell, a couple of weeks."

"Okay, let's have it."

"I've got a new woman in my life. It's been a month now, and I'm telling you, Charlie, I've never—"

"And the wife knows?"

"Charlie, of course. Of course, I'm going to tell her. But I had to tell you first."

"Why?"

"'Why?' the man asks..." Travis toasted me with a forkful of pie. "Because it's Bonnie Dressler."

V

THE NEAREST THE CITY That Never Sleeps ever sleeps is the way its people close their eyes to the lunatics that regularly canter its streets muttering to themselves. I was forever one of them, and now I am one of *them*. It is forty-some blocks to my apartment, and I was unable to cover any of them without barking snippets like "*That kind of image does not end with the session...,*" "*One point is an accident, two points is a line...,*" "*Came out 'you look ravenous'...,*" "*Men's room's over there...,*" "*Rabbi Chaffkin saw no moral contretemps...,*" "*Never thought I'd be my own story...,*" "*I don't know, you tell me...,*" The sidewalk yawned. Nothing it hadn't heard before.

That last one, *I don't know, you tell me...* I yelped over and over. It was the last line of our last and only exchange. I had to get out of there. Veselka. My glorious Polish Cordon Bleu now shuttered.

Maybe I made it through ten minutes of Travis Waldman's fuss-filleted narrative of the tracking, tagging, and banging of Bonnie Dressler.

"And the best part?" he had begun from the side of his mouth, now strangely shielded by the back of his hand. "My faith in my deepest instincts has been restored. Well, maybe not the best part. Because the woman knows her way around a prick. I don't have to tell you. Hah! Maybe I do. Hey, sometimes, being an enabler has its ironic merits, right?"

I jerked his hand down from the side of his mouth. "Travis, how am I an enabler?"

"I don't know, Charlie. You tell me."

Maybe I would recompose the infrastructure of this high-speed betrayal when I stopped sputtering, but now, just past Forty-ninth and Third, I was still in present mid-spew. Is recompose even a word? Right now, anything containing "compose" seems delusional. Repiece. That's what I will do. Repiece what Travis just told me. I know repiece is not a word. Somehow, a word that did not exist before now, a word unspoken, befits the situation.

The last six blocks, I've made three stops. I went into LaMaganette, ordered a bourbon on the rocks, then left ten dollars on the bar and walked out when the bartender took fifteen seconds to answer the phone. At Fifty-third and First, I sat at the counter, ordered a cup of coffee and had however many sips it took to slip a spoon into my pocket. I am now leaving D'Agostino's on Fifty-sixth and First with a pint of some Ben & Jerry's weapon of muscle mass destruction, which I intend to eat with my stolen spoon on the street, a block and a half from my apartment.

Two things stop me. It is the second week of December. And it occurs to me that only crazy people eat ice cream out of the container in the street a block and a half from their apartment the second week of December. And I am not crazy.

I put the ice cream in the freezer and turn my breakfast table chair to face the window on the second week of December. *I don't know, Charlie. You tell me*, I said to myself for the last time. Okay, I'll tell you.

The Bonnie Dressler background tale I laid out before? The phone calls and the playful talk and the horridly misread dinner and the more horridly misread confession to Jennifer? Slightly incomplete.

Shit.

Dead in the middle of everything, May, 1998, my mother had her hip replaced. During the three days she was in Brigham Women's Hospital, I had to stay at Israel Putnam Village with my dad. She would convalesce at a rehab for a week after that, then come home, and my younger sister, Alison, and her family would handle the back nine of her recovery. But for those three days, I had old man duty, which was basically making a couple of meals and driving Ducky Traub to see his wife in the hospital and intermit the awkwardness between them with banter from their own lives, which they would then correct. This is a gig I have had since birth. Not the cooking or driving. The entertaining demilitarized zone.

This was the condition on which my mother agreed to have the hip surgery: I would drive up from Washington and stay with Ducky. Alone. Jennifer was thrilled. "Nice to know Gwen Traub can actually be threatened by another woman," she said. Jennifer always got along well with my mother. She deferred to her constantly, like the thoughtful heathen shiksa she was. Her behavior was respectful, above reproach and generously sweetened with real affection. And Gwen had no choice but to respond in kind, which I am sure infuriated her more than the fact that son-stealing was not prosecutable.

I left after work on Wednesday, when Bonnie had filled the satellite screen in an open cream-colored shirt and offered this possibility to Rod Richmond and the in-studio panel: "*You know what point hasn't been raised? Maybe Monica was good. Maybe she was good at it. Maybe the President was simply delegating. I don't know, but speaking for other Jewish women out there, some of us have a reputation for that kind of expertise..."*

Staying with my dad turned out to be a nice break for me. Mind you, this was eight years ago, in the time when all I did was worry about the wrong thing and not know I was doing it. Thought I was being self-stimulating and challenging and whatever else we say to pass the time between catastrophic thoughts.

My father was still very much sound of mind. He had retired as a marketing executive with a retail health and beauty aids chain in 1992 and spent an enjoyable year selling high-end personalized tote bags and cloth belts part-time until he committed the Class A felony of walking with his sample kit into a store where his wife was shopping. "I will not be married to an old man with a bag," Gwen Traub had ultimatummed. Ducky turned in his samples, though we can all agree he was still an old man with a bag. Since then, he had tried painting, ceramics, bridge, yoga, and a couple of book clubs before he settled on a leisure activity he could embrace: awaiting further instructions.

I'm being smug and I should watch that. My dad was not inert. Five days a week, he would normally get a lift from a fellow Israel Putnam villager to the health club, swim for a half-hour, then sit in the steam room long enough to watch the toxins run out of his body like a golf gallery moving onto the next tee during a sudden-death playoff. Now, I was his ride. He was fine with it all. Even the clipped exchanges with his son.

On the third and last day of my visit, we were finishing up in the steam room before we headed out to the rehab. By then, I was determined to stay in for the full Ducky Traub shvitz cycle. I figured if I brought in a newspaper I could be distracted enough to not feel like a side of ribs in a smoker.

"They don't like you to bring stuff in to read," he said.

"Really? Who?"

"The people."

"Why?"

"They feel it cuts into the...camaraderie," he said with his head back and eyes closed.

"But dad, it's just you and me."

He opened his eyes. "I don't want to get yelled at."

You're going to have to believe me on this. In all the time I knew my father, he had never said anything of personal exposure that landed within 500 feet of that line. I was out and back without the newspaper in seconds. He smiled. You're going to have to believe me on this. Before that, I never remember a gesture on my part that had come within 1000 feet of his approval.

I sat with a towel draped over my lap.

"You got a girl?"

"What, Dad?"

"A girl. You got a girl?"

"Yeah, Dad. Jennifer. My wife."

"I know Jennifer."

"Is that what you mean?"

He had said something like, "I'm being a wise guy." I think that's what he said. He might have said, "I don't know, Charlie. You tell me."

I know what I said. "Were you ever unfaithful to Mom?"

"Nah."

"Not even when you were overseas in the service?"

The eyes closed. "I had her picture in my wallet the whole time."

That was it. Does any son think, *I wish I'd spent more time with my dad in the steam room?* Any son other than me?

We got to the hospital an hour before my mom was discharged to rehab. Alison was already there. And her kids. And my dad became Grandpa and I was staring at another family's visit. "Charles Traub, Jr., you are hereby relieved of duty," Gwen Traub proclaimed.

It's a straight shot to I-95 South and DC, and yet, forty-five minutes later, I was parked on Mass Ave, half a dozen blocks from Sacramento Street in Cambridge. 22 Sacramento Street. That's where we sent the checks. *Ms. B. Dressler. 22 Sacramento Street. Cambridge, Ma. 02138.*

I would call from a phone booth. It was May, 1998, and only assholes had cellphones. I would tell Bonnie I was visiting my parents and get the pesky truth portion of the call out of the way. I would say the *Washington Post* had contacted my office the day before about me doing a first-person piece for an upcoming Sunday Arts section on how I had hired her. And just to give it the proper soupçon of imitation karma, I would go on that I had just called the *Post* back and when I told them Bonnie and I had never been in the same room, they, not me, declared, "Let's make that the story!" That's when I would get adroitly accommodating and tell them, "You'll never guess where I am. Boston! Let me see if she's available." And so, here I was, just me, just being of service, seeing if Bonnie Dressler was available. Seriously, who gets hurt?

I sat in my 1993 LeSabre on Mass Ave for an hour and did the kind of heavily edited introspection readily accessible to a forty-four-year-old man plotting a mistake. At one point, I decided I needed a joint. No problem. Just turn the LeSabre around, head back toward Harvard Square. Surely, someone would be able to help me. Surely, nothing had changed in Harvard Square in the twenty years since I last scored weed. Besides, and more to the point, what would I do with it? I couldn't roll a joint if Jimmy Cliff's life depended on it. Never got the hang of it. Those duties had belonged to my old roommate Tuck Davenport, my old dealer Little Eva. And Jennifer. And that is what lurched me out of it. The laughable notion that the one person who could help me out would be in the way when I was high enough to call Bonnie Dressler.

I made good time on I-95 and walked into the house around eight. Jennifer gave me an uncharacteristically tight hug and said, "I expected you much later. If I'd known, I would have, you know, showered." "Showering" was her highly crackable code for being clean enough to entertain guest tongues. As I recall now, staring out the window at the second week of December, she showered the next morning. Early the next morning.

It hardly competes with the true tale of The Chassid and The Dominatrix, so I had left out that last part when I told Travis Waldman this story. It was my answer to a session-opening question toward the end of our first year together. "*Charlie, had you ever considered acting on your feelings for Bonnie before she came to Washington?*" At the time, we had dismissed it as ham-fisted fantasy. Or I had. We never discussed it further. But that's where Dr. Waldman got the idea. The fake article. That's how I enabled him.

As for the specifics, all we have is the version he had just given at Veselka. And how can you not trust that?

Travis said he waited two weeks after I had stopped seeing him to contact Bonnie, as if honoring some sort of probationary period before the duplicity clearance paperwork came through. "That kind of image does not end with the session, Charlie. It never did," he offered in his throat-clearing opening. Thanks.

She was still teaching at Simmons. He introduced himself over the phone and requested an interview for a paper he was working on for a psychology journal. The paper: "If We Let It, Can Oral Sex Teach Us?" The journal: Really, does it matter?

The premise of this scholarly work, and why I'm taking even a moment to give credence to this elaborate grift of desperation is beyond me, was that therapists never fully explore a patient's oral sex history because the same taboos, ambiguities, and misconceptions about the act are already in place for them. Travis humbly divulged that Bonnie had laughed when he told her about the piece, which was the Bonnie I knew. But Dr. Waldman ("*Feel free to Google me! Travis Waldman. Or Travis A. Waldman. My last piece was 'The Magnificent 7 Points to Avoid Depression.'*") cannily went on to remark that his research had only uncovered three worthwhile examples of late twentieth-century artists who had fearlessly pulled back the psychological curtain on getting and giving head: Lenny Bruce, Susan Minot, and Bonnie Dressler. And that hooked her enough to Google Travis, then agree to one interview. On the phone. *Look I'll be in town next week to interview Susan Minot, why don't I stop by? Is there a good time?*

Susan Minot had written a book in 2002, *Rapture*, which should have been subtitled, *Blow Job: The Novella*. She had family in Boston, so it wasn't a stretch. Bonnie had actually met her at some Kennedy School cheese and crudité backslapper in the early nineties. And not only had she heard of Susan Minot's book, six of her friends might have sent it to her for her birthday.

"Charlie," said Travis as he sipped his cold Veselka coffee, "one point is an accident, two points is a line..."

That made their first meeting a breathless ninety minutes. An hour of Bonnie Dressler telling her life story up through and including her time on *Beltway Today with Rod Richmond* and the town cryering of fellatio that defined it. "I felt like I was just saying something my girlfriends would have said to me. You know, if I had girlfriends," was Travis' account of Bonnie's explanation. Again, that sounded like Bonnie. And her self-effacing candor turned him on as I hadn't allowed it to envelop me. The last thirty minutes of the, uh, interview, consisted of Travis reading selected paragraphs from *Rapture* and asking, "Does this ring true?" At the end, she said, "Dr. Waldman, you may want to rethink this paper as a half-hour pilot for Cinemax."

"I didn't even get it and I laughed!" he confided. "Of course, now I do."

Well sure, now.

I was trying to listen and not be distracted by the glee with which Travis told of the second meeting. I know, I know. How could there have possibly been a second meeting? Three days later, guess who happened to be back in Boston? Guess who decided to show up at Bonnie Dressler's office and come clean? And by come clean, apologize for wasting her time on a paper he would never write...before knitting another falsehood about Susan Minot double-crossing him by deciding to collaborate on *her own paper* on the *same topic* for a *competing* psychological journal with a *more decorated* therapist. A lie of self recanted with a lie involving a stranger. The psychopath of least resistance.

And Bonnie bought it. Which didn't surprise me. It was the only thing that came out of Travis' mouth that didn't surprise me. It surprised him. He patted his moustache and giggled that Nancy-faced sock-clad purr of his and said, "I guess I was convincing."

Now that he was out of my ideas, Travis stumbled briefly. We should all stumble so. As Bonnie rose to thank him and show him out, according to Travis—oh, what the fuck, I'll use his words: "She stood up from her desk, away from the one of those green banker's lights, and the angle of the ray hit her waist, where her maroon silk shirt was half tucked into her gray slacks. And I swear, Charlie, I meant to say either 'You look luminous' or 'You look ravishing.' But it came out, 'You look ravenous.'" And Bonnie Dressler said something like, "You know what? I am. Buy me a burger and we're done."

Something like that. That was when I had stood up at Veselka and shoved my chair hard into the table and looked around. "Men's room's over there," Travis had said, stabbing banana cream detritus.

It is now fifteen minutes later and I have just finished cleaning up what's left of the ice cream I threw against the window. I felt it, I did it, I know why, so no need to examine. And now, strangely, I feel good enough to continue.

I stood and arched over Travis, gripping the top of the chair like a bike messenger, a hover which told him not to stop talking, oh no, but simply to pick up the pace. So, I was blessed with hearing there was another phone call to Bonnie, then two more dinners, followed by the check-in with Rabbi Chaffkin, who we now know saw "no moral contretemps" and the Penthousian denouement of "I never thought I'd be my own story..." And the Big Finish. Back of the hand to the side of the mouth. Locker room chestnut ("...the woman knows her way around a prick...") to moral compost ("Being an enabler has its ironic merits..."). That maddest dash to "I don't know, Charlie, you tell me."

That was it. I had to get out of there. Too late? I know, but I'm new at this.

And now, you tell me. What do I have here? What is my move? Call the police? "Hello, Midtown North? My ex-shrink stole my fantasy! Describe it? Uh, uh, 1998. Mint. Uh, uh...I'll call you back."

I repeated my imaginary call to the police out loud, even picked up the phone and pantomimed dialing the number. It made me laugh. And then I did it again, but this time I added the cop at the desk saying, "*Sir, settle down. Did the man physically take your fantasy, or did he act out on it?*" And then I looked quizzically back into the dead receiver at what the fake cop had just said to me in my voice. Now that, that's acting out. I collapsed in the chair and giggled like a kid with a secret. I was exhausted and sugar-crashed and looked out on the second week of December.

A man had behaved badly. So what? Seriously, so fucking what? I know I'm tired, but now anytime I try to go in a righteous rageful direction with what I just heard, I end up tripped by what I already know about myself. Travis had taken something that never really belonged to me except in self-centered fancy. And what's worse, he had IMPROVED on it. Bad judgment to tell me? Absolutely. Worse than my decision to tell Jennifer about the Bonnie tryst-not? Not even close. Had he violated the patient-doctor relationship? Not if the relationship was over. Not in his mind. And really, whose opinion counts here? The guy who got blown by Bonnie Dressler, or the guy talking to himself?

What can I tell you? Now every time I think about never seeing Travis Waldman again, I am happy and grateful. And frankly, I think the ending of my Bonnie Dressler story is better. It's real.

I'm tired.

So, how about this? I got angry, I left, I laid it all out and reacted to that. I saw the behavior and the behavior saw me. And now I'm happy, grateful, and tired. And whatever is next doesn't happen until I wake up.

What if I am not crazy? You know what? I'm not.

WHAT THE FUCK WAS THAT?!? The phone. The phone scared me. Oh yeah. I'm fine.

"Hello?"

"Traub?"

"This is Charlie Traub, yes," I said.

I heard the High Holidays shofar-like g-flat of an old Jew blowing his nose. "Sy Siegel," he said, but much too soft and hesitant to be the guy I knew. "So, your mother left *ahem...*"

It sounded like *Your mother left me.* I felt bad. "I'm sorry, Sy."

"Is that some particularly robust strain of Harvard stoicism?" That was more like it.

"No, I mean it. She can be a little pugnacious. You probably left some food out. Don't worry."

Sy Siegel's place on the phone was taken by an old man weeping. It couldn't be him.

"No, Traub" the voice said. "She left. She's gone. Go grab the dark suit."

VI

IT IS A LONG drive to your mom's grave if you don't need to think about what you'll say at the funeral. I left the next morning because I was in no hurry. And I slept well. One of Travis Waldman's "Magnificent 7 Points to Avoid Depression." (You know, in addition to medication and therapy). So, I'm not depressed. Terrific.

If I was speaking to Travis, I might tell him to add another point to his "Magnificent 7." #8: *Wait until the morning after you've slept well to ask your sister how your mother died.* I called Alison just before I hit the Merritt Parkway. "She slipped in the shower and hit her head," she said.

"That's odd," I had said.

"Well, that's what happened. I don't want to talk about it, Charlie. You know what you're going to say?"

"At the service? Yeah."

"I don't want to talk anymore. Everything's done. I'll see you this afternoon." And she hung up. So, we need to amend #8 to *Wait until the morning after you've slept well, and showered, to ask your sister how your mother died.*

I would have loved to cheer her up, but that wasn't my gig. Alison and I had always been more colleagues than brother and sister. She handled all the administrative details of being a child of Ducky and Gwen Traub. I was in staging and production. My gig was cheering up my mom. And I had lost my gig.

By the way, that's the opening line of my eulogy: "I lost my gig." I told you I was ready.

So, I've been using the drive to try and think of something that would cheer up Sy Siegel, a man I had met a little over a month ago and was convinced would not only be able to entertain my mother, but me. And now, I need to come up with material. For this stranger. Why?

Harmony.

That's it. Harmony. Can't be anything else. That's my wellspring. That's what has motivated almost every decision in almost every relationship I have ever had. No more examination is needed. We're done.

Look how quickly I answered my own question. How fearless. How unfiltered. Seriously, other than the inner dialogue, I am integrating in real time. This must be the essence of the non-psychological life. Shrink thyself. To thine own shrink be true.

He'll want a story about Harvard. He'll want a story about Harvard that speaks ill of Harvard. And a story that somehow from its innocent beginnings careens far enough out to victimize me. And not some elite, precious, too-clever-by-an-eighth Ivy miscreance that ends with Daddy at the police station. I imagined three Venn diagram circles: **H, Bad H, Me** and they intersected crisply at the stocking incident.

I'll tell him about the stocking incident. Let me see if I remember this right. I had just finished my sophomore year. I had patched together a good bit of work for the summer. A bartending job five lunch shifts a week and a number of odd jobs through the student employment agency. Weekend moving, night catering, and custodial work at three department office buildings in and around campus.

The janitor gig was a dream. Fifty dollars a night for the three buildings. Two-fifty a week for what amounted to maybe eight hours of work. Maybe. And I think I'm counting the fifteen-minute walk over from my bar job. During the school year, maintaining these buildings was a thirty-hour-a-week job. But no one loves the academic calendar more than a teacher. The faculty borough of Harvard Square traditionally evacuated after June fifteenth as if it had called an exterminator. Those who remained after the Mass Ave exodus were either saving money for next year's time-share or quarantined by a working spouse or a child in summer school.

My buildings housed the staff of the English, Anthropology, and Sociology departments. I would key-jangle in around 6:30 or 10:30, depending on whether I had taken the T downtown after my shift to watch the Red Sox. The English and Sociology buildings I could barrel through in about forty-five minutes using a method we in the custodial business referred to as "ash and trash," which is exactly as it sounds. In my case, it took the time I could open an office door and see the wastebasket and ash tray in their Ides of June positions. Once a week, I backhanded them with a feather duster in case my bosses at the Harvard Student Agencies sent forensics in to see if I was showing up.

Between June 16 and Labor Day weekend, I saw maybe four people in the three buildings. Two regulars and a fast-thinking couple. One of the regulars was a brow-ridged, dimly-lit, ear-haired grunter who never left his desk in the anthropology building because he was either finishing his thesis or because he was a display. The other was the secretary of the English Department, Anne Grand. Anne Grand had the cheek to expect her office vacuumed three times a week. She left a note for me my second night: *I will assume you are planning to vacuum every other night. I may take a vacation. You may not.* Our paths crossed a few times. The exchange was always the same: "*I'll come back in an hour?*" / "*That will be fine.*" She looked exactly like someone named Anne Grand should, as if her almost rhyming name tapped a monochromatic chime: light skin, light hair, bangs, glasses, tan cotton skirt, and espadrilles rushing home to feed at least three cats. Forgettable, except we had a deal, and I tend to remember deals.

You should have seen me with the vacuum. I had that Jack Lemmon *Odd Couple* ballroom dancing move working. I must have picked that up originally to entertain my mother. Must have. No other explanation. She would say, "Rhonda Lee had to leave early. Give us a little dance on the living room cah-pet before your fah-thah gets home." Rhonda Lee was the housekeeper who always had to leave early. Come to think of it, they all did. Until I went away to school. But until then, away I went to get the Bissell upright and do the dance, like some imaginary pool of judges hadn't yet selected the semifinalists for Most Dutiful Eleven-Year-Old Boy. I must have figured out early on that if I did what I was told I would be asked to do less. Another deal. So, the least of my chores looked like this: keep your room clean; empty the wastebaskets; dance with the vacuum once in a while. Ash and trash.

The fast-thinking couple was more fast-thinking uncoupled. A renowned-in-his-field sociology professor and a woman who might have been one of his students if she hadn't been busy taking his order at the Oxford Ale House. I stumbled in on them around 2:00 A.M., long after the Sox had lost to the Angels in extra innings, and just after the professor had switched on his desk lamp and proclaimed loudly, "Well, uh, Mimi, we've looked everywhere. Call Fred, Professor Skinner, tomorrow and tell him I don't have his bird feeder." She gave me a *Can you believe what an asshole?* look on the way out, and I wanted to say, "Maybe seventy-one-year-old BF Skinner left his bird feeder at her place." But I didn't, because I thought of that line just now.

The following fall, I was trying to fill out my schedule with one of Harvard's alarmingly plentiful offering of gut courses with minimal requirements (paper and a final, or better, optional paper and a final). There, in the course catalogue, under Social Sciences, was a twice-a-week lecture from the same professor I had chanced upon. B. F. Skinner's bird feeder docent. The name of the course: Adaptation to Life.

(I hope I can get through that part of the story without Sy interrupting me and going off on some dismissive fit about B. F. Skinner being a dilettante and paying off cops to stay out of the loony bin because he wanted to give pigeons the right to take the civil service exam.)

As the faculty began to stagger back after Labor Day, my custodial livelihood's powers to charm waned as the hours grew. The Harvard Student Agencies asked me to stay on until the second week of September, when I could train someone eager to make seven dollars an hour. No problem. In the spirit of harmony, I was always accommodating. I didn't need to attend a lecture twice a week to learn how to adapt.

Except I never made it to the second week of September. The Wednesday after Labor Day, I was cleaning the Sociology offices just after 6:00. I was hoping to finish all three buildings by 10:00, and that way leave four hours for bar drinking and ten hours of sleep before my first class.

I started on the third floor of the white clapboard house at 11 Kirkland Place and ashed, trashed, and corn broomed the first three offices, which were mercifully bare floored. The fourth office belonged to Virginia Prexel-Hayes, a Philosophy and Ethics professor whom space issues had forced out of Emerson Hall and onto the third floor of 11 Kirkland Place. Professor Prexel-Hayes was the foremost authority on the eighteenth-century English theological philosopher William Paley in either the world, the country, or on the third floor of 11 Kirkland Place. She had a large oriental rug and too many end tables, and if I was lucky and her light was out and the wastebasket was half full, I could get by with a shuffleboard shot from the carpet sweeper, a whack from the feather duster and pushing her chair in tight to the desk.

The light was out. I was lucky. And her door was open, which was not uncommon, especially among the offices at 11 Kirkland Place. A kind of empirical field test to see if the janitor would be sufficiently acclimatized by his strata to know to lock up when he finished an office. So, the open door was odd, but not odd enough to register. Professor Virginia Prexel-Hayes, fifty-year-old leg propped against the windowsill in the beginning of a hurdler's stretch, was odd enough to register as I flicked on the light.

Virginia Prexel-Hayes shrieked loud enough to wake William Paley and make him rethink his thoughts on contempt prior to investigation.

I'm stunned by how well I remember the exchange thirty-four years later.

"How dare you!"

"I'm sorry. Your light was out."

"I know damn well it was out."

"Well, that usually indicates there's no one in here."

"And you don't knock?"

"Not after hours when the light is out."

"So, you just saw me fixing my stocking and thought you'd get a better look."

"Ma'am, I didn't see you..."

I might have said, "Ma'am, you have to believe me" or "Ma'am, I apologize." The problem was I said "Ma'am." That turned out to be the first of three impeachable offenses. I did not call her "professor" or "Professor Prexel-Hayes." I did not acknowledge the title she had earned.

"What did you call me?"

"Professor Hayes. Professor Prexel. I'm sorry, Professor Prexel-Hayes."

And then, and I can't tell you why except to say that I had no reason to stay, I turned off the light and backed out. Even though I had bestowed her proper title, I was way short on squaring my tab. I had not acknowledged the stocking adjustment. And much worse, I had not acknowledged that she had a leg worth acknowledging during a stocking adjustment in the dark.

She ran after me into the hall.

"Are you a student here?"

"Yes," I said. It would prove the one time that mentioning Harvard would close a door.

"Write down your name and your undergraduate house. Your semester just got really, really shitty."

I was placed on non-academic probation for the semester, which meant I could do no extracurricular activities, including working for the Harvard Student Agencies. And I could not look at a full professor adjusting her stocking until January. The dean was sympathetic. I was not the first undergraduate speciously disciplined by Professor Virginia Prexel-Hayes. Gum chewers and inappropriate gigglers were also ticketed. The dean referred to her as a "claims mill." He may have even patted a thick folder. Don't remember. But man, I remember "claims mill." It was the first time I had heard that expression. I hung onto it and never stopped using the phrase, but rarely in its intended image. It was how I dismissed anyone who trafficked in outrage, whose pointed fingers entered a room ten seconds before they did. Lyndon Larouche? Claims mill. George Steinbrenner? Claims mill. Anita Bryant? Pitchwoman/claims mill. Newt Gingrich? Fucking claims mill.

You know who could dismantle a claims mill in two minutes? Bonnie Dressler.

Let it go, Traub.

So, I ended up working for the Harvard Student Agencies under the name of Tuck Davenport, my roommate. The HSA had no problem writing checks to someone else, provided they wound up in his checking account, and as long as I played along and answered to his name. They set me up with a job bartending at the Faculty Club. You got called in several days a week to handle a reception in one of the upstairs function rooms. A decade before the word "aerobic" lunged into the lexicon, two hours of nonstop drink-slinging for the Neiman Fellows or the Friends of the Nathan Pusey Library Extension Project was a cardiovascular avalanche. The attendees would line up in front of the portable, minimally stocked bar. Once served (in each hand), they would head to the back of the line, in what geometricians might call a sot parabola. Whatever conversation rose above glass tinkling was solely between you and your direct line mate. After two hours, a Faculty Club manager would flick the light and, drenched through my crimson waistcoat, I would wheel away the portable bar to groans, boos and the occasional Socratic question, *What the fuck?*

My gig at the Faculty Club ended quite suddenly when I showed up one day and saw that I, Tuck Davenport, was working a reception for the sociology faculty. Not what you think. I begged one of the seniors working the main bar (a cushy, quiet two-man slot that paid twice the function room rate for a third of the work) to switch with me for double-pay. He cleared it with the manager and I looked forward to spending my shift washing glasses, my back to the main barroom in case Professor Prexel-Hayes stopped by early to bang one back before heading upstairs.

My bartending partner was a charismatic chin model who I immediately recognized as Stevie Coolidge, a three-year starter on the football team.

"Steve Coolidge," he needlessly introduced himself.

"I know," I said. "Uh, Tuck Davenport."

"You write for the *Crimson*?"

I had to think. Tuck had completed the six-week byline audition on the Harvard daily paper the fall before, pre-upholstering his résumé. I smiled. "That's right. Sure, last—"

I never got to finish. Stevie Coolidge pinched the flap of skin below my chin and dragged me outside behind the kitchen. He picked me up and threw me into the dumpster as if I was an empty case of Cutty Sark.

"Thanks for calling my ten-yard punt against Brown a 'boomer.'"

I stayed in the dumpster until it was dark enough for anyone who might walk by to mistake me for anything but an undergraduate. Virginia Prexel-Hayes never showed up to the sociology department reception.

Come on. That has to be good enough for Sy Siegel.

e

IT WAS NOT SY'S intention to meet me at the entrance to Windgate Point, it just worked out that way. I had barely locked the door of my rented Impala when he quick-shuffled through the automatic front doors, chasing after two bemused local policemen, waving a battered baseball hat replete with military clusters—scrambled eggs—on the bill and TOP GUN stitched across the crown.

"Hey fellas," Sy yelled. "You forgot to illegally search under the button on my cap!"

The larger cop stopped and turned back. "Mr. Siegel, were we disrespectful to you?"

Sy dropped the TOP GUN hat as if he was suddenly unarmed. "Oh, I see. Now we're going to playact in front of the decedent's son."

The cops looked at me. "Is that right?" said the smaller one.

"Yes. I'm Charlie Traub. Hello, Mr. Siegel."

"Traub." He picked up the hat and turned away to weep and eventually blow his nose in between "TOP" and "GUN."

The smaller cop tried, "Mr. Siegel, why don't you go inside and sit down and wait for your friend?" Sy was clearly getting ready to compose himself long enough to turn around and bark back some invective containing the words "fire hose," "dogs," or "rubber bullets." Luckily, two women from the kitchen (one I recognized from my dad's bedroom) emerged and walked him back inside. By then, the larger cop had moved close enough to me to talk in that earnest policemanhush.

"Sorry for your loss, Mr. Traub," he began. I think I said thanks. "Your friend, Mr. Siegel, has had a rough last twelve hours. He's clearly distraught. He clearly feels responsible. But from all we can tell, he did everything right and never panicked. It was just a freak accident with your mother."

"Yeah. She fell in the shower and hit her head," I said, echoing what Alison had told me.

"No, sir. She slipped." The cop was correcting me like a relative.

"And did Sy hear her slip," I asked. " Or did he walk in on her later?"

"Oh no, sir. He was there."

I was just about to ask *What was he doing there?* but I figured it out. So, I said, "Oh" or "right."

"He was in the chair," said the cop.

Okay, this explains why h—CHAIR!?!? Whatever is three towns over from figuring out what happened, that's where I was. The cop put his arm on my shoulder.

"We see this more than you think," he says. "Older couples. They want to be intimate, but they don't want to use the bed. You know, memories. Besides, they think it's safer in the shower. It's a chair. What can happen in a chair?"

Why am I laughing? I know why. I'll tell you in a second.

"Thanks, officer. Sorry I'm laughing."

"Believe it or not, Mr. Traub, I've seen this reaction a lot, too."

I barely get out "Thank your partner" because I am wiping my eyes and lightly convulsed. I am laughing because all I can think of is my father's favorite expression of disdain when I was growing up. I'm not even sure of the connection, but it's all I can think of. "Charlie," Ducky Traub would say, "you won't be happy till you break it."

It takes me a good ten minutes to compose myself enough to walk inside Windgate Point and go to the front desk. I don't even know where Sy Siegel's apartment is. The only thing I know is that my little stocking story will not fly.

℮

SY SIEGEL IS IN apartment 235. I don't bother to knock because the music is so loud he won't hear me. Mozart. I know zero about classical music, but I recognize this piece. Years ago, my left shoulder and elbow went numb for days. I went to a chiropractor who told me to listen to Mozart for an hour a day in my right ear and it would reconnect the circuitry in my left side within a week. "What if it doesn't?" I asked him. Not "*Why?*" I went with "*What if it doesn't?*" This is why I'm a producer, not a journalist. The chiropractor had an answer. "If it doesn't, you get to listen to Mozart for a week." So, I did. Took three days.

"You don't knock?"

"Would you have heard me, Mr. Siegel?"

"What?"

"Let's turn the music down."

"Fine," he said.

"I didn't figure you for a Mozart man."

He spun the volume knob to the left like he was pouring out bad milk. "I don't program the radio station, Traub."

One of the things I'm working on is not hanging around to talk with people who don't want to talk to me. That's going well. The other side of that, not hanging around to listen to people I don't want to listen to, that's not going well. But you know that already. You heard what happened with Travis. "Okay then, Mr. Siegel," I said. "Maybe I'll go to my mom's apartment and see what we have to do. I just came by to see if you had a ride to the funeral tomorrow or if you wanted to talk."

I started to leave when Sy Siegel sniffed, "That's nice of you, Traub."

"Well, you were nice enough to call me."

"Come on," he said. "We'll sit in the kitchen."

The kitchen was the same size and layout as my mother's, but with two noticeable differences. There was only one chair-backed stool by the eat-in counter, which I was motioned to.

And my mother did not leave the door of the microwave open so she could have easy access to the dictionary inside.

Sy opened his harvest gold refrigerator and pulled out a tri-colored, four-tiered parfait glass of Jell-O that looked less like dessert and more like the prototype for Tom Ridge's terror alert chart.

"Jell-O?"

"No thanks."

"Sure?"

"Yes."

"Come on," he said, tilting the glass to catch the sunlight that wasn't there and have it reflect off the plumb-dead symmetrical layers of red, orange, lime, red. "It's Jell-O..."

Wait. Maybe it was strawberry, orange, lime, raspberry. Is it any wonder my mom had been nuts about him?

"Mr. Siegel, that is really gorgeous. But I'm going to have to pass."

Sy Siegel slammed the refrigerator door shut and stormed off into the next room, muttering, "Big Harvard man won't eat my Jell-O." I thought that might have been my cue to leave, but he came back shortly, dragging a small cane chair that he angled against the dishwasher just right so he would be speaking directly into my waist.

He wiped his eyes a few times and I waited. For what? An explanation? We must have sat there ten minutes. Finally, Sy stepped on my foot, not lightly, and said, "Why?" I was torn between "*It was an accident,*" and "*It was her time*" and luckily I didn't have to say either. His foot eased up for a second, just resting on top of mine, but here again came the pressure, and he said, "Why...don't you look like her?"

"I look like my old man."

"I saw your old man. You don't look like him."

"Not lately." What was I going to say? "My sister Alison looks like my mom."

"Traub, I've seen your sister. Not a match. The board goes back."

"Did you just quote a line from the old game show *Concentration?*" I asked, fully intending to use it the next chance I got. Maybe the eulogy...

Sy got off my foot and stood up. "I'm sorry if I startled you by not being some detached, crackpot Marxist all the time."

"Mr. Siegel, I loved it. I might cop that line tomorrow. Don't worry, I'll credit you."

He looked at me, and I realized that I had been listening too carefully to what Sy Siegel had been saying to ever look up and identify if he was angry or confused. "I don't fathom you, Traub," he began. "Your mother is dead. It was an accident, but I was there."

"I'm glad you were."

"Are you that fucking sophisticated?"

A man like Sy Siegel really shouldn't curse, but I let it go. I needed to hear myself answer his question.

"No, Mr. Siegel, I'm not. But this is where we are. What happened, happened to you. I know me, and I'll be dealing with it on the drive back to New York." *How did I know that? I know it's true, but how did I know that right then?* "But that is days away. I got the eulogy and dealing with the apartment. And being another guy without a mother. That's a big club."

"And not a restricted club," he said.

I stood up, laughing, and put my hands on his unfrail shoulders. "Now, who's sophisticated?"

He slumped back in the small cane chair and started crying.

"Do you want me to stay?" I asked. He shook his head. "Want me to come back in an hour or so after I look through her stuff?" He nodded. "Want to hear a humiliating story about me at Harvard when I come back?"

Sy Siegel took his hand away from his face and looked up. "Very much so."

VII

D ID I HEAR A cat on my way out of Sy's apartment?
This is not important, except it would make me feel
better. I don't feel bad right now, and I won't until I walk into
my mother's place and try to figure out where to start. So, I
have about thirty seconds. It would make me feel better to know
Sy Siegel was not alone, and that he had retained a pet despite
being involved with Gwen Traub, one of the preeminent cat-
haters of the Postmodern Era.

My mother hated cats for two reasons, and if you asked her
for any more, she would say, "That's all I need." The global reason
she hated cats (and this is only the domestic variety) was simple:
When a cat enters a room, it commands everyone's attention
and ends adult conversation. She felt the same way about infants,
but when pressed, she would diplomatically blame the parent for
bringing the kid in. The only instance, incidentally, in which she
would blame a parent.

The specific reason was uttered once. When my sister Alison
was about to turn ten, she asked for a kitten for her birthday. My
mother said it was out of the question.

"Are you allergic, Mom?" I asked, as any provocative twelve-year-old would.

"I wish I was," she said. "No. Twenty years ago, when your father and I started seeing each other, we spent the weekend at the Schlays in Scituate. Well, we got up Sunday morning and all I wanted to do was sit on their porch after breakfast and do the puzzle in the *Times*. I put the magazine down for one second and that cat of theirs, Mitzy or Bitzy, flopped on it and wouldn't get off. And if anyone got close, you got such a scratch. Your father and I had to go back into town, but they were sold out."

That was it. Gwen Traub never so much as smiled at a cat after that. She also claimed never to have used a public restroom, but who can check?

Shit, I have to call Alison. The cops had left the door unlocked. I grabbed the phone in the kitchen rather than fumble for my cell.

"Hello?"

"It's Charlie. I totally fucked up. I completely forgot about this. Mom wants to be buried with HER family."

"I know. It's done."

"Really? She told me in complete confidence when Dad died. Made me promise."

"Yeah," said Alison. "I made the same promise to her. And so did the mortician, Brezniak, as she was leaving the cemetery."

"What did Brezniak say?"

"'Gwen, it's not supah cawmmon, but fah you, it's a lawk.'" Who knew she could nail the Boston accent?

"Whew," I giggled. "And what did he say?"

"Charlie, I'm not doing the accent again."

"Sorry."

"You in the apartment?"

"Yeah."

"How does it look?"

"I just got in. Some water on the carpet. I'll try to start an inventory. We'll whack everything up later."

"I did the inventory yesterday," she huffed. What did I tell you about Alison?

"Lovely. Well then, I guess it's nap time for me."

"Fine. Is Jennifer coming?"

"I don't know."

"Well, what did she say?"

"What?"

"Jesus, Charlie, did you make any calls?"

"Just this one. To tell you I was going to call Brezniak and get his boys to dig another hole at the cemetery in Quincy. But I guess it's done. What was the line, again?"

"Christ, what the fuck is with you?" Alison's voice began to teeter. "Call your ex-wife. And tell Sy he better get his shit out when I'm not there." Big inhale before she threw up a last-second heave, "And blot the carpet with a towel." *Click.* A lot of tribes say "goodbye."

By the way, I am happy to answer the question "What the fuck is with you?" when it is not meant rhetorically.

The last time I had spoken with Jennifer may have been when she said, "I like this guy" about Travis. Well, did I have a story to tell her now about her guy. If only it involved someone other than Bonnie Dressler.

You already know that Jennifer always got along with my mother. She was as reverent in front of her as she was blisteringly insightful behind her back. She used to say, "Can you see your mother going into the bathroom and putting on lipstick before Clinton gives the State of the Union?" Now that you mentioned it, yes, I could. But only her bathroom... Ha! Great. That's two things I can't bring up.

I threw a towel down on the carpet and blotted up the water left from when whoever had pulled my mother out of the shower and loaded her onto whatever I had been spared from seeing. Which would be the third thing I won't talk about with Jennifer. I looked through the refrigerator and found an apple, a small wedge of Brie, and enough V-8 to make myself an exceedingly generous mix-in-the-bottle-then-shake-vigorously Bloody Mary.

"This is not a tough call," I hear myself say. I believe this, and am an apple, a wedge of cheese, and a Bloody Mary away from being its disciple. This is not a tough call because we are no longer married.

For all of her years of passion and service to an array of noble causes, Jennifer Bright (She's Jennifer Lindmiller now. No, Lindenmiller. No, Lindenmuller. Never took my name, which made a lot of the divorce paperwork easier.) was more than Bright enough to know she was no match for the power of honest fantasy. Or unbidden fantasy, honestly related. Or bidden fantasy, recapped with thoughtless candor.

Now, you can ask, and you probably have, "So, that was it? *Bonnie Dressler...thought perhaps...blow job...pack a bag?* You mean saying something stupid is now grounds for divorce?" Jennifer was not Mr. Siegel. She didn't want a humiliating story about me. And if I didn't know that after almost twenty years of marriage, what promise lay in knowing it now? So, what do you do? Go to your girlfriends and sob, "I can't believe it. All these years, and my husband's been telling me the truth." You can't. You can't because if you're Jennifer, you don't have those kind of girlfriends. You tell your husband to leave, and a month later, you work up the guts to tell him it was the right decision. And he doesn't disagree with you because he doesn't disagree with you. And he doesn't disagree with you.

Let's try that again. She told me to leave, and a month later, she had the courage to tell me she had made the right decision. And I didn't disagree with her because I didn't disagree with her. And, as I learned later from Dr. Waldman, I did NOT disagree with her.

So, yes, saying something stupid is grounds for divorce. Especially if you have no children. Twenty-two years together, nineteen married. No children. No accident. No coincidence.

"You were married nineteen years and never had children. I have to ask why." Travis would have to ask near the end of every other session for the first few months.

"Never wanted them." I would always answer.

"Why?"

"We just wanted to be with each other."

"Well," he'd exhale into his glasses, "I believe you. So," he would look for something to wipe the fog off, "where's Jennifer?" Drove me fucking nuts.

And he might have kept asking me if I hadn't one day answered, "Where's Jennifer? She's gone, Chief. Get over it. I have. This ain't about her." I probably should have just got up right then, shook his hand, thrown my coat over my arm and headed out. But to where? To start over? Start what? Over what? So I stayed, and Dr. Waldman and I went to work on the sink full of dirty dishes that was my unexamined need for harmony. Sure, every once in a while Travis would interrupt for a wildly non-pertinent parable, like the woman in the concentration camp who kept swallowing and shitting diamonds for four years so the guard wouldn't find then. But mostly, we stayed on point.

Mostly. The dishes-in-the-sink analogy is not some gem I just unearthed. I made the reference three months ago, with at least ten minutes left in the session, and Dr. Waldman said, "That's an interesting phrase, Charlie. You paint a vivid picture, and I'd like to pursue it further, but it reminds me of a joke, and we have just enough time for the joke..." And off he went:

A man buys a motorcycle from his cousin. He knows the motorcycle is ten years old, but it shines like it's brand new. The man says, "How do you keep this motorcycle in such great condition?" His cousin says, "Well, since you're buying it, I'll tell you. Every time it rains, cover the motorcycle with Vaseline. That way it will never tarnish, it will always look brand new and will last you a thousand years. Just remember, every time it rains, cover the motorcycle with Vaseline." So, the guy hops on his new bike, goes to pick up his girlfriend. Now, they're on their way to the girlfriend's parents' house for his first dinner with the parents. Before they get there, the girlfriend says, "Look, we have a little rule in my house. Anybody who talks during dinner has to do the dishes." The man figures it's a little strange, but he'll go along with it. So, they get to the house and walk in. There's dishes on the floor. There's cups and saucers hanging from the ceiling. There's bowls and plates with food caked in them. There's one room just filled with dirty silverware. Dishes have been wallpapered over, carpeted over. The dishes have not been done in this house since World War II. So, they sit down to eat. The guy is looking at his girlfriend, and he's real horny. He figures, hey, nobody's talking anyway, grabs his girlfriend, rips off her clothes, throws her on the table and in front of the mother and the father, fucks the girlfriend right on the table. Nobody says a word. So, they keep eating. The guy's still horny. He figures, hey, the mother looks pretty good—grabs the mother, rips off the mother's clothes, throws the mother on the table and in front of the father and the girlfriend, fucks the mother right *there on the table. Nobody says a peep. Now, they're having coffee. He looks out the window. He sees it's starting to rain. It's starting to rain all over his new motorcycle. The man jumps up and says, "Hey, does anybody have any Vaseline?" And the father says, "All right. I'LL do the dishes!"*

THAT WAS WHEN I began to think that our sessions had become a little too conversational. As for the need for harmony, mine is no longer unexamined, just under-resolved. Come on, look at me. Here I am, sitting at my dead mother's desk, calling my ex-wife's house in Alexandria, Virginia, with the perfect words to say to the answering machine.

But someone named Bettina picked up the phone. "I'm the nanny," she said. I think I knew about that. I think. No, I knew. They had adopted a year ago. Mom told me and I reacted like she had said the Celtics had just acquired Raef LaFrentz. I introduced myself and told Bettina I needed her to hang up and let the machine pick up, but not before giving me the name, age and, if the name was new-millennium odd, the sex of whoever she was taking care of.

Jennifer's voice was on the outgoing message. *It's Jennifer... and Morris. And of course, we're screening your call...* When did she get so funny? *Beep.*

"Hi, it's Charlie. Funny message. When did you get so funny? Forget it. I know the answer... I'm calling to tell you that Gwen died. Yesterday. The funeral is tomorrow morning. Don't even think about coming up. I'm just telling you because I thought you'd get a kick out of the fact that she's being buried with her family in Quincy. No, this is me calling to thank you for getting along with her all those years as few women could. Or men. She was really fond of y–"

I got cut off before I could finish the perfect message, which would have been something like, "So, thanks. *Say hi to Morris, and kiss, uh, Gretel for me. The nanny told me her name...*" I was about to call back, but that was cut off as well. By Sy Siegel shuffling past the open door and yelling, "I know you want to take a swing at me. Go ahead!" I stuffed the phone in my pocket and stood up in time to catch him lunging at me, eyes and nose red from scouring his face with a handkerchief or a piece of paper towel.

I moved him back to a chair, like a cut man. "If you keep doing shit like this, Mr. Siegel, you're not going to get the Harvard story. Now, what time do you want me to pick you up for the funeral tomorrow?"

"I have a ride."

"Somebody from here? One of Mom's friends?"

"No. A former student of mine."

"You were a teacher?"

"Professor, you little shit." I don't know why, but for some reason, that made a lump in my throat.

"What did you teach, or profess?"

"Perception."

I nodded to stifle a laugh while Sy Siegel pulled a folded piece of paper out of his pocket.

"I thought," he said as he handed it to me. "I thought, well, in case the boy could use a trenchant piece of verse tomorrow."

I opened up the note. Read the line. Here comes the lump's big brother. "Thank you, Professor," I choked out.

He waved with his back to me when I called after him in the hall to ask if he knew how to get to the funeral home or that the cemetery was all the way out in Quincy. I'll slip the address under his door later. I'll write it on the other side of the piece of paper he just gave me. I know he'll want it back.

Sy Siegel had handed me the wrong note. I'm sure he had jotted down some appropriate lines of elegy from Horace, Lincoln, or Paul Robeson. Somewhere. Somewhere else. But on this piece of paper, retraced in bold ballpoint, were just three words: Get cat food.

Get cat food.

I don't know. Maybe I'm in shock because I'm standing in my dead mother's house. Maybe I'm distracted because my ex-shrink is fucking a woman I told him about in session. Maybe I'm delusional because I decided I want to be John Feinstein without accepting that the position has already been filled—by John Feinstein.

You know what? It's none of that. I'm okay. A little tired. There is nothing to delve into right now. Leave the delving to the delvers. Sure, I have things to do. The things that are in front of me. Clear Sy's stuff out of my dad's bedroom. Bullet-point the eulogy. Take a nap. Reread Sy's note.

Get cat food.

For someone in his third month of trying to lead a non-psychological life, is there a more succinct notion of what that life is than "Get cat food"?

Chop wood, carry water, get cat food. I want to run after Sy Siegel and break the news to him that he's a Buddhist. Instead, I lie down. On my mother's bed. Which, for the moment, is just a bed.

ε

How does ten and a half hours of sleep sound?

And I would have kept going if a dream hadn't awakened me. Pretty straight forward. A woman was yelling at me. Right up in my face. So, I bit off her nose. Felt good for a second, then I was terrified she'd sue me and I'd lose everything. Did the woman look familiar? Perhaps, but once they lose a nose, they could be anybody. Not a match, the board goes back.

It's just after five in the morning. My only interpretation of the dream is that it was my alarm clock. I scrambled the four eggs left in the Gwen Traub Estate refrigerator and then got the luggage cart outside the maintenance locker room in the basement. The cart was five years past rickety, but Windgate Point needed to keep it around and wheel it past potential residents who thought they might be moving into a hotel rather than a facility that required a $50,000 deposit and a soft cough. I figured I'd stack Sy's cartons and give one of the porters a head start and save on tip money. Push the rack back upstairs to Mr. Siegels's apartment, *por favor?* Ten should do it. I guess I was still worried that the woman in the dream was planning on suing me.

I only loaded five or so boxes. So, I'll be into the porter for twenty. I had cleared enough space to sit on my father's bed and eat my eggs with the plate resting on the last carton at the foot of the bed. All the other boxes had been slavishly labeled: "Letters to Commentary (1974-89)," "Correspondence with Students I (1947-65)," "Worthy and Unworthy SS Verse," "Tax Returns (missing 1967, 1969, 1975-1981, 1996-present)," "Owl Club Ruling/Settlement (1972)."

That's right, the Owl Club. One of the exclusive male-only final clubs at Harvard. The son of a bitch went to Harvard! That he was involved in my mother's accidental death, that I can let slide. That he's a hypocrite, well, now we have a problem. The kind of problem I relish. I will wait to confront Sy Siegel on this. Say, ten minutes after we get back from the burial. He'll be exhausted, and I should finally have an intellectual edge.

The last carton is unmarked and much less academic looking. I didn't move it because I'm pretty sure it might belong to my father. It is a square, unflapped white corrugated cardboard case emblazoned with the bloody red shield that was the unofficial Traub family crest: Smirnoff. I am not an archaeologist, but I would carbon-date the box circa 1979. Just a shot. I remember my parents making the move to Stolichnaya just after Reagan's first inauguration. Or in response.

It looked like the kind of box I had kept my albums in at prep school before I switched to the much more serviceable plastic handled Hood Milk crate for my four decidedly non-Owl Club years at Harvard. It took me however long that period lasts when curiosity flips to rage to cut through the homemade-bomb tape job on three sides of the top edge of the box. Was Ducky Traub ever that nuts? Surely my dad must have wrapped one gift in his life or taken one trip to the post office. This was the work of an amateur archivist, and much too inaccessible for Sy Siegel's filing system.

Wrong again.

Sitting on top of a stack of old issues of *Sports Illustrated*, newspaper clippings, and Red Sox yearbooks was a letter stamped "Return to Sender" and Sy Siegel's old address in Brighton. The letter had originally been sent in April 1981 to a television station in San Francisco, KRON. Its intended recipient had been Tony Conigliaro. Former Red Sox outfielder Tony Conigliaro. The top of the envelope had been gashed by a letter opener, sparing me of consulting the moral compass I never carried at six in the morning.

Dear Mr. Conigliaro,

I am a former Harvard professor and published author teaching folklore and mass psychology at Simmons College, just down the street from Fenway Park.

I have followed your star-crossed career avidly and have always thought your story, your definitive story, more than merited a book. Not just some jock hagiography, but a scholarly examination of what has happened in the 14 years since your injury and the six years since you played your last game.

While I believe that what occurred on the night of August 18, 1967 was a tragic accident, I also believe that what befell you three years before that night and in the decade that followed was a medical malpractice cabal financed by the Red Sox, Major League Baseball, organized crime, and the plastics industry.

Of course, your participation in this project would be invaluable. That said, I can understand if my approach is too unflinching and the psycho-serendipitous turmoil of what I might unearth be too unappetizing for your hand to willingly grip the spade. Either way, a few academic presses are interested, and I plan to proceed. I am sure you are aware of the esteem in which New England holds you. That may warm you like a windbreaker as you read local scores in the Bay Area. But trust me, you have no idea how much of a hero you could be.

I await your response like a belt-high 3-1 fastball.

Sincerely,
Sy Siegel
Professor/Activist

Ɛ

IT IS NOW 8:00 A.M. and the porter, Enrique, just knocked on the apartment door. I tell him to store the luggage cart and everything else downstairs for twenty-four hours, then unload it in front of Mr. Siegel's apartment, all while stuffing two twenties into his shirt. He hugged me and said he was sorry he was never able to teach "Mrs. Gwen" how to work the cable remote. There may be a tear or two on the on the lapel of my dark suit. It could be sweat.

In less than an hour, I had emptied my dad's bedroom and set the loaded luggage cart, the bridge table, chairs and Canon copier in the hallway outside the door, awaiting Enrique. It took five minutes to run up to Sy's apartment and post a note with directions to the Brezniak-Rodman funeral home in Newton. It's much too cold for anyone other than me, Alison, and the rabbi to make the cemetery. When I came back, there was another ten minutes looking in one carton on the luggage cart to confirm what I already knew. That Sy Siegel hadn't gone to Harvard, but his teaching career there ended shortly after he threatened to sue the Owl Club for dithering on admitting a Jewish student, a Varsity Crew coxswain named Daniel Winereb. By 7:30, I had pulled my dad's bed from out against the wall and my lower back from out between lumbar disks No. 4 and 5. The hot shower helped a little. I put on the dark suit and may have reaggravated the injury pulling up my zipper. I do things like that.

No, that's wrong.

I wrenched my back before all that, walking barefoot in the underground parking lot and balancing my car keys in one hand as I loaded the Smirnoff box into the trunk, then spun quickly when I thought I heard someone. The spin did it.

But you know what? Bring on the pain. I have Tony Conigliaro safely locked in the rented Impala. Tony C.

I can be John Feinstein.

VIII

GOOD MORNING.

I don't want to frighten anyone, but when I walked by the casket just now, I'm pretty sure I heard my mom say, "How's the house?"

The house is good, Mom.

Thanks everyone for coming out this morning, braving the cold weather and trying to find parking on Washington Street during the holiday shopping season. Mom, I know you can hear me. I had to circle the block three times. You're better off here.

Thanks for laughing. It means a lot. Especially today.

I, uh, I lost my gig.

If you ask my mother—and go ahead, ask her—she'll tell you that I have been making her laugh since I was one and a half. She'll swear the first complete sentence I ever uttered was, "I gotta get outta here!" If I live to be a hundred, I'll never come up with anything half as good as that.

Gwendoline Zimmerman Traub didn't live to be a hundred. She fell six weeks short of eighty. Whew, that was close. If you know anything about Gwen Traub, if you ever stood off to the side for one moment—in a tee box, on a driving range, in a fairway, never in the rough—and saw her take that slow, perfect backswing, stop a half-second at the top as if to pose for someone making a mold for a trophy, then uncoil in measured fury and joy at a hapless golf ball, you know that eighty is an unacceptable number. Three years ago, she walked onto Sterling Acres in early May, maybe half a dozen rounds under her belt for the season, and shot her age. Seventy-six. Shot. Her. Age. When she told me, in an almost mumbled aside, the way she always delivered good news about herself, I was thrilled. "What did Dad say?" I asked. My father Ducky was on his way out, but certain outside stimuli could still rocket him back to the here and now. Taming Sterling Acres in seventy-six blows would do it. "What did Dad say when you told him?"

My mom harrumphed. "Him? Your fahtha? He said, 'Gee. It must be nice to play alone.'" And then she laughed. She laughed the laugh she lived to give up. And the laugh I lived to get. That was my gig. I lost it.

My last shrink called me an Oedipal winner. By the way, I'm cured now. I'm not sure exactly what that phrase means. Oedipal winner. I haven't poked my eyes out. I ain't blind, but I might as well be. I know precious little about my mother. Like most doted-upon children, I assumed she sprang fully formed from the head of Zeus, or David Ben-Gurion, nine months and a week before giving birth to me. Not true. I'll tell you what I know. The best part of delivering a eulogy is that the deceased gets no time for rebuttal.

Gwen Zimmerman was born February 7, 1927, in Milton, the fifth of six children, to George and Betty Zimmerman. Her father rode steerage from Austria to Ellis Island at the age of six, and by the time he was nine, he had saved enough money to open his first paper mill in Turners Falls. Three years later, at the age of twelve, he hired Betty Levinthal as a bookkeeper. They were married ten days after that, and for the next four decades concentrated on the paper business before starting a family. That's the story. Who are we to dispute it?

My entire childhood was filled with tales of Grandpa George. By the time I was aware of him, he was eighty-nine, chewing up meat and then throwing it under the table. I barely knew anything about my Grandma Betty until two years ago, when Gwen Zimmerman Traub looked out the window at Windgate Point and told me, "I loved my mother even before I knew she was my mother. My brothers and sisters tell me when I was six months old, she walked into the living room, and I crawled off my nanny's lap and yelled, 'Mama!'"

I have no original material. This is my long way of saying that, thanks to her, I now know I loved my mother before I knew she was my mother.

Gwen Traub leaves with one defeat on her record. Did you know she was turned down for admission to her number one choice of college, Sarah Lawrence, because they didn't accept Jews back then? So, she was forced to settle...for Radcliffe.

She was always the smartest person in the room. She still is. She could parry with authority about history, literature, art, politics. Especially politics. One night shortly after I got out of school, I came home to visit her. I had finished working on my third campaign, third losing campaign, and breathlessly told her I had decided to run for office one day soon. I was going to do it. And Gwen Traub, first female officer in the Massachusetts chapter of Americans for Democratic Action, volunteer and serial donor to Jack Kennedy's first run for Congress, cohost of a weekly radio show with former Governor Chub Peabody's wife, the same Gwen Traub smiled and said, "Why would you want to do that? So you could win and then be in charge of an employment agency?"

Do I need to tell you that I never ran for office?

Speaking of the radio, eight years ago, I was on a local morning show talking about political ideology and the media. I know what you're thinking, *How do they come up with these unexplored topics?* I came in the day before and set mom's radio to the right station. I did the interview in the studio, forty-five minutes. Forty-six, if you count all the phone calls we had to take. Again, I stopped by the house before heading to Logan to catch the shuttle back to Washington. Forty-four years old and still desperate for the early reviews. "What did you think, Mom?" I asked. "Well," she said, "I enjoyed the first few minutes, but then you started talking about people I didn't know, so I shut it off."

Did I mention I had been in therapy and was cured?

Maybe I *was* cured. What now, now that I lost my gig?

I aspired to her level of knowledge, wit, and chase-cutting candor. It was the noblest and least attainable of pursuits. So, I made her laugh. She would want me to quote Goethe or Cervantes or Keats today, and I would want to quote them as well. Who wouldn't strive to be the intellectual she was? But the line I keep thinking of comes from Sue Anne Nivins, the Happy Homemaker played by Betty White on *The Mary Tyler Moore Show*. The cast is gathered for the funeral of Chuckles the Clown, when Georgette, Ted Baxter's wife, whispers, "I don't understand why people send flowers to a funeral." And Sue Anne Nivins pipes up, "Well, what would you suggest they send, dear, fruit?"

Whew. What happened? Did everybody leave? That line killed on the drive up from New York. Of course, I was alone.

Eight years ago, I got divorced. That's right, ladies, I'm available. The reasons were, as they always are for two people who had been together almost twenty years with no children, both complicated and uniquely un-unique. When I told my mother (this time I didn't stop by the house) that Jennifer and I were splitting up, she needed less than no time to fasten the button of her thoughts. "You know," she said, "she never forgave me for crying at the wedding."

"Mom," I said. "I was there. You didn't cry at the wedding."

"Is that right?" she replied. "Well, then that was probably it."

That, by the way, is the only example I could come up with of Gwen Traub being mistaken. I am aware of the stories that I was in and almost nothing else, and it is too late to ask. Too late. And I thought my timing was good. But that's the way my mother wanted it and I was too willing to oblige. She knew everything and felt nothing out loud, and that was wasted on me.

Wait. Now I am mistaken. One night when I was sixteen, mom and I were watching the film *Downhill Racer*. It is safe to tell you this now, but she had a gigantic crush on Robert Redford. If they had invented stalking during the 1970s instead of the 90s, she might have dropped golf and taken that up in his cause. But there we were, in the den, watching the scene where Robert Redford's character, an Olympic skier named David Chappell, goes home to Idaho Springs, to visit his father, a poor dirt farmer. They're in the kitchen and it's a stilted, tense half-a-conversation. Robert Redford spends most of the time eating the last crumbs of a box of Ritz crackers. For me, that move was very distracting and ruined what might have been an important scene. At the end of the scene, because I felt that way, and probably more because I saw a rival for my mother's affections, I said, "Jesus, what a terrible actor." And she stood up, turned off the TV and said, "He comes home, all he wants is the approval of his father, and all that's there is a box of Ritz crackers!" And she slammed the door on her way out. So, scratch the part about feeling nothing out loud.

Three months after she shot the seventy-six, my dad passed away. My mom played alone for a while. It wasn't nice. Depending on what calendar you use, she had taken care of him for five years or fifty-five years. So, talk about losing one's gig, here was the reigning champ. I'm sure I could have been much more sympathetic, more compassionate in the aftermath of dad's death, but I guess those qualities do not lie among the spoils of being an Oedipal winner. All I cared about was my version of harmony. My gig. She would stop laughing, or she wouldn't start, and it would be time for me to get off the phone. "Ma, you okay? Good. All right, call you next week..." Luckily, she found Sy, who was caring, stimulating, and more than a match for her in intelligence, independence, and fierce wit. Maybe that's when I lost my gig.

Sy was there at her sudden end. To call my mother's death an accident is to call intimacy an accident and to dismiss passion as a fluke. I respectfully disagree.

Thank you, Sy. For all you did, and all you would have done.

So now, she's back with Ducky. I think. I hope. And I'm jealous because I can't hear them talk. That was the great joy of being their son.

Once I realized they weren't talking about me, I relaxed and enjoyed it. I spent a lot of my youth in a bedroom a wall away late at night, with my face jammed into the pillow so they wouldn't hear me laughing. I knew I was funny, but they were always funnier. Here's an exchange I heard one night, while I was home on vacation from prep school. I wrote it down and kept it for the last thirty-seven years. I never knew why. Evidence, I guess. For legal reasons, the speaker is not identified.

"You'll never guess who I saw today."

"Who?"

"Marty Callahan."

"Ugh. Did he have any idea where he was?"

"No." (rasping, snorting sound)

"You look like Jerry Nachburg."

"My new best friend."

"Good luck to him."

"You know who's a complete dumbbell?"

"Who?"

"Merle Kaniznick."

"Don't you think she's more of a simp?"

"Why? Because of Lenny?"

"Yes."

"He's a bad guy."

"He's a thug."

"Yeah. The worst."

"Well, you two used to be big pals."

"I think you're confusing me with you."

"No, that's something you're famous for."

"Well, you better stay away from him."

"Lenny?"

"Yeah."

"But I saw Merle."

"Well, where do you think Merle is going after she sees you?"

"Merle has no idea where she's going."

"Speaking of which, are we going to this thing Wednesday?"

"We're supposed to."

"Jees, how come?"

"How do you expect me to answer that?"

"Well, what are we supposed to do?"

"It's a cocktail party."

"Ugh."

"All your buddies are going to be there."

"Who?"

"Marvin and Belle, Lou and Anita, Harry and Eilene."

"Those are your buddies."

"Since when?"

"Since I saw you talking to them."

"When did I ever talk to any of those slobs?"

"Calling them slobs is not going to change anything."

"You're being very protective of your friends."

"Said the person who accepted the invitation."

"When?"

"Wednesday night."

"Oh, you mean to the thing that somebody said, 'Marvin, do you need us there early?'"

"I was saying that as a joke for you."

"Good one."

"Didn't you see me wink at you?"

"No, I missed that. I was too busy trying to stay away from Sharon."

"Grossman?"

"No, Felkin."

"What did she want?"

"Who knows. 'Well, my daughtah, dih-dih-dih, and then my son, dih-dih-dih, and then we took the two ferrets up to Connecticut, dih-dih-dih.'"

"Did she have the teeth going?"

"That's what I was doing."

"You used to do it better."

"Well, maybe I feel sorry for her."

"You know, I feel sorry for her, but—"

"Don't waste your time."

"Speaking of wasting your time, you know who was standing behind me in the bank?"

"Who?"

"Chuck"

"How'd that go?"

"How do you think? I'm ill."

"That's funny. I heard you two had gotten very chummy."

"From who? One of your friends?"

"I heard you two were cooking up something big together."

"I think you've been spending too much time with those people you hear things from."

"Well, you seem to drop everything when they're around."

"Yeah, like Denny Gilmartin?"

"Did he join the club?"

"Sure. Thanks to all the business you gave him."

"I gave him? You called him."

"I called him, but he saw you coming."

"Well, he was in the pro shop buying the ugliest shirt they have from your buddy, Jackie."

"My buddy? Hey, I'm not the one he let return those club covers."

"You should have seen the two of them. The brainpower as they tried to figure out what size it was."

"Or what day it was."

"Forget that."

"Which shirt was it?"

"It was a Norman Wickman original."

"The one he wore at the Member-3 Guest?"

"No, after."

"That's what I mean."

"Yeah, but in powder blue."

"When did he get so smooth?"

"When he hooked up with your best best pal, Jackie."

"You're not going to let me forget the raffle tickets, are you?"

"Give me one more year."

GEE, I THOUGHT THAT would go much better...

I will miss her terribly, but I have to wonder if for me, my mother's death is the ultimate acquisition of harmony. I pray that she finds a corner of happiness in that corner of heaven where she can pick her head up from the *Sunday Times* puzzle or a never-published work of Naipaul, take a sip from the glass of vodka that has no bottom, and look down at all of us long enough that we feel her gaze, and we can look back up and say, "Ma, I got the funniest story to tell you."

I guess it'll have to wait.

Thanks for listening. My sister Alison also prepared something... Where'd she go?

IX

YOU HAVE TO BELIEVE me, I never saw Travis. I never saw him while I was up there, watching my eulogy carom off the walls of the main chapel at Brezniak-Rodman Funeral Home. I looked out, but committed none of the fifty or so faces who stared at me to memory, their slacked mouths waiting for something, anything they might recognize about the woman they knew. The woman they had shown up for. Not this attention-eating creature I had built in the spare room above my right mind. Couldn't place anyone in the audience. None of them looked familiar. Not even the three or four I had mentioned BY NAME in that reenacted transcript of my parents' bedtime evisceration of their fellow members at Piney Lea Country Club. I didn't see my sister Alison leave, but you already know that. The rabbi and a few others used the phrase "storm out," but is it really a true storm out if you don't hear heels clicking against carpet? And if the husband doesn't leap up and follow her out? Boy, is that guy in trouble. Jonathan. I wouldn't want to be him. I never saw Travis until I had finished all my apologies. That's right. A twist on tradition. All the mourners lined up, and I had to apologize to them. *"Of course she was lovely. I was trying to convey that. I'm* sorry if it came across otherwise. I'm sorry you don't share my sense of humor. Yes, yes I believe if she was alive she would have been laughing. Yes, perhaps it was fortunate that she wasn't. Well, I think turning over in one's grave is just an expression..."

Sy smiled. Through the whole thing. It might have been his joy at being the least uncomfortable person in the room. It might have been my shout-out at the end, with a side of exoneration and a hat-tip to still being able to get his freak on in the shower. It might have been the attractive fortyish brunette who sat with him, locked her arm inside his and judiciously held him back until all the ill-wishers had put their objections on record, received their regrets, then regifted them to Alison.

"Maybe if you'd come by more, you would have seen she wasn't like that."

"I hope your son has better manners."

"Couldn't keep it in your pants, could you?"

"I'm Merle Kaniznick. I'd rather be dumb than mean."

"I'm Norman Wickman. I never wore powder blue in my life. It was Ducky who wore fag shit like that."

"Gwen used to say how funny you were. What happened?"

"My name is Anita Wishner. My so-called slob husband Lou couldn't make it. He's dead. Have a nice day."

"Hey, sonny, can I ask you something? Why didn't you just yell 'Hey, they were fucking in the shower!' What, all of sudden you have tact?"

ℰ

CAN I TELL YOU something? Nothing anybody said landed. Although I apologized to every one of them, by the third complainant, I had stopped trying to set the record straight about my remarks. Two reasons. Every time I began to even think about feeling badly, I would look over and see Sy, arm locked with the pretty brunette, using his free arm to wave the next dissatisfied mourner though and conduct a mythical band. The Righteously Indignant Philharmonic. And I was too distracted by Travis, who hung back by the entrance to the chapel, leaning against a wall, cleaning his fingernails with the edge of a business card, as if waiting to pick up an envelope of cash because I had lost a bet on my mom. Over eighty and a half.

When the last one of Gwen Traub's Windgate Point neighbors and the old friends Alison had called (those local contemporaries who can't read the label on a cereal box but can make out the **Helios** bold type of a death notice) had about-faced their walkers or been promenaded by their aides toward the elevator, Sy Siegel quick-stepped up. He hugged me and said, loud, "Don't listen to these diasporantic dilettantes. They're all playing checkers and you're playing chess... Well, we're playing chess. You nailed it. You rose to her level. I see it. You're not just some Harvard fairy pulling your pecker on the corner."

"Shhh! Jesus, Professor Siegel," the brunette weakly objected.

"I will not be silenced!" he whispered. "Traub, this is one of my former students, now a shyster. Polly, what's your handle now, Trombley?"

"No, Shyster." Pretty quick, this one. "Is your name Charlie Traub?" she asked.

"Yes."

"You know my sis—"

In the middle of this, Jonathan, Alison's husband, the guy I didn't want to be, ambled by against his will. "Alison—your sister—wants to know if you're coming to the cemetery."

"Why wouldn't I be going to the cemetery?"

"Charlie, give me a break here."

"Five minutes?"

"Make it ten. They're trying to clear everyone out of the parking lot before you leave."

Polly, who I wanted to hear more from, had marched Sy back a few paces when Jonathan came over. He yelled, "Watch it, Robespierre!" and she laughed and backed him up some more. And now I'm staring at her. She is petite and smoky with a well-thought out wedge of chocolate hair atop an expensive royal blue silk suit that she never wears as often as she'd like, so let's bust it out for a stranger's funeral. She is as playful with Sy as I thought might be possible, which is instantly arresting. And there is a familiarity to her, which I may have made up because she knew who I was. Tell you what I'm not making up: my mom's hearse is idling outside and I am...I am horny. I would like to tell Sy to keep Polly occupied until I get back from the burial to Windgate Point. What's that, an hour and a half, tops? Maybe more. I'll want to jump in the shower...

As far as I could see, Polly Trombley had one bad quality. She had backed Sy up too far. There was an opening.

"So, Mommy's gone."

"Hello, Travis."

"Hey, I'm an orphan, too!"

"Travis, what are you doing here?"

"I came to see how Charlie was holding up. How is Charlie holding up?"

"Charlie's okay. I mean, I'm okay."

"Is that your professional opinion?"

I needed a crowd. "Sy, Polly, this is Travis Waldman. My old shrink. Travis was about to tell me how he got here."

"Doc, can I ask you a question?" Sy said.

"Of course."

"Were all your socks destroyed in a fire?"

We all looked down, where Travis had crossed his feet at the ankles, first position, just enough to reveal that day's hosiery malfeasance—purple socks with five afroed silhouettes under the bold, bell-bottomed serifed seventies script that read "Good Times."

Travis waited for our heads to come up. "No. Why?"

"We had a couple of guys working on the Frank Sargent grant like you," Sy huffed.

"What do you mean 'like me?'"

One thousand-one...one thousand-two...one thousand-three...one thou—

"Pastel-driven," Sy replied. *Exhale omnes.*

Polly asked Sy if he'd like to sit down. I would have replaced "sit" with "lie," but that's just personal style. Man, I wish she would keep talking.

Sy held up a finger. "In a moment," he said. "First, I'd like to hear how this Briggs-Meyers troller managed to find out about Gwen in Manhattan. That's where your shingle wobbles, isn't it, Herr Doktor?"

"Total coincidence, Sy," said Travis. "Do you prefer Sy or Professor?"

"Professor," Polly and I answered for him.

"Okay, professor then. I came in yesterday to meet my girl—lady for dinner. She was running late, so I ended up reading the entire *Globe* in my car. I saw Gwen Traub in the notices." Travis nodded toward me. "Suddenly, huh?"

I think I said "Yeah" too loud. Then Travis put his hand on Sy's shoulder. "How about how this one doesn't blame you for what happened in the shower with his mommy? Do I do a good job, or what?"

I was still so lost on the word "lady," I collided my question. "So, you had dinner and spendayed the nover, stayed over?"

"Natch. By the way," Travis dipped his voice, "Ms. Dressler sends her regrets. But she had three student conferences this morning she couldn't get out of."

"Uh huh."

"And the last thing we all need here is more awkward."

"Uh huh." That was Polly.

"Especially you, Charlie. If you want, you and I could ride together to the cemetery. I've done sessions in stranger places. Or if you just want company."

"Excuse me." Polly again. "Travis?"

"Yes."

"You mentioned a Ms. Dressler. That wouldn't be Bonnie Dressler, would it?"

Travis underbit his top lip, a gesture of feigned embarrassment that you could hitherto only see on display in a community production of *Baby Doll*. "Why yes, it would be," he said, followed by the stage whisper to me, "So much for avoiding more awkward."

"Bonnie Dressler, the Simmons professor?" asked Polly.

"Who else?"

"Bonnie Dressler, who used to work with Charlie in Washington?"

"Polly, I don't think you're helping."

"Travis," she said, "Bonnie ain't here."

"You're telling me," he said.

"No, I mean she's not in the country."

"*Cómo?*" said Sy, which made me laugh until Polly shushed us both.

"Miss Trombley..."

Polly unlocked her arm from Sy, smoothed the royal blue silk suit and added ink to her eyes. "You need to stop talking,

Dr. Waldman. And it's Mrs. Trombley. Bonnie Dressler is in the Dominican Republic. On her honeymoon. She's been there almost two weeks."

"I'll take that seat now," said Sy.

"In a second, Sy. Bonnie married a developer she's been seeing for three years. Mark Hynes. Nice guy. I know all this because I was at the wedding. As her maid of honor."

She grabbed Sy, who wanted to be sophisticated enough not to teeter, but couldn't. "Charlie, little help here." We backed Sy into a chair while Travis did nothing but move the back of his left hand to rest under his chin. I didn't miss this move. Polly did because she had her back to Travis while setting Sy down. She still had her back to him and was a little winded as she continued. "I am also," she puffed, "Bonnie's sister. Polly Dressler Trombley." She swung around, petite arm extended. "Nice to meet you."

Travis dropped his left hand from his chin, as if the downward force would bring his right hand up to shake Polly's.

"Charlie!" someone yelled from the back of the chapel. Jonathan. "We're waiting."

"Need a minute here, Jonathan."

"Haven't you done enough today?"

"Wait!"

Polly withdrew her hand from Travis. "I am also," she said, "her lawyer."

The thought of killing a man in a funeral home in the presence of a lawyer and a witness, saving everyone a world of time and suffering crossed my mind only as in-flight entertainment. I am, by nurture, a coward. But you knew that before the eulogy, I'm sure. I did nothing but stare as I had been stared at minutes before. Then the moment was further lost to a monstrous throat-clearing cough, the kind of rumbling mucus Klaxon horn that was unheard in this country before it arrived via steerage in 1903, which was discharged from just behind Jonathan. We looked up.

"Folks," said the rabbi. "I don't mean to be indelicate, but I have a 2:30 in Brookline."

"We should go," said Travis. Polly grabbed his wrist as he turned.

"No," she said. "We should talk." And then to me, "Go." No need for a DNA swab. This was Bonnie Dressler's sister.

I turned to Sy. "You want to ride out to Quincy?"

He bounced up. His color was back. His mouth had never left. "Okay, Mac," he chuckled. "Your funeral."

X

I GRABBED ONE OF the floral arrangements on the way out. The plan was to throw it into the grave before we started shoveling. I would give that honor to Alison, a combination ceremonial first pitch and non-ceremonial attempt to coax a smile out of her. And it would. There is no more vivid communication between siblings than the unspoken. I would pull the flowers out from behind my back. Alison would hug the cache of carnations and lilies and whatever the hell else there was (in three decades of hurriedly sending flowers over the phone, I had yet to take note of what the sales rep listed was in the mix I had chosen. "Yeah yeah, great... Ready for my credit card?"), and she would instantly be reminded of two innate ardors: our mother's love of flowers and our father's love of presenting his wife with pilfered centerpieces.

Weddings, bar mitzvahs, award dinners, silent auctions, birthdays, tea dances, museum receptions, golf outings, people's friggin' homes. No vase or pot was safe around Ducky Traub. Even the health and beauty aid conventions he attended on the road, where he would jab a handful of anemones into an open-end of his carry-on bag so it would take one move to hold it in his teeth as he walked into the kitchen and said what he always said, just more clenched: "Dees ar fah you."

My dad had a couple of moves like that. Here's another: Forgetting Valentine's Day and running upstairs to put last year's card from my mom to him into an envelope, draw a heart that looked like a kidney, then hiding it somewhere in the refrigerator. By the third year, it's funny. By the fourth, a tradition. And you have no idea how cheap a Valentine's Day card is by February 15.

"These are for you." My dad never apologized. Never sought forgiveness. Just wore down those he loved into begrudged acceptance of him in manners alternately unapologetic and unforgiving. I just figured that out walking to the car.

I don't bother to examine why I am thinking so much about my dad on the way to bury my mother. As you know, I'm trying not to do that anymore. Besides, I don't have the time. I open the trunk of the rented Impala to toss in the flowers and I see the Smirnoff box. Luckily, Sy has already walked around to the passenger side and not looked back. He is waiting for me to unlock the door. I slam the trunk down, unlock all the doors, and throw the flowers in the back seat.

"Chevy? Figured you for something in the Jap family, Traub."

"Sorry to disappoint you," I said. "You need help?"

"Do you?" said Sy.

"I mean getting in the car."

"So did I," he said. "No, actually, I just meant 'Do you need help?'"

Where does a person go to get his conscious mind's filter removed like that? Surely, Sy was not born with such a precise scalpelish tongue. My dad would have been no match for this guy. Verbally. Intellectually. Forever a baton pass behind in a relay of wit. Sure, Sy was everything my father was not, but that meant he had never sold anything more solid than a theory. He had never lifted anything heavier than a student aspiration.

Ducky Traub had known how to operate in the free market that Sy Siegel choked on. He still did. Even dead three years, Ducky Traub had just eliminated his competitor. How come I feel like my mom did not die, she was relocated? Sure, she was being buried with her family, but who was alone now? Who won?

Have you noticed I haven't even brought up the notion of what the ongoing discourse must be like between Travis and Polly? You want to chalk it up to grief or emotional paralysis, knock yourself out. I cannot begin to imagine how that scene is unfurling because I cannot get past the fact it has nothing to do with me. That, and the other two facts: my former shrink is nuts and Bonnie Dressler has a sister. Everything else is just conversation. Conversation that I am not in. Believe me, I'd love to fixate on it, I'd crave the distraction, but I have directions I need to follow to the cemetery in Quincy, and they're a little involved.

We get in the car, and Sy fastens his seat belt as no human being under seventy-five can do. One move. *Click.* He's fine. He accidentally killed his girl, who happened to be my mother, but he's fine. You want to lead a non-psychological life? Follow this guy in the passenger seat. The guy who just asked you, in sixty percent taunt, "Do you need help?"

"You know what, Sy, I do need help. I'm thinking of writing a book about Tony Conigliaro. What do you think?"

ε

IF PEOPLE REMEMBER ANYTHING about Tony Conigliaro, it is only the details most vivid and least interesting. *"The ballplayer who got hit in the head, right?"* they will say with the same cadence they would reduce the story of Lot to: *"The salt wife guy, right?"* Here's what I know, and it is not nearly enough. Tony Conigliaro grew up in Revere, Massachusetts, twenty-five miles north of where my rented Impala is right now. This is how I remember the beginning of 1964 in Boston. Everyone is still crying over Jack Kennedy, then girls start screaming over The Beatles, then the screams die down around the middle of March for three weeks, then they're back up again in April for Tony Conigliaro. He is nineteen and already in the big leagues, playing with the hometown Red Sox. Home run on the first pitch he ever sees at Fenway Park. Then the next season, 1965, he leads the American League in homers. Thirty-two, I think. Movie-star handsome, TV-star accessible and jock cocky. On his nights off, he starts singing in nightclubs, mostly Beatles stuff, and he even records a couple of 45s, which chart locally and are bought by every woman in New England under twenty.

Then it's August 18, 1967. Five months into his best season, Tony Conigliaro, crowding the plate as he always does, can't get out of the way of a high, inside fastball from Angels' pitcher Jack Hamilton. Can't. The ball crashes into his left cheek, just below his eye. He lies in the hospital for eight days, and everything you read is bookended by two ghoulish measurements: how close the pitch had come to killing Tony C. and how close Tony C. might be to coming back.

He sits out the entire 1968 season while his vision slowly retraces its steps from the outskirts of 20/400. We hear he may return to the majors as a pitcher, but that has to be the scribbling of some wag who read way too much Malamud. He's back in right field for Opening Day, 1969, in Baltimore, when he breaks a 2-2 tie in the tenth with a two-run home run, then scores the eventual winning run in the twelfth. I am fifteen and relieved. Not so much that he's okay, more that he'll still be okay in seven years, when he's thirty-one and I join him in the Red Sox outfield.

He has the finest season of his career in 1970, thirty-six homers and 116 RBIs, and the Red Sox reward him. By trading him. To the Angels. I don't know, you tell me. Look, I know baseball can be ironic. And thoughtless. But baseball does not mindfuck in public. Not usually. Trading Tony Conigliaro to the team that almost killed him is like sending George Wallace to finish his rehab in the Bremer family's guest room.

The Angels had the nickname emblazoned on the back of his road jersey. **Tony C.** Now, he's a cross between lounge act, capo, and some guy in a twelve-step program. He becomes another afterthought in the Orange County sun and retires after half a season in Anaheim. He holds a press conference after his plane lands at Logan Airport in Boston and says, "This is the end of Tony C."

Now explain this. Four years later, four years out of baseball and running a nightclub and notching whatever blondes are left in Greater Boston, he somehow wins a spot on the 1975 Red Sox roster as a designated hitter, and, in eye-rubbing redux, hits a home run on Opening Day. Seriously, explain this, other than a promotional ad for the Make-A-Wish Foundation. This time, the comeback sputters until June. Tony C retires for good. And the story begins.

For the next six years, he bounces around as a TV sportscaster and occasional color man on NBC's *Game of the Week*. The letter I found from Sy Siegel had reached the San Francisco affiliate a few months after he'd been let go as its fill-in sports anchor. On his thirty-seventh birthday, Tony flies back to Boston to try out for the full-time job as color man on the local Red Sox telecasts. It's more confirmation hearing than audition. Tony C is still an epic hero in New England, albeit Achilles, and the job is his to lose. He's still cocky, fit, and handsome like a guy worth leaving your husband for, if you had a husband. No one is asking him about the eye anymore. He's going to be a home team baseball analyst. The blind spot is implied.

Two days after the audition, his brother Billy, another former major leaguer, is driving Tony to Logan to catch a flight to San Francisco and start preparing to move back home. On the way to the airport, Tony Conigliaro suffers a massive heart attack that leaves him with permanent brain damage. He's in a coma for months, and then for the next eight years, if you're paying attention, the only news you ever hear is about him moving a couple fingers or saying half a sentence to an ex-teammate. Those are the last eight years. He's dead at forty-five.

What did I tell you? Not nearly enough. This is where Sy comes in.

$$\mathcal{C}$$

"YOU KNOW ABOUT KEVIN Scappatola?" Sy said.

"Who?"

"Do you know about the smoke bomb?"

"What smoke bomb?"

"My God, Traub," he said. "If I had arresting privileges, you would be in stir with no chance of seeing a judge for telling me you were going to write a book about Tony Conigliaro and not knowing about the smoke bomb."

"You can drop me off at Central Booking on the way back from the cemetery."

Sy Siegel undid the top button on his shirt and unlocked his seat belt. I was going to ask him if that was necessary, but with a man this committed to his thoughts and words, every action is necessary. "The night he got beaned, George Scott led off the fourth inning with a hit and was thrown out trying to stretch it into a double. It might have been a close play. Somebody threw a smoke bomb onto the field and the game was stopped for ten minutes."

"And it wasn't long enough and there was still smoke on the field when Tony came up?"

"You want help, or do you want votes?" I shut up.

"Reggie Smith was next. He was a switch-hitter, so they wanted the lineup to go right left right left right against Jack Hamilton. So, Tony was batting sixth. Reggie Smith lined out to center. Then, Tony came up. First pitch. Thud. Like dropping a cantaloupe on linoleum. Sure, there was some residual smoke in the outfield, but the problem was the delay. Hamilton went back to the dugout and sat down for ten minutes. His arm clearly stiffened up. He never warmed up enough when he got back out on the mound. The pitch got away."

He looked at me. "How do you know, Sy?" he half-mimicked. "I know because Jack Hamilton bought a hydrocollator pad the next day at a Rexall near Sancta Maria Hospital, after he had tried to visit Tony. The family wouldn't let him in."

"Kevin Scappatola?" I had to ask.

"He was either the hospital spokesman at Sancta Maria or the pharmacist's assistant at the Rexall. It's in my notes."

I wanted to lie. Or at least play ignorant. *"Your notes, you say?"* It would have been easier. It would have been justifiable to the point of misguided compassion. But it was not possible now. "That's why I brought this up," I said. "I opened a carton by mistake when I was moving your stuff and saw you had all this material on Tony C." I looked at Sy and waited for outrage, but he was staring through my head, out the driver's side window, eyes dancing as he mentally rummaged through the same carton. He wanted me to stop talking. So, I did.

"Do you know about the rolling pin?"

"No."

"After his first training camp with the Red Sox, Tony got permission to go home to Swampscott, where his family had moved, and pick up his car before reporting to the minor league team in Wellsville, New York. He showed up on time, but with a cast on his arm and missed the first six weeks of the season. The day before he was supposed to leave for Wellsville, he broke his thumb after he punched some guy in the face. There are a couple of versions of the story. He either saw the guy talking to his girlfriend outside the high school, or the guy saw Tony talking to his girlfriend and gave him a hard time. Doesn't matter. By either account, Tony shows up at the guy's house, rings the doorbell, the guy answers and he flattens him."

Sy pushed my shoulder. Here comes the big point. "And in both versions, while the guy is lying on the ground, his mother runs in from the kitchen screaming and starts hitting Tony with a rolling pin." Another shoulder push. "On the head."

"That story sounds a little apocryphal, Sy."

"When did you get hired as a Red Sox stooge?"

"When did you become such a baseball fan?"

"I am a fan of justice," he said. And then, slowly, "On. The. Head."

"So, you're saying even before Tony Conigliaro was hit, there may have been something wrong with him."

"Yes."

"Which the Sox covered up."

"Yes."

"Why?"

Sy laughed. "Why? Why did the Tigers cover up two ginzo muscleheads stomping on Mark Fidrych's arm in a Cleveland hotel room after he dated a mob boss's *gumare?*"

"That happened?"

"Of course it happened. Christ, I cannot believe I am talking to the same intellect that hatched and served Gwen's eulogy."

I just remembered where we were going.

"Sy," I said, "we don't have to talk about this now."

"No, we don't," he said. "But where should we be now? Unless you need to unburden yourself over some other property of mine you've robbed, is there another discussion?"

"Not unless you need to unburden yourself over what you robbed from me, Professor." I don't usual parry with guilt's edge, but Sy had either snickered or buckled his seat belt, which smacked of dismissal. And I was already angry for having missed the cemetery exit off the Southeast Expressway and had to double back. The old man picked the wrong moment to try on the victim costume.

We did a quiet mile and a half on the access road. Quiet. Harper-Lee-after-1960 quiet.

"You know about the mental episode," he finally said.

"Mom?"

"No, Tony C. with the Angels."

"Where did you get this?" I said.

"If I gave you a name, would it matter?" In that moment, Sy Siegel sounded much too close to Travis Waldman when we had the "How am I an enabler?" / "I don't know, Charlie. You tell me..." exchange. Which made me think about where Travis might be in his dialogue with Polly Dressler Trombley. Charlie, stop. Listen to the old man. What passes for his truth is much more useful now than whatever you might conjure up between a woman you just met and a guy you never knew.

"No Sy, I guess it wouldn't."

"Why are we stopping?"

"Because the cemetery is right there, and I'd rather not wait."

Again, the seatbelt clicked Sy free. "The Red Sox knew they had damaged goods," he began. "That's why they kicked him loose for nothing. They also knew that they would be pilloried for getting rid of one of their most popular players. But, and this is crucial, they were well aware there were other issues, psychological issues, rolling pin-related issues, which could be ignited by any adverse stimuli. So, they decided to make him part of a field study. Let's trade Tony to the team that almost killed him. Let's see how that plays out. Let's get off the hook for this time bomb, but let's insure that it is a time bomb.

"They only had to wait half the season. Just before the All-Star Game, the Angels were playing in Oakland. Tony came in hitting two-twenty-ish and had four home runs. He had missed many games with a pinched nerve in his neck, the Rosetta Stone of psychosomatic injuries, and had complained to the *Sporting News* that someone had stolen his little black book. Of course, all this endeared him to his new teammates, who thought they were getting a cleanup hitter and a leader, but wound up with a guy who was only making headlines for dating Mamie Van Doren. And only had four more home runs than Mamie Van Doren."

"Hah! Sy, is that line yours?"

"If I gave you a name, would it matter?"

"No." I need to remember that move the next time anyone ruins my rhythm with an unnecessary question.

"The game in Oakland wound up going twenty innings. Tony went 0-for-8 with five strikeouts, but he wasn't even in the ballpark when the game ended after one in the morning. In the eleventh, he struck out and tried to run to first when the ball got past the catcher. Which is fine, except there was already a man on first."

"So, he's automatically out." Bad move by me.

"If only you'd been there that night!" Sy said. "The home plate umpire yelled at Tony not to run, that he was already out, and Tony got into a loud argument with him. It happens. Long game. The greenies are wearing off. You forget the rules and you feel shown up. Embarrassed. You lash out. You don't even need to be a ballplayer to do that."

Sy waited for me to say, "So, that's the mental episode?" Come on. I just came from my shrink making up an affair with the woman I had devoted forty percent of my sessions to in front of her sister at my mother's funeral. So, keep talking, professor. There are no hands up.

He went on. "Now, it's the nineteenth inning, still no score. The Angels get their leadoff hitter on. Here comes Tony C to sacrifice him to second. He tries to bunt at the first two pitches and misses, so the manager, Lefty Phillips, takes off the bunt sign, as he should. But Tony squares to bunt again, misses, strike three. Off comes the batting helmet. He tosses it in the air, then takes a swing at it and sends the helmet halfway down the first base line. The first base umpire immediately throws him out of the game. Tony fires his bat just over the umpire's head. Lefty Phillips and a couple of players had to escort him off the field.

"He was on the 8:00 A.M. flight back to Boston. As he left the hotel, on his way to the airport, he told the writers who covered the Angels, who were just getting back from the park, that he was quitting. That his eye had never gotten better. By the time he landed at Logan, he had reworded 'quit' to 'retire.'"

Now I had to interrupt. "And then, ten years later, he had the heart attack that caused the stroke that eventually killed him as he went to the airport. Why did things always happen to him on his way out?"

Sy smiled, "I see the smart Traub decided to show up. Unless you answer that question, you don't have your book. You just have another Harvard literary circle jerk."

"So, if I follow the letter you wrote that I found in the box, you believe he was seriously injured by blows from the rolling pin and that, not the beaning, is the starting point. And this was all covered up by the Red Sox..."

"...who wanted a hometown hero after Ted Williams."

"Major League Baseball..."

"...who needed another good-looking Italian star after DiMaggio."

"Organized crime..."

"...because nothing substantive happened in the early 1960s without organized crime, the backbone of an efficient debased society."

"And the plastics industry."

Click. The seatbelt was back on. "Come on. Gwen is waiting for us."

"But what about the plastics industry? Does that have something to do with batting helmets?"

"I needed a fourth," he said.

"A what?"

"A fourth. In journalism, you need two confirmations to support a fact. In a conspiracy, you need four participants."

"So, you made it up?"

"Oh, so now we're defending DuPont? Say, let's bury Mom in Delaware and pick up your cut."

Alison was standing next to her car inside the cemetery entrance, hands on hips. And it was not hands-on-hips weather. *These are for you...* would not work, even a little. The hearse was already at the plot. She jumped back in the car and Jonathan slowly pulled out. We followed respectfully in distance only.

"Traub, you must not tell anyone about the conspiracy rule of four."

"I'll take it to the grave."

Sy coughed. "You know that was my way of apologizing," he said.

You know what? I did.

XI

NEW YEAR'S EVE IN my dead mother's bed. That's what looms for me.

I know, I know. The funeral was a week before Christmas, and now I'm talking about New Year's Eve? What happened to the non-psychological life and living in the now?

It's still ongoing. It's just that the last few days have been so in the now, I haven't had the occasion to stop in the present and process. The hecticity alone, which isn't even a word. But I've been so busy I haven't had the chance to look up the right word. So, hecticity. A lot of phone calls, a lot of "Come on. What? Seriously? Come on." Four drives back and forth to Manhattan. Four. And too many lawyers. This is my way of saying I missed Christmas, fell asleep on my mom's bed after the last round-tripper and was making my second pot of coffee twenty-one hours later when it dawned on me: Nobody was singing anymore.

So, what's that, ten days to cover? It's better this way. And as good as I usually feel about not having a family, I feel that much better now because I can be immersed in all the shit that needed and needs my attention, all the distractions, and there's no "Sorry, kids. Daddy missed Christmas." I cannot tell you how thrilled I am to have missed Christmas. So, to Windgate Point, Sy, Alison, Polly, Bonnie, Travis, Tony C, Avis Leasing, American Express, McLean Hospital, and all the lawyers, thank you.

Let's open with the bad news. Polly Trombley is still married. I assumed she was by the fact that she goes by a name other than Dressler, but I was hoping she might have liked the sound of "Polly Trombley" and retained it long after the loser was out of the picture. You cannot do any better than Polly Trombley. Polly Trombley sounds like the name of the broad Dick Tracy would dump Tess Truehart for. But no. She's quite married. Which, I'm going to say it, just blows because this girl is Bonnie Dressler without my baggage.

In fact, I said that to her.

"Are you still married?"

"Quite."

"You'll pardon me, but that blows." I left out the Bonnie-Dressler-without-my-baggage assessment because, even living in the now, there is enough room to remember that no woman likes being compared to her sister.

"Well," Polly said, "maybe it won't work out." Sadly, she remembered to laugh after that. Then she added, "I do know a few women like me. If you're going to stay around, I'll be happy to set you up."

I need to add that this exchange was at the end of our second conversation. After she had filled me in about Travis committing himself and I found out that I needed to remain at Windgate Point.

When Sy and I got back from the cemetery, Polly was in the lobby of Windgate, writing on a legal pad with the quiet fury of someone trying to get it all down before the judge came back from recess. I apologized for keeping her waiting, but she was sorry we'd returned so early. She wanted to have all the preliminary paperwork done. So, there's paperwork. A lot of it. Get used to this. I had to.

The burial was quick because of the weather and the rabbi's fear that I might speak again. Sy stayed in the car with the motor running to keep the heat on and cover his sobs. I knew more intimate details about Tony Conigliaro than I did about Sy Siegel, and yet to watch him cry when I could not was strangely nourishing.

There were the nine of us—Me, Alison and Jonathan, their son and daughter, only one of their spouses, two grandchildren and some kid annexed from the daughter's second husband's first marriage—chattering while the rabbi raced through the graveside prayers like he was auctioning off the casket. As we walked quickly back to our cars, Jonathan said, "Alison, your sister, would like to see you." Just like that. Not Alison. Alison, your sister.

"Can I get in to see her?" I said.

"Give me a break here, Charlie," Jonathan said for the second time in the last hour.

Alison, my sister, rolled down her window and got this out before the annexed grandkid screamed to put it back up.

"You take care of the apartment. I'm done with it. And I'm done with you." Window up.

I think you can understand why I feel particularly close to Sy these days. And it should be no surprise that when he pressed a nut and bolt in my palm and closed my hand around it, I dutifully ran back and placed it on the top of the Zimmerman family headstone.

The drive back was quiet. I haven't owned a car since I moved to New York, so I value the spirituality of driving as a commuter cannot. I don't know if it is spirituality. Is the feeling that when you're driving "they" can't "get" you spiritual? Well, that's what it is. So, I was content not to be talking. Didn't mean I didn't want to listen. But Sy only spoke three times in forty minutes. Twice he said, "Okay, Traub," which I could tell merited no response. Then, when we were a mile or two away from Windgate Point, he tapped me and said, "Get cat food."

"You mean that? You want to get cat food?"

"Traub, I know it's been a tough day, but what else could I possibly fucking mean?"

I couldn't tell him that *Get cat food* had become my mettā mantra after he had mistakenly handed me the slip of paper he thought had scripture or doggerel on it. That it was the essence of doing what was in front of you and only what was in front of you. The Egyptians worshipped cats. And they had zero shrinks.

Meanwhile, forget all that. Sy Siegel had said fuck! Again! Which made the possibility of leaving him even sadder. Can't tell you why. Remember, I don't stop to examine that stuff. Get cat food.

We picked up five cans of Fancy Feast mackerel (*"Why don't you get more, Sy?"* / *"Because I don't eat cat food."* *"Why just mackerel?"* / *"Because, again, I am not an aristocrat like you, Traub."* *"What is your cat's name?"* / *"Why? Are you hiring?"*) and Sy spent about three seconds in the lobby saying hello and goodbye to Polly. If Windgate Point ever kept such records, no resident ever made it up the stairs faster than Sy Siegel at that moment. He was done with people until further notice, or five cans.

Polly and I sat in the small study off the lobby for at least an hour and a half. I never thought to ask her into mom's apartment. Never occurred to me. It does now, but at that point, our first extended talk, I was maybe a little too *get cat food*-y, like I had dropped mom off at the beauty parlor.

"I lied a little," Polly began, sounding fifty-percent less lawyer and eighty-percent more guy. "Bonnie is out of the country, and she is in the Dominican, but she is not on her honeymoon. She didn't get married. She's been seeing the developer, Mark Hynes, for a few years, and yeah, I like him, but you know the type. Shit, you *are* the type."

That's right, Bonnie Dressler is not married. I would have put that under the heading of good news—hell, sometime journalist that I was, I would have led with it—but Polly continued.

"I tell Bonnie all the time I'm doing this once, marriage. If it doesn't work out, I'm gay. I tried. You're witness. Who needs it?"

Believe me, I appreciated how familiar Polly was being, and I would have loved to have a waiter come over and take our order, but my mind told my face to furrow, and she got back on point.

"I lied a little. I knew about Travis," she went on. "Not that he'd be here. Jesus no. I mean I was aware of him. Bonnie called me after he showed up unannounced the first time six weeks ago and said that even though she'd been quite clear and succinct with him, she wanted me to be available in case he showed up again. Nothing ever happened, until today. We figured it was over. Message received. And Bonnie meant in case he showed up at her office again. Not at a funeral. I was here as a favor to Sy. Complete coincidence. When I realized you were the same Charlie Traub, I was going to try and find a moment to ask you about Travis. I never expected him to pop by, let alone walk into the conversation and implicate himself."

"I am completely confused," I said. "I'd tell you what I know, but I think what I know is all lies."

"So, lie to me," she said.

And I did. I wound up telling her most of what Travis had told me about dating Bonnie the last time I saw him at Veselka.

Most, because if this wasn't a need-to-know situation, then I need to take an adult ed. course in how to identify one. The romance scenario Travis broad-stroked that night turned out to be utter fallacio. The only time Polly and my versions matched was the fact that, yes, I knew Travis, yes, he was a psychologist, yes, his name was Travis, and yes, he had originally contacted Bonnie to interview her for a journal article.

"You know there was never any article," I said.

"I do now."

"That was all a guise to meet her. The fake article."

"How do you know?"

"He told me," was what I said. Come on. What was I going to say then? "How do I know? Please. I know because Travis got the idea from me. I almost used it as a ruse to see Bonnie eight years ago. When I myself considered dropping a toe into the River Tryst? You know Bonnie, your sister..." Bonnie, your sister. I would say it just like that. Like Jonathan. "Alison, your sister..."

"He told me," I said.

"Why would he tell you the truth about that and make everything else up?"

"Polly, he's the shrink. You're the lawyer. What can I tell you? I'm just a guy who gave him a name in a session." Need to know.

"Yeah," she said. "What about that? Bonnie said he told her that you said to call. And never mentioned you were a patient."

"What about what? You want me to explain why Travis would willingly conceal that I had been his patient? I would guess that might have made their first contact a tad awkward. No more awkward than right now, though."

"Sorry," she said. Less than five minutes in and I get an apology? Who couldn't fall for this girl?

Now, I made Travis' lies work for me. Two reasons. What happens in a session is confidential...and thus uncorroboratable. I made up another word. Kill me. Second, I was still working under the delusion that Polly might no longer be married.

"You want to know how her name came up," I said.

"You don't have to tell me." She made a point of dropping her legal pad to the side and capping her pen.

"There's very little to tell." I wish I always chose my words as well as that. Or the deliberately casual synopsis that followed.

"Yes, well, okay," I began, "one day in session, a few months after I had started seeing Travis, he asked about what I was most proud of in my career, and I talked about *Beltway Today* and finding Bonnie Dressler and convincing her to go on. He remembered her and got very excited, so I told a few stories about some of her greatest moments, which he loved. Who doesn't want the approval of their shrink? I'm sure I was quite animated. I had good Bonnie stories, as I'm sure you do. He asked if my wife was jealous. I said no. He asked if Bonnie came between me and my wife, and I probably said something wry like, 'My wife and I came between me and my wife. There was no room for anyone else.' And that was it. I saw him another year. He did nice work, as you can see. I liked him. When we ended in October, we agreed we would keep in touch. We had two meals. One in November, which was a little weird, but why wouldn't it be? The last one at Veselka a few weeks ago, when he told me he and Bonnie were, uh, involved."

(By the way, that line, the wry one, "My wife and I came between me and my wife..." I actually said to Travis when we were a few chapters into our mostly twenty months of using Bonnie Dressler as a reference point. And he said, not for the first time, "You know, Charlie, it's a miracle you're not more fucked-up.")

Polly held up her hand when I hit the word "involved." "And the next time you saw Travis," she said, "or he mentioned Bonnie was..."

I looked at my wrist with no watch, "About three hours ago."

She picked up her legal pad and started to read. As nuts as my non-professional encounters with Travis Waldman had been, they were half-speed, no-contact drills compared with the talk he had launched with Polly. He admitted that when confronted with the details, his pursuit of Bonnie and his insistence they were an item might be looked at as harassment, stalking, or, at the very least, in his words, "Jehovah's Witnessy." He was not sure whether he was infatuated with Bonnie, or viewed her as a threat. A threat, you say? Yes, a threat to his relationship with—are you sitting?—ME! And that really, when you think about it, if he was following anyone, it was me. Because he was. How do you think he got to the funeral home? Travis went on about his wife catching him throwing her toothbrush in the toilet and getting thrown out of Shea Stadium for punching Mr. Met in his giant styrofoam head and dressing up like a dominatrix to roleplay with one of his patients (So there really *was* an orthodox Jew with lower back pain. What a relief.). He kept repeating: "This might be a medication issue" and "Hey, it seemed like a good idea at the time."

Polly looked up from the pad. "If he used those phrases once, he used them six times," she said. "He must have talked for twenty minutes nonstop. I waited for him to finish, and I asked him, 'Travis, are you suicidal?' And he said," a glance at the pad, "'What do you need me to say?'"

"He wants to go inside?" I didn't want to ask that, because it was obvious that's what he meant.

"Jesus, where were you an hour ago? I had no idea that's what he was inferring. We had that same exchange three times before he got frustrated or sympathetic and said, 'Your first commit, dear?'"

Travis would agree to go in, but only to McLean Hospital, the legendary psychiatric facility in nearby Waltham made famous by Sylvia Plath. Although I would think if Sylvia Plath was an alumna, you might want to keep her name out of the brochure. There were two voluntary admittance routes into McLean. One was to have a policeman or psychiatrist fill out a Section 12A and be committed through a local emergency room, provided there were beds available. The other was finding an opening in "The Pavilion," McLean's discretionary evaluative residential unit, which advertised in the *New Yorker* like it was a place you went when Canyon Ranch was booked. Polly gave Travis forty-eight hours to gather his things in New York and come back. If he could not secure lodging in The Pavilion, she would pull local cop-and-shrink strings through a Section 12A.

And that's where they left it. Again, I did not want to, but I had to ask Polly if she was worried Travis wouldn't return. She stood up and smiled. "He's coming back. You and Bonnie are here," she said. It's nice to be teased by a stranger. Especially when she follows it with, "Maybe you can help me with one last thing. We're all settled, and as he was leaving, I said, 'Travis, you know you may need insurance at McLean. Do you have any insurance?' And he said, 'Oh, I got a helmet.' What does that mean?"

It was the first time I had laughed since Sy said fuck. I told her it was a Jack Nicholson line from *Easy Rider*. (Fonda or Hopper: *You're gonna need a helmet*. Jack: *Oh, I got a helmet*.) And then I kept laughing, long enough for her to start laughing at me laughing. Two days later, Friday, we met at a Starbucks in downtown Waltham a few hours after Travis had been processed in. No cops were necessary. The Pavilion had a bed and Travis had the $40,000 required for a two-week discretionary evaluative stay. The Pavilion did not take insurance, so dress was helmet-optional.

Like Travis, I had also made the round trip from New York, except I checked in at Windgate Point. (For at least another week. I'll get to that.) Starbucks was when I coughed up my inquiry if Polly was still married and as disappointing as her answer was, I was strangely comforted that she might fix me up with someone like her and even more strangely comforted that Travis was going to be close by for the next two weeks.

Travis' transition went decidedly more smoothly than mine. When Alison told me I was responsible for Mom's apartment, I figured it would be a couple of phone calls and then two days of bubble wrap and packing tape. That was before I found out Mom had signed a three-year lease and Windgate Point was in no hurry to collect $7500 a month from a new tenant. And that was before I got a look at my Mom's will, which made me legally responsible for the apartment.

In the middle of those two revelations, I met Phyllis Soriano, the Executive Manager and Admissions Director of Windgate Point. "What happened to that lovely tall lady, Natalie, who helped my folks when they came here seven years ago," I asked.

"She died three years this June."

"I'm sorry. I remember the residents loved her."

"If you let them, they will," said Phyllis Soriano, "And that is how they kill you."

And that was the warmest part of our first chat.

Phyllis Soriano was mid-forties, jeans and blazer, inundated with bracelets, and hovered over her desk like she was at a makeup counter and in a hurry to be served. She was running a facility in a business that makes no money for older men who don't want to hear about being in a business that makes no money. Even though she had given me a smile when I came into her office, it was clear she viewed that gesture as inefficient and not cost-effective.

I was not in her office long. And I went in knowing this was going to be a challenge after Sy referred to her as Batista when I told him I needed to see how flexible Windgate Point was about leases and turn-around time. Come on. Someone dying with years due on their apartment? At assisted living, the precedent is when that doesn't happen.

Turns out this is how these joints make their money. Other places are worse. They make you buy your apartment, then when Grandma dies, you sell it back to them at the price they tell you, which smells like market value 1979. At Windgate Point, you rent, so the game is how fast you can get a new tenant in there. You, not Windgate Point with its five-year waiting list of active seniors with self-disposing income. And not just any tenant. An admissions department-approved tenant. Approved off the waiting list you have no access to. By the admissions department, housed in the advanced Jazzercise class body of Phyllis Soriano.

So, if I wanted to move the apartment, I had to be on call at the apartment. "I've seen this take a month, I've seen this take a year," she said. "But I have a good feeling about you."

Are you ahead of me? You probably are, but I will act as if you're not and recount in clueless chronology.

I drove back to Manhattan and packed up enough things for a month. Clothes, my computer, Lipitor. Everything I thought I needed went into an old, bulky, elements-beaten leather suitcase I had first grabbed from the attic when I went off to prep school. Sy saw me lugging it down the corridor and said, "Hey Traub, did that valise come with an accent?" Fine. I'll hang around with him and start the Tony Conigliaro book and show the apartment. Except that I went to the reading of Mom's will and not only was I not splitting the money with Alison, I was on the hook for the place.

"This is not the will I have," I told the attorney. Eric Fitts. Remember that name. Or we can go with Lawyer1.

"Well, let's see it," he said.

"My copy says Alison and I split the money, there's no mention of thirty-three percent each, with the remaining thirty-three percent going to her children. And no mention of my having to pay the rent on Windgate Point. I'm not sure they had even moved to Windgate Point when my version was drawn up."

"I'm going to need to see that."

"I don't have it here."

"Well," said Lawyer1 Eric Fitts, "you need to get it."

And now, we have the second round-trip to Manhattan. Just long enough to open my safe deposit box and review my copy of the will with the second of too many lawyers, Glen Edelstein. "Doesn't look good," he said. Okay, then. *Seven hundred fifty dollars and no cents.* Pay to the order of Lawyer2. Actually, what Glen Edelstein said was if the new will was properly executed, which it probably was, I then had to prove that Alison exerted undue emotional influence on Mom to make the changes. Or that Mom had cognitive difficulties and didn't understand the changes. Please. You've met Gwen Traub. She and cognitive difficulties never crossed paths. And exerting undue emotional influence was her home turf, not Alison's. So, *nolo contendere in loco parentis* and *ave atque vale.* Thanks for stopping by.

Alison was not at the second meeting with Lawyer1. Eric Fitts would speak for her if I had any issues. I showed him my copy and said I wasn't going to contest his version. He said that was wise and amicable and I may have said, "Are you saying that, or is my sister saying that through you?" Nah, I didn't say it. Too Tennessee Williams. And the meter was running. So, when everything got whacked up, I was looking at $300,000, minus however many months' rent I would have to pay at Windgate Point and whatever taxes there might be. And I'm sure this guy, Eric Fitts, charged for undercoating. Which means Alison had re-edited me out of about $150,000. Fine. And I don't mean fine okay, I mean fine as in that must be what you owe when you've been delinquent in paying proper attention for thirty years. So now, fine okay. I get it. Actually, Alison's kids get it. They split $300,000. I'm choosing to move forward as if my cut is going to her daughter, whom I much prefer. What's her name? Hang on, hang on, I got it... V-something... Veronica! No, Victoria. Your Uncle Charlie loves you, Victoria, and your two children. I mean one.

It looked like things were going to go my way on the apartment. Phyllis had two prospective residents off the waiting list. Two couples both eager to see the place. They were also both on their way to Florida. Everyone on the waiting list was either on their way to Florida or there already. So, this was a big break, according to Phyllis Soriano. And it would have been a big break, if it hadn't played out in the following fashion. "*Great. Bring them by.*" / "*They can't make it today. How's tomorrow?*" / "*Fine.*" / "*Bad news, Charlie. Looks like a blizzard. They're taking an earlier flight.*" / "*Both couples?*" / "*Yeah.*" / "*Can't they stop by on the way to the airport?*" / "*We should have thought of that?*" / "*We?*" / "*Okay, you...*"

By the time I could actually get in to see Phyllis, I could not look in the mirror. I knew I had the smile of someone desperate for diplomacy while both eyes worked peripherally for the next unforeseen foray. A look favored by the lunatic on the go. And I was on the go. Avis had called. I had kept the Impala a week too long and they wanted it back in Manhattan by 6:00 P.M. that night or my rate would jump Shylockingly.

So, Boston-NYC Round Trip Number Three. Actually, Three and Three A. Me dropping off a car and leasing the last available subcompact in Manhattan for a month at a remarkably fair price is not interesting (even though who knew Avis had leasing?). It wouldn't even be blog-worthy for those people who post daily about the barista's attitude when they sent their cappuccino back for more foam. I wouldn't even mention it except while fighting the oncoming blizzard in my snug Kia Rio on the Merritt Parkway, somewhere around Stamford, I realized I had left the Smirnoff box with Sy Siegel's Tony C archives in the trunk of the Impala. So, trip Number Three A. The Avis attendant had saved it, and got the holiday $100 I would have given my doorman if I had seen my doorman one of these last two shuttles.

Remember what I said about the spirituality of driving? Turns out I'm full of shit. The snowstorm lived up to the hype and it took me six hours to get back. I limped into Windgate Point with the Smirnoff box in a death grip and needlessly fumbled for the keys to my dead mother's apartment.

Door unlocked. Light on. Cigarette smoke. And a window cracked open to a blizzard howl soundtrack was sucking none of the smoke out.

"So, that's it?" Phyllis Soriano said, stubbing the cigarette into a vending machine cookie. "Things don't break right for Charlie, and he splits?"

There was half a bottle of wine left and no empties lying around, so it wasn't one of those situations. It was the other one. She had a black knit dress on and boots under a leather trench coat and had done a better job on her hair and makeup now than whoever had worked on her midday. She must have come from somewhere.

"Were you somewhere else tonight?"

"Yeah. The third floor. We had the holiday 'Jeopardy' tournament and a string quartet."

"Oh."

"Somebody does not look at my bulletin board."

"Yeah," I said. "That's another one of my things. That, and splitting." Nothing. "When did the party break up?"

"Nine...twelve," she said.

"Well, which was it?"

"9:12."

"You haven't been here since then, have you?"

"Nah." Sip of wine. "I worked for a couple of hours. Found some more possibilities for you on the waiting list. Came by around midnight. You left the door open." I had. "Left. Came back with the wine. Was gonna give you till two-thirty." Slug of wine. "Wanted you to see the boots."

She kicked up a well-kicked leg. Serious boots. Off-duty boots.

"Very nice."

That was the last thing I said or did that would come under the heading of "smart," "diplomatic," or "self-aware." Forget being beyond fatigued from all the driving and the nattering of lawyers or screaming snow hip-checking a Kia Rio. Or the unavailability of Polly Trombley. Forget all of it. I lost track of time these last ten days because I didn't want to think about the jackpot that might be Phyllis Soriano.

Here's what I did not do: fuck her. And it remains to be seen if that was a mistake. If I am still showing people this apartment in May, mistake.

Here's what I did do: kissed her for a while. Asked her if there was a Mr. Soriano after I had been kissing her a while. Stopped kissing her after she made a remark that I needed to keep the door locked so "Certain unhinged assholes don't use the place to indoctrinate the help." Referred to Sy Siegel as my friend. Walked her to her car and invoked my mother's death as the reason we were not naked. Nodded when she said, "Well, you need a little time. A little."

All that, and twice had this sleet-driven exchange while leaning into her driver's side window: "Why can't we say, 'I have many other people interested in the apartment, so you need to commit now?'" / "We?" / "Okay, you." Twice.

So, you tell me. Good shape?

Wait. Eight-thirty the next morning, covered in Tony Conigliaro clippings, I am awakened from a solid hour of sleep by Phyllis and Mr. and Dr. Rachel Blech. Seriously. Phyllis, five hours after driving off un-laid, looks so refreshed I swear she must have turned one of the card rooms into a meth lab. That is the only reasonable explanation. And Mr. and Dr. Rachel Blech? Are you kidding me? The Rachel Blechs? Where are they from, the third panel of a *Mad Magazine* strip?

Nice people, the Blechs. I spent most of our time together matting my hair, adjusting my pants and palm-ironing the shirt I'd been wearing for two days. At one point, as they wandered into dad's bedroom, and I came out of the bathroom with a glob of toothpaste under my lip, Phyllis whispered, "What kind of man reads *Playboy*?"

Again, nice people. He's a retired movie producer, she's a retired internist. And they were maybe fifteen years older than me. No way they were seventy. I never asked if they were looking on behalf of an elderly parent. I didn't have to.

"We like it," said the doctor. "So, February?"

"Okay, I'll eat a month," I said, which got a nice laugh.

"No," Phyllis half-chided, "Next February. 2008."

"Oh no," said Rachel Blech, "I thought we were clear. February, '09." Bigger laugh.

Phyllis looked embarrassed enough and hustled the Blechs out at a pace that convinced me she had made an honest mistake. But how does someone who gives every indication of hyper-competency pull a rock like that? Again, I'm going to go with card room/meth lab.

"Pull a rock" is an old baseball expression for screwing up. It had jumped out of one of the Tony C clippings before I nodded off. It is a wonderful image, though way off literally. You want literal "pulling a rock?" You be me, an hour later, coming out of the shower, looking out my mom's bedroom window and seeing Sy Siegel and two kitchen workers (dishwashers?) rolling a State Fair-sized boulder out from the woods onto the snow-covered back lawn and no more than ten feet from where I'm watching. They never looked up. Sy, making his natural hunch work in his favor, cleared the snow off the rock and the two kitchen workers kicked the ground clear and then broke out entrenching tools to de-sod a cup and saucer-like indentation. One more revolution of the rock, then *thud*. In. Then a quick blanket of snow for camouflage. The entire mission took ten minutes.

The next time I looked at that rock, the snow had been cleared off and the word FREEDOM had been painted on in bold, yet asymmetrical, letters. Sy had run out of space before passion. So, it looked like **FREEDO**m. But the point was made and the flat white enamel was dry. He had probably done his work in the dark, when I was somewhere on the I-84 interchange, on the last leg of Boston-NYC Round Trip Number Four, returning from Lawyer3.

After the Blechs left, I realized that I was going to be here a while. I needed to settle up with the network, which was under the impression I was a shiva away from returning to my freelance executive producer gig on the weekend news show. I don't usually use the word freelance. It sounds unstable. But being a freelancer has its benefits. You can declare yourself a corporation and pay your own taxes. You can take other freelance work. You can come and go as you please. Actually, you can only go as you please. This I learned when I called in and told the network things had gotten complicated and I needed to take a three-month leave of absence to get my mother's estate in order. The network guy, the guy who hired me, didn't take it well. His name isn't important. Let's call him Jeff, just because there are a lot of guys at the network named Jeff. He's not my boss, because I really don't have a boss. See how I've carved things out? Well, (Jeff) went nuts.

"First, you're taking six months off, then you change your mind, now we're all set, now you tell me you need three months? Jesus, did you get some girl in trouble?"

"No, (Jeff). And it might not be three months if I can get this straightened out. I just didn't want to leave you hanging."

"Forget it," (Jeff) said. "We're done. I'll produce the fucking show. I started in news. I could use the money."

I asked him if we could talk in person, and he told me if I got to his office by 2:00, he'd give me fifteen minutes before he left on vacation.

On with the tie. Back in the Kia Rio. I-90, I-84, I-91, the Merritt, the Bruckner, the FDR. In midtown by 1:30. At his assistant's desk by ten-of. Sorry. (Jeff) left at one. No, he never mentioned you'd be by. Isn't that odd? The assistant probably said "Isn't that funny?" but I'm trying to get through this and just the notion of anyone choosing to call that level of narcissistic yo-yoery "funny" might trip the launch codes on all that unconscious rage I've heard so much about. So, I'm staying with "Isn't that odd?"

I drove from the network down to Sixth and Broome and the Producer's Guild of America, the union I had joined while in Washington, when I was younger and brighter about driving around a city Christmas Eve day. Aside from the Professional Golfers' Association of America, the Producers Guild of America is either the second most powerful organization in the world named the PGA or the least powerful. Before you decide, consider this: Do Tiger Woods, Phil Mickelson, and Ernie Els get free screeners of Oscar-eligible films? I didn't think so. I broke up an office party of three to inquire about what it took to file a grievance, which sent me and the Kia Rio thirty blocks back uptown to meet with Lawyer3, Balvinder Singh. Let me just say this before I continue: If another kid ever asks me for career advice, I'm going to tell him to quit school and devote his life to buying a parking garage in Manhattan. That's all. Here endeth the mentorship.

Balvinder Singh was too kind to be a labor attorney, but I'm making a list, so he's Lawyer3. He stood in the doorway to his office so he wouldn't start his meter and said, "It's the holidays. All of you white people are nuts. Call this guy when you're ready to come back. If he's still an asshole, we'll try something. But from what you told me, your rights as an independent contractor are slim. The only thing a grievance would accomplish is you'd never work for that network in that building again. And you wouldn't be able to look out the window and see the giant Christmas tree." Ah, The Tree. Now you know the network. Balvinder Singh shook my hand and told me to go home to my family. I did not correct him.

Here's another thing about Manhattan parking garages: They won't let you take a nap in your car. What a racket they've got. That was the plan. That was my best thinking. That was my answer to "Go home to your family." Crap out in a subcompact. But I wouldn't have been able to do it even if I did get some kind of racket dispensation. There were two messages on my phone, which I had left in the driver's side door handle of the Rio. One from Phyllis, a bit miffed that she had brought another wait listee by mom's apartment at two o'clock and I was not there, and downright furious that she had come back at four with another bottle of wine and still no me.

"Really, Charlie? Really?" I said to the rearview mirror after I listened to her voice mail a second time. "You want to do this? Why don't you put a bow on it and fuck her in the shower chair?" Now you know why I wasn't eager to talk about this as it happened.

The second message was short and as familiar as the blind side can be. "*Charlie, it's Bonnie. I'm still away. But this is some segment you've produced here, Ace.*" And her number.

I made no calls on the last leg of Round Trip Number Four. I can thank another snowstorm and the tenuous one bar on my uncharged phone for that. And exhaustion fecklessly cloaked in one of those five-hour energy drinks. And the realization that if I ever made it back to Windgate Point, I would have nothing but time. Time for all of it, whatever "it" was. Jesus, now I sound like Clinton. And Bill Clinton helped end my marriage.

Convexed over a Korean-made steering wheel, forty-miles-an-hour astern of a stranger's taillights, I can only afford to consider that which is directly in front of me. And if that is not the non-psychological life, then I don't know what is.

I'm beginning to think I don't know what is.

Do I have to tell you the door to my mom's apartment was locked and I'd left the keys inside? It was just after nine when I got back, and Sy was able to get Enrique the porter to let me in for $200 ("Traub, just because I'm a Marxist, it doesn't mean I don't believe they're not allowed to test what the market will bear.") That's when I collapsed and missed Christmas.

Now we're caught up to New Year's Eve in my dead mother's bed. All that's left to cover is the last few hours. I just came from Phyllis Soriano's office, where she summoned me to meet Lawrence Bollinger, the attorney for Windgate Point. Lawyer4. Lawyer4 informed me I had to vacate my mother's apartment by January 2. I was not a resident of Windgate Point and therefore not allowed to live there indefinitely. It was a liability issue. The good news is the couple Phyllis had shown the place to *WHILE YOU WEREN'T THERE* was available to move in July 1. And the even better news, I would not be charged with breaking into the apartment Christmas Eve.

"I have a good feeling about you," said Phyllis, same subject, completely different object this time. I caught Lawyer4's open collar and ringless left hand. She was moving on. And I would too, if Windgate Point would simply let me out of the lease, oh, say, January 3.

Lawyer4 said that was not possible. Instead of begging to differ, I asked for his card and told him he would be hearing from my lawyer. Whoever that was.

Right now, it's Polly Trombley, who says she'll call me back with a good name. It might be expensive. "Less than $45,000?" I asked.

"Oh Christ, way less. Maybe ten grand. Where'd you get that figure?"

"Six months' rent."

So, that makes Polly Lawyer5 and the new guy when he calls Lawyer6. Meanwhile, I'm sitting here on the floral print couch like the last squatter in the last apartment before they can blow it up and build the new off-ramp. I might as well go back to sleep. I have nothing but time.

Before I drop off, you know what? I could really use a session. I should have seen Travis while he was here...

It's now five hours later. The phone woke me. Polly. Lawyer6 did not get back to her yet, but The Pavilion did. He hasn't even finished his two weeks, but Travis ain't going anywhere. The Waltham police found him naked at the Shell station, asking for directions to the cracker factory. Out came the Section 12A, in went Travis to the wing at McLean where they take insurance.

So, I got that going for me.

XII

YOU WON'T BELIEVE THIS. I did it again.

The last time, I let ten days pass before it dawned on me that I had to think about all that had transpired. I'd say "all that happened," but did anything really happen? You tell me. So, here we are, and once again, I let things get away from me. Just a little. Last time was ten days. This time, uh, ten months. I was about to give myself shit, but then it occurred to me. Ten months and not a peep. Isn't this the non-psychological life I've been yakking about? The life I strove for when I first strode out of Travis Waldman's office last October? A year ago. And now, I'm just now getting around to giving the last ten months some thought. If this isn't an unexamined life, then you haven't been paying attention. Or I haven't been paying attention, which I'm pretty sure might be the point.

The sun has put a fresh coat on the left side of the ocean, which is moving West in an orderly line, as if being admitted for festival seating. I already have a page of such musings about the sea, which is the kind of thing everyone must do when they come out here to Montauk. Yeah, I finally made it. Tuck Davenport gave me the keys after Labor Day, but it took me six weeks to get myself out here. I made a decision, and then there was nothing in my way. So, I came out to walk the beach, stare at the water and whatever else. So far, all I've got is the page of sea musings. Here's another: *The sun is out making coffee and the ocean is agitated, as if jostled into doing an errand before football comes on.* Right. It sounded better before I wrote it down.

You need to get to Montauk in October. Go ahead and disregard everything else I may have said, but grab this and hold it close: Montauk in October. Sixty-five and sunny. Chance of rain, twenty percent. Chance of assholes still here from the summer, zero. The Atlantic retains its August temperature for another couple of weeks, so in between the local surfers and surf casters, you can have an entire undertow to yourself. And all the horizon you can eat.

I've been here a day and a half, and I'll stay until I get tired of reading, drinking coffee, and staring. Which could be anywhere from a day to two months. I'm going back to the network the first of the year, just as the 2008 Presidential primaries begin to unfurl and the network people think they have to have me. That was not the decision I had to make, whether or not to go back. That took maybe five minutes into a phone call I got at the end of the summer from (Jeff). I said yes right then. So, the free union lawyer knew what he was talking about. Just sit back and it'll work out. It did work out. It was all working out. And then, yesterday, I got the call from Travis' wife and I made my decision and now I'm here. So, I'll read and stare and drink coffee and jot down my sea musings (Just thought of another one: *The ocean is now going 90 degrees to the right, as if embarrassed by the wrong turn it made yesterday*.) Shut it down, as they say in the big leagues. Until then, we should catch up.

You have a lot of questions, I know. Maybe you don't. Maybe you're pissed off I let so much time go by. *We really cared about some of these people, Charlie. We don't even know if Sy is alive. Or if Travis is still inside. Why should we give a shit now, ten months later, when you're just getting around to letting us in? Ten months later? Ten months? Are you kidding? What kind of a selfish prick does that?*

Sy is alive, Travis is why I'm out here, and one of the things I've begrudgingly faced in the last ten months is that yes, I can be selfish. Prick? That's your word.

Am I selfish because I am not attending Travis Waldman's funeral the day after tomorrow? No? I didn't think so. Okay—and remember you answered "no"—Am I selfish because I refused to give his eulogy?

The world needs many things. It does not need another eulogy delivered by me. There is no way Travis' wife, Muriel, knew I was out of the eulogy business when she asked me. We have never met. She called yesterday and introduced herself and sounded remarkably composed for a woman who had lost her husband due to litigation-worthy complications after routine shoulder surgery. She sounded more like a business manager than a wife.

"I'm really sorry, Muriel," I said.

"How sorry?"

"Excuse me?"

"Charlie, I'm not going to lie to you," she began, which made her the only one in the Waldman family who could make that claim. "I need someone to speak at the funeral. Travis was pretty much estranged from the rest of his family. You were his only remaining patient, and his only friend."

"A eulogy?"

"Yes. You were his only choice."

"You discussed this?"

"Again," she said again, "I won't lie to you. We didn't discuss it. Actually, you're my only choice. I was hoping for someone I've never met. You know our marriage was not the best."

I lied. "That never came up."

"Well," exhaled Muriel, "you were the only one who didn't know."

What was I supposed to say? "Muriel, I'm sorry for your loss. And from the sound of your voice, probably sorrier than you. Maybe you hadn't heard I retired from the funeral tribute racket after my effort at my mom's funeral simultaneously could not have gone any better or worse. Travis was there, but I'm sure you don't know that. Look, when all was said and done, I was no longer your husband's patient and certainly not his friend. If anything, for a while, he was my patient. You want a stranger to do a eulogy? Backhand a fifty to the rabbi on your way in. If you're even using a rabbi."

I didn't say any of that, because only a selfish prick would uncork a stream of candor like that. What I said was, "I can't, Muriel. I'll be out of town." To which she replied, "Look, we can move the date." Which made me quite sure she wasn't using a rabbi. Which would have brought the backhanded eulogy fee down to $40.

So, I had to say no.

"Muriel. I'm sorry. This is no." I never remember saying anything like that my entire life. *This is no.* It felt okay. Didn't have to think about it. Still don't have to think about it. I ain't doing it. That's it.

But that, that thought, that cross-conscious search to remember if I had ever said anything in my life like *This is no.* That. That made me recall what I hadn't thought about the last ten months.

So, I ain't doing it. The eulogy. Come on. To attempt to piece together and make sense of someone else's life and the only accessible route is through my relationship with him? My relationship? With him? Me? What the fuck have I been trying to NOT do for the last year? *This is no.* Again, come on. Give me a break. Give me the break I don't normally give myself. Give me Montauk.

Here is what I try to do. I try to get my needs met by being available to others. It is an imperfect pursuit, but it requires no analysis. It requires no guide. I keep quiet and await further instructions. It's a little more nuanced than the union lawyer's advice to sit back and wait for it to work out. A little more active. First, I get to the next thing in front of me. Sometimes, it's a gig. Sometimes, it's an errand. Sometimes, it's a person. Sometimes, it's a feeling. If I stay quiet (which is exhausting), the answers come. The resolution appears. All because I was available. And then it's on to the next thing. And there's no post-game wrap-up. There's no rearview mirror. There's just the next thing. I'm a self-cleaning oven.

That's it. I shrink myself. Does that make me selfish? At times. Like when I say "no" to take myself off the hook rather than my ex-therapist's wife. Shrink thyself. Don't ask, "What if I'm not crazy?" as I did when I left Travis that first time. Ask "So what if I am crazy?" And only ask it once.

Remember what I said about me alone is better that way? Near the beginning. I meant it, still do. Although now I know I meant "on my own" more than alone. I am alone for the first time in ten months. And on my own. Nothing came to pass the way it was supposed to come to pass. It looked like I would be planted indefinitely in some cheesy cable sitcom of a life: Divorced fifty-two-year-old in his dead mother's assisted living apartment, helping his wacky old Marxist neighbor write a book about a ballplayer everyone forgot while not fucking the woman in charge. I won't lie to you. There was a little bit of that. Maybe a month's worth, which is nine weeks less than it would have run on TBS. The short version is Windgate Point let me out of the lease early because I turned out to be exactly who I was, a potent combination of my mother's son and Sy Siegel's friend. But all that did was close one door.

Listen to me. Teasing with a slice of the story. It's as if I'm already back in network news. *The ocean is hissing only slightly derisively, another wave of adverbs.*

I'm flinching.

This is not going to work this way. Hemming and musing and being cute. There is nothing to frame. You want to be available to others? Be available to the last ten months! You want the next thing in front of you? THIS, the last ten months, is the next thing in front of you. *Stop flinching and catch us up!* Catch yourself up. Shrink thyself.

℮

THE NEW YEAR BROKE not without incident. The $7500 my mother was paying in rent included a meal a day, so it stood to reason I was entitled to a choice of soup, salad, heart-healthy or aorta-be-damned main course and clichéd or sugar-free dessert. My third night in the dining room, my constant supper companion, Sy Siegel, nudged me, flicked his head two tables down and said, "Ruthie Gulkis ordered the roast pork. Get ready." Sure enough, fifteen minutes later, Ruthie Gulkis festooned the carpet next to her chair with a projectiled reassessment of her entrée. The second vomit was accompanied by a noise that sounded like she was identifying herself: RUUUUTHIEEEE!!!

The two women I recognized from the first day I had met Sy, Desiree, and Enid, dropped their trays, grabbed buckets, and dashed to the table and began the furious clean-up. "Those girls have maybe three minutes before we have a chain reaction," said Sy. Ruthie Gulkis gingerly rose to shuffle back to her apartment and have her coffee and sorbet delivered later by her aide, a linebacker-sized Ugandan woman who was just now bringing her walker over to the table's barf-free port of call. Before she left the dining room, Ruthie opened her purse, fished out a $20 bill, laid it on her chair, then threw up in her open purse. Ten people mumbled, "Feel better," twenty never saw it, and twenty more missed it and coughed.

"Wait for it," muttered Sy.

As Enid, greyhound-sleek with low-hanging earrings, hustled off with the bucket, I watched Desiree, round and deliberate, clear the table, tablecloth and all, and not touch the twenty on the chair. She returned with a rag and a plain white envelope. She wiped down the table, re-situated the centerpiece and the salt and pepper shakers. Then she placed the twenty inside the envelope, sealed it, and wrote on the outside before slipping it in between pepper and poinsettia.

"What did she write, Sy?"

"Gracias, no," he said. And before I could ask why, he rose hunch-first, walked over to the empty table, held up the envelope and yelled, "Gracias, no? GRACIAS, NO!!!!??!! How long are we going to stand for this shit?" More mumbling, much more coughing, interrupted by a cherrywood-haired woman (whose name I later learned, though probably could have guessed, was Henriette Fishman), who told Sy, "So, don't have the pork."

Desiree, busy fishing a rogue ice cube out of someone's water, ambled back to the table, reslotted the envelope and helped Sy away by the elbow. Just in time, as a particularly viscous hack was trilled, a phlegm clarion to signal the arrival of Phyllis Soriano. She smiled and nodded at the diners like a Stalag Kommandant overseeing the delivery of Red Cross packages, grabbed the envelope off Ruthie Gulkis' table, tapped it to her forehead to salute Sy's back, pivoted as no one in that room could and headed home.

(That Kommandant analogy occurs to me just now. At the time, I half-stared at Phyllis Soriano, who looked intractably sexy, and thought, *Nice going, Charlie. You could have had that, instead of the pork.*)

"So, they're not allowed to take any money?"

"You can give them something at Christmas," Sy said. "If you give them too much, the aides blab to each other and the residents complain they're being shown up. But look around. Get your head out of John Harvard's ass for a second. Do you think any of these people remember peeing on the rug while they're doing it, let alone six months later? But they'll remember when Enid brought them butter instead of Promise on a Tuesday in April and that'll be enough for a holiday stiff. And when they throw up, it's the food, not them. It's the kitchen's fault. It's out of the aide's jurisdiction."

"This is crazy," I said. "That's like saying if Ruthie Gulkis had fallen in the dining room, Enid or Desiree would have had to take her to the hospital."

"Or reset her leg."

"So, tell me this, Sy. How come when Ruthie threw up in her pocketbook..."

"That's the aide's mess."

"Well of course." I said. "Eminent domain."

Sy tapped my wrist hard, where I wish a watch had been.

"Hey, prig. Lose that tone. Your mother and I fought hard for that exception. Five months ago, the aide would have left the purse on the table. That was an enormous victory."

It was the first time either of us had mentioned Gwen Traub since the trip back from the cemetery. Sy often talked about my father. It was the oddest thing. And Sy, who never said the same thing twice, repeated himself when it came to Ducky Traub. "By the time I came here, your dad was pretty gone," he would begin. "But friendly. Friendly like a speedboat salesman. I usually stay away from people like that. Most people. You have none of that in you. You're guarded and elitist and distracted. We had a guy like you in my outfit in the service. Turned out he was autistic. But your father, whenever he saw me, would say the same thing. 'Hey, Sy. You gonna watch The Boys tonight?'"

"Red Sox, right?" I cannot say for certain, and I don't know what people do where you're from, but I'm pretty sure the notion of calling the local big league team "The Boys" originated in New England. The proprietary familiarity was much too provincial for the rest of the land.

"Unless it was October through April," Sy said. "Then he was referring to the Bruins. Which he pronounced 'Broons.'"

That was right. That's how my dad and other hahdened Bostonians of his generation had said it. Broons. Like the other, unnecessary syllable had been added on during the thirties by the WPA.

"There are so few men in this joint," Sy would go on. "They really should turn it into a women's prison. He must have seen me reading the *Globe* sports section one day, and that was it. 'Sy, you gonna watch The Boys tonight?'"

"What would you say?"

"I never had to answer him. Either he would say, 'Let's root 'em in' before I could talk or Gwen would shush him and say, 'Ducky, don't bother Professor Siegel. He's brilliant.' And really, who was I to disagree with her evaluation?"

"How long after my old man died did you start seeing each other?" I asked him that night.

"Seeing each other? What, now you're a Boston College coed?"

"Said the man who wants to turn the place into a women's prison."

"I was attracted to your mother because, as the man said, she understood that those who deprecate direct action and pin their hopes on the powers-that-be are untrustworthy allies and even worse leaders."

"George Novak," I said. "*America's Revolutionary Heritage.* Essay on the Emancipation Proclamation. 1962."

Sy Siegel's smile yanked on his vertebrae, briefly rendering him six inches taller and twenty years younger. "1963," he corrected. "I see somebody read the book I gave him and sat patiently on his sandbag."

"What do you want me to do, Sy?"

"Carry on your mother's work. We need to present a petition with every resident's signature that they are willing to have their rent raised two dollars a month to create a $2650 courtesy fund for dining room cleanup."

"That's it?"

"That's how we get in."

"In where?"

Sy returned to his hunch, where his spine conveniently contoured to its normal arc of conspiracy. "That's it, Traub," he said, "play dumb. We can make that work for us." I knew I could go door-to-door at the assisted living facility collecting signatures for the petition unencumbered. The attorney Polly referred my case to, Lawyer6, had informed Phyllis Soriano that my mother's January rent was being held in escrow. Any further communication, written or otherwise, between Windgate Point and me must first go through him. That helped a little. What helped much more was the first time Phyllis and I passed in the corridor. She wobbled briefly on her almond-colored high heels. I knew then that this situation was more awkward for her than me. Or that's what I decided. It gave me the freedom to view her only as an object of lust. To know that I was still capable of such hormonal fury at fifty-two was encouraging and the fact I hadn't acted on it invoked the kind of Jesus-applauding pride they must shoot for in Week One of those teen abstinence classes.

Herein, in the corridor-passing body of Phyllis Soriano, lay the essence of the non-psychological life: It's not what I'm feeling, it's what I'm doing. And sometimes, it's not what I'm doing, it's what I'm not doing. That. That is the essence. Until I come up with the next essence.

You want me to explain what I just said, don't you? Okay, but if the logic starts to unravel, it's on you. I'm good with it. This is working for me. It has to be working. Look who's sitting in Montauk in October.

What's the first thing a therapist says after you tell him some story? "How did that make you feel?" I am trying to live the non-psychological life. So, I have eliminated that question. What I do is action. What I feel is distraction. I'm not saying I don't have feelings. I'm not saying I don't pay attention to them. I just don't trust them, because I know they are a distraction. I accept it. I entertain my feelings, but I don't entertain them for so long that I have to put hors d'oeuvres out.

And my feelings entertain me. Let's try this. Ever been to a parade? No? Doesn't matter. Here's what happens. You stand on the sidewalk and a band marches up, stops, plays a short song, and then marches another block or two, where it stops again and does the same thing. That is not the end of the parade. Before you're done, a hundred other bands are going to stop, play, then move on. That is the procession of my feelings. They distract me and move on. And I don't move with them.

Parade, feelings, move on. Can I walk up the analogy to Phyllis Soraino with less subtlety? It's not what you're feeling, it's what you're doing. And sometimes it's not what you're doing, it's what you're not doing. And I was not doing her.

So, what was I doing? The next thing in front of me. Literally. Remember the boulder that Sy made the workers roll onto the back lawn. **FREED**om? We had some January rain, which washed away the layer of snow weakly hiding it. Phyllis made the maintenance workers roll it back into the woods. Which meant that six mornings a week, I got up at 5:00 A.M. and lugged it, six inches on each side at a time, out onto the back lawn and re-plunked it in the trench. The entire process took about forty-five minutes, which is all the cardio and weight-training you will ever need. I was not thrilled that the very people whose rights Sy was fighting for had to undo my work every day, but they understood. They must have, or they wouldn't have left the **FREED**om boulder propped up on a small rock, where I could start my pre-dawn Sisyphusian Pilates with decent leverage.

I rolled that boulder every day except Sunday for six weeks until Windgate Point relieved me of my lease. I haven't touched a stone in months and if I was the kind of guy who thought about what I missed, I would miss that terribly. But I can't think like that. Can't even think of all the imagery quarried in me and my rock. Those were my mornings. Boulder rolling, back to sleep till eight, coffee and eggs and pickles, listen to Sy read the *Times*, then off on Petition Patrol till lunch. I got every signature of every resident for Sy's petition. One-hundred-nineteen names willing to pay $2 a month as a vomit-cleaning deposit. And Lawyer6 billed me an hour to reformat the top paragraph so the document read more civil and less disobedient.

Sy and I had the drill down. He told me we needed to make our rounds between ten-thirty and noon, when, as he put it, Windgate Point was still pre-gulag. We saw ten residents a day, six days a week. And we saw everyone at least twice. The first visit, the petitionless one, was my idea. There were three acts to the petitionless visit. Act One: Sy would introduce me and I would first tell them how fondly my mother had spoken of them and that I was putting together a collage of remembrances in quotes and wondered if they would like to be part of it. "No pressure to come up with anything now," I'd say. "I'll stop back in a week or so." Act Two: As we pretended to leave, I'd ask how their toilet was running and if they wanted me to take a look at it. I am not nor have never been a plumber, but I know how to massage the internal organs in the back tank of any commode. This was a big hit, although the word quickly went out that I was available for picture hanging and lightbulb replacement. Three over-perfumed widows, Dellie Baron, Brenda Tsitoris, and Lana Stone, had me stop by with a stepladder and test their smoke detectors. I had a standing appointment at 4:00 P.M. with Brenda Tsitoris for eight straight days until she fell handing me a nine-volt battery. "Traub, what can I tell you?" said Sy. "They think you have a nice rear end. I don't understand it. If anything, it's barely utilitarian."

Act Three of the petitionless visit was the gift of graft. Again, we would be about to leave, and I'd ask if they needed me to pick up something for them at the Star Market. Before they could give me an item, Sy would interrupt and say, "Traub, we're not headed that way. But we're going by Martignetti's Liquors. Low on anything?" That part, Martignetti's, the hangar-like liquor warehouse in Brighton, was Sy's idea. And mass-psychology expert he once was and Marxist he never stopped being, he knew the universal language of hooch. Nobody, not one Windgate Point resident, said, "Nah. I'm good." They all put in orders. If they drank, they rattled off their usual. If they didn't (maybe ten women) I would say, "I thought my mom mentioned something about having a sherry with you." And Sy would huff on cue, "Christ, Traub, Mrs. Schauss (or one of nine other European Union-approved surnames) told you she doesn't entertain." To which every Mrs. Schauss-type invariably responded, "You know, I should have something around for when I entertain."

Whatever it was—liquor, wine, beer, brandy, sherry—Sy and I made sure we spent between twenty and twenty-four dollars. That way, when we returned ten days or two weeks later with the petition, the fix was in. No level of dementia could erase the simple math that two dollars a month times twelve months is twenty-four dollars. If my summer stock-worthy throat catch ("My mom... Hang on... I'm sorry... This is embarrassing...") over carrying out Gwen Traub's wishes for humanizing the facility that housed her and the staff she loved didn't seal the deal, the offer of the even-up trade, bottle for signature, did. Sy had told me going in there would be maybe fifteen tough nuts. He was right. Everyone else signed and paid for their delivery. Fifteen opted for the Martignetti's honorarium, and one of them, Dennis Duggar, made Sy sign the petition for him as penance for calling his alma mater, Dartmouth, a trade school.

Duggar was the only man at Windgate Point who dared tangle intellectually with Sy.

"This gives me great pleasure, Professor," Dennis said as he clutched a fifth of Jameson's and watched Sy practice on a piece of scrap paper. "And when they come to arrest you for forgery, and they will, I promise I will visit you in jail."

Sy looked up. "What else can I sign to make you not come?" he said.

So, figure the whole thing cost me $450. Which works out to just over three sessions with Travis, who dropped his in-locked ward rate ten percent to $140.

I'm lying about faking the throat catch. Maybe the first few times, but after that, my heart always beat my mouth to it.

We had all the names by February 8, but Sy waited until Lincoln's birthday to present the petition. His bow to symbolism, even though he frequently referred to our sixteenth President as an "errand boy," was costly. In the four days between the 8th and the 12th, two Windgate Point residents, Marcia Gorson and Walter Teplitsky, had the bad taste to take enough turns for the worse that they needed to be relocated to the nursing home down the road, which invalidated the petition. And when Phyllis Soriano ripped up my mom's lease on Valentine's Day, that made three names that didn't belong on the record.

Phyllis gave me two weeks to clear out and took the security deposit my dad had left in lieu of February's rent. And Lawyer6 only charged me $5000. So, I made out big. For about half a day.

Here's another thing about the non-psychological life. Your issues get smaller, your conscience gets bigger. As Phyllis slowly tore asunder the pages of my mom's lease (and we'd have to go back to Fawn Hall, Oliver North's secretary, for the last time shredding had been this alluring), she smiled and said, "Mr.

Traub, you are welcome at Windgate Point any time. As a guest. Not an accomplice. Any further righteous agitation will be done without you. Are we clear?"

We were. I was getting bought off for a month's rent. $7500. And me, the liquor mule, already on the hook for $450 in beverages, had no room for umbrage. So, to the $7500 I had saved I added another $450. It came to $7950. And then I told Sy management had blinked. In exchange for my moving out, which was what I wanted all along, the dining room cleanup courtesy payments would be funded by Windgate Point for three years without any additional charge to the residents' rent. Three years at $2650 per year. $7950. A separate account would be set up that would disperse quarterly checks of $330 to Enid and Desiree. Although he would not have access to the account, copies of monthly statements would be mailed to Sy for oversight. After three years, he could revisit the issue of the rent surcharge with management.

That was the second-to-last time I lied to him. My motives were noble both times, and if what I did ever bothers me, which it won't because the non-psychological life comes regret-free, but if it ever does, I will settle up when the time comes. Not at the funeral. Before that. Because you've heard I am out of the eulogy business.

When I broke my settlement news, Sy was overjoyed. "Lovely work, Traub. You and I will behave for a few months, gathering interviews for the Tony Conigliaro book. Then, in the summer, when Batista shaves her legs and leaves early, we start to set up the workers' pension."

"Sy, I promised Phyllis, Ms. Soriano, that once I moved out of this place I would no longer have any business dealings with the staff or the administration," I said. "That was the deal."

Sy Siegel winked at me. "Okay, Charleen." I would have laughed if I hadn't thought about how much funding a pension might ruin me.

And it's not like I didn't have other expenses. There was the move and putting all my mom's stuff in storage. And all the sessions with Travis while he was locked up at McLean. At $140 per. And even though I got the network corporate rate, I lived in a hotel two and a half weeks before Bonnie Dressler let me stay at her place.

I know, I know. She let what at where?

ع

BONNIE WAS BACK IN Boston after the first of the year, but we didn't see each other until early February, when we had lunch at a seafood place in Kenmore Square that should have been better. There were a couple of canceled meals before we were finally able to sit down. She backed out first because she had to take her son Boggs, now seventeen, condom shopping. A week later, I begged off after Sy and I spent eight hours in the emergency room at Newton-Wellesley Hospital after he had a gallbladder attack from eating three homemade chili rellenos that an appreciative Desiree had dropped off. Most revolutionaries would have stopped at one deep, deep-fried pepper-and-queso torpedo. Rather than draw attention to himself by calling 911 and having an ambulance show up at Windgate Point (which happened with a regularity yearned for by most of the residents), Sy banged on my mom's apartment at two-thirty in the morning and whisper-yelled, "Traub, my own men are trying to poison me!"

At one point, Bonnie floated the idea of inviting her sister Polly to lunch with us, and when I stammered, she said, "Yeah, best to work up to that level of awkwardness."

She showed up in yoga pants, a zip-up sweatshirt underneath a calf-length parka, red hair in a ponytail poking shyly through the back of an adjustable white Red Sox hat. So, forget about me jumping up for a big hello. No way. She recognized me, and I didn't know it was her until she pushed the bill of the cap up just enough.

"You look great," I said.

"Bullshit. I just look a little better than I'm supposed to look, " she said. "I got the baseball hat/ponytail/no-makeup move from my son's girlfriend. It's tremendous. Everyone thinks I had work done."

"That's a good way to save a few grand." Nothing.

"You look like you lost weight."

"You're being kind."

"Maybe," she said. "We only met in person the one time."

We didn't talk about the one time until the next time. The dialogue at that first lunch never ventured back in past tense further than the two postponed meetings and that morning. If Sy and her son Boggs had been there, they would have been horrified with how readily and exclusively we used them as conversation props. Bonnie spent a solid ten minutes detailing the mother-son condom shopping experience like she was polishing a bit for her first HBO stand-up special (*"Only a man could write the copy on those packages and avoid prosecution for deliberately false and misleading statements."* / *"What am I supposed to say when my kid holds up the extra-large, 'You'll grow into it'?"* / *"When did they come up with the flavors? It's a nice concept, and I don't want to nitpick, but they have every flavor, except cock..."*) and the rest of her allotted time bragging about the kid. Listen to this. She gets him into some ultra-competitive, gifted-only private school. I can't remember the name. Not important. The school has a requirement that all students take a year of mechanical drawing. The only way out of it is if you're in the band. Her kid goes up to the band teacher and says, "I'm supposed to be here." The band teacher says, "What instrument do you play?" The kid can't play anything, can't read music, but he notices an empty chair next to an Asian girl playing the clarinet. Boggs says, "I left my clarinet at home," and for the last year and a half, he's sat next to the Asian girl and copied everything she did.

"Didn't the band teacher know?"

"Of course he did," Bonnie said. "But you think he's going to let a brilliant little fucker like that get away?"

Baseball-capped and child-protective, she could still sound like Bonnie Dressler. But it was just sound. Familiar, but not urgent. She might as well have been someone else, and in many ways, she was. I got to see her move around, which was new. She sent her salmon back as I have never seen an entrée sent back, excusing herself from the table, carrying her plate back to the kitchen, putting her hand on the waiter's shoulder and smiling. She veered off for the ladies room, and when she returned to the table, she was greeted by a piece of key lime pie. "The salmon will be on the check, but this won't," she said. "So, the lawyer in me gets justice and the carb-counting gal gets dessert with no paper trail."

I had no expectations for the first meeting with Bonnie and she met all of them. Believe me, I understand the irony of claiming to live the non-psychological life and now examining the last ten months as if it were an emotional autopsy. And you don't have to point out the half-ton paradox of my visiting my therapist in the nuthouse. I get it. We all get it. But in making the case for the self-shrinking technique, I am really onto something with this no expectations gambit. Shortly after I unpacked at

Windgate Point, I discovered that I would get through whatever I was trying to get through more humanely if I anticipated no outcomes. None. You cannot drive back and forth as many times from Boston to New York as I did over the holidays if you think issue deliverance is going to be on either end. Whenever I found myself starting to project a result, I responded two ways. I either looked at the clock on my cell phone and said the date and time out loud to myself, or I imagined myself standing at my destination, laughing. I can't recall how or when I came up with those moves. And I won't, because I don't think like that anymore. But I know they both worked. Ten months later, they still work.

That's why just before Bonnie showed up at the seafood place, I looked at my cell clock (February 10, 2007, 12:34 P.M.) and imagined myself laughing. And when I started theatrically recreating Sy at the ER or Sy's sardonic reading of the *Times* that morning, it dawned on me, as things do when you have no expectations, that Bonnie Dressler no longer worked for me. This was not me on the other end of a phone or satellite feed saying, "What have you got for me?" and coming back with "Yeah, that's good/do that/move that up front/close with that." Suddenly, I had a responsibility to hold up my end of a conversation.

Have you done this? Held up your end of the conversation? It is exhausting. No wonder I spent the greater part of my life asking questions rather than answering them. Seeking harmony rather than risk honest discord. And yet as exhausting as it was, when it dawned on me that Bonnie Dressler was no longer working for me, I could relax. It sounds contradictory, but relaxing amidst exhaustion is an ideal state for me. A less-than-ideal state is being less than candid. Which I am right now. Let's face it, what made me relax with Bonnie was the clear notion that we weren't going to talk about what happened until the next time. And which really made me relax was that nothing had happened, until I got home and told Jennifer.

"Okay, Charlie," she said, leaving a heaping forkful of key lime. "Let's try this again, in a week or so, and you can tell me what you said or what I did to make your ex-shrink such a fan of mine."

"I'll bring the spreadsheets."

Of course, it would have been great to discuss my breakthrough realization with Travis. Not only the fact that Bonnie Dressler no longer worked for me, but the very *idea* of Bonnie Dressler no longer worked for me. So, had it all been about power? Me, Charlie Traub, Mr. Harmony, Mr. Acquiesce Before Ruffle, suddenly testing my dominance as an employer? Could I have been that big of a creep, or worse, that big a cliché? It doesn't matter because I don't look back in that way, I don't dwell in that place. I dwell in the present. And in the present, that day, I wanted to drive straight from the shitty seafood joint to McLean, sign in, meet Travis in the second-floor card room, and somewhere around our third hand of gin, loudly whisper at him, "Hey genius, why the fuck did we never talk about the likelihood that this whole thing with Bonnie might be a classic case of a boss taking advantage of his bossness? Shouldn't this have come out in, oh, say, session three?" I thought about doing it. Hell, I was due for a visit anyway. But in the parking lot, as I watched Bonnie throw off her baseball cap in the safety of her Hyundai, I just looked at my cell phone clock, read "February 10, 2007, 1:56 P.M." out loud and began to imagine myself laughing. Except I already was.

The nuthouse sessions with Travis never quite were. As I gave away just now, they were visits. The staff at McLean would have never allowed a current patient to be seen by his former patient. So, I became Travis Waldman's only friend in Boston. If anyone asked, that was my title. I was approved for visitation by Muriel, Travis' wife, who came up once a week to see him. Our paths never crossed until I got the phone call about doing the eulogy. The fucking eulogy.

Did I say they were visits? That's not right. What would you call a walk or five hands of cards where the visitor, *the visitor,* does this for forty-five minutes: "Uh-huh... Uh-huh... I see... And who is doing the talking here?... Let's walk over here... Well, that blows... Did you play a card?... How'd that make you feel?... Anything else?... See you next week..."

You'd call it a session. It's a session.

So, when I saw Travis after the first lunch with Bonnie, there was nothing to say, as there had been the first three times I had seen him previously. That day, we were approved for a ride out to Target in nearby Watertown.

"What do you need at Target?" I asked.

"A couple pairs of shorts."

"Underwear?"

"No, shorts."

"Travis, why would you need shorts in February?"

He waited until we were in the middle of the store. Have you been to Target? Of course you have. I hadn't. I can get a little chest-painey just thinking about the place now. I was not prepared for the vastness. It is not a store, not a chain. It is an alien craft, which deftly touches down amidst other stores, other chains. It will one day return to its Crab Nebula home when its fuel tank has been topped off by the souls of consumers. Until then, just get your shit and get out. Do not gaze at that blood-red hypno-wheel logo too long. Do NOT! Too late. They just got you.

That people get lost in Target so easily is not a coincidence. That is the whole idea. I was sure Travis had brought me there to ditch me. Wrong again. He just wanted the space to walk around, with only merchandise staring at him.

"When I was eight years old, my grandmother turned eighty," he began. "My mother's mother. Martha Malinkopf. There was a big party at The Pierre. She threw it for herself. Her husband, my grandpa, Grampy Ike, was pretty much out to lunch by that point. Grandma oversaw the family fortune—parking garages, strip malls, apartment buildings—and doled it out piecemeal to my mother and her three siblings. She rented the downstairs ballroom at The Pierre, hired a twelve-piece orchestra and put my mother in charge of inviting her 200 closest friends and acquaintances, even though by the time someone makes it to eighty, there's only about sixteen people left. Basically, you need to keep addressing envelopes until you get to 300 and figure a third will send regrets or not show. So, that's what my mother did for two months. I would see her sitting for hours in the den or the kitchen, making calls or scratching off lists. It was the only time in my life I ever remember seeing her work. You know, work work.

"No, that's incorrect. We had moved from the city to Great Neck the year before, so she was busy working on that. The move was a huge adjustment for me. Seven years old, and I had to learn how to ride a bike and shower in the middle of other boys. I had no siblings. The only penis I had ever seen was my father's. And I never really saw it. I was too distracted by his testicles, which were huge and covered in powder."

Now we were on the escalator, headed for the second floor.

"A couple of weeks before the party, my mother comes home with a box from Brooks Brothers. 'I have your outfit for Grandma's party,' she says. I tear open the box. Inside is a navy blue collarless suit with white buttons and short pants. And knee socks. Charlie, I love outfits. I love the word 'outfit.' But when I was eight, I was just starting to feel normal in Great Neck. I was no longer the new kid. I was still considered weird and funny, but I had made some friends and won a couple of fights. I could talk to the girls. And thanks to badgering my mother, I was finally wearing what the other boys wore at school. I can assure you the other boys were not wearing collarless suits with short pants and knee socks.

"My mother and I went back and forth every night. She would tell me, 'Nobody from school will see you' and 'This is a special occasion' and 'This is what your grandma wants.' I would beg her to change her mind. I bargained with her. What about the jacket with long pants and the knee socks underneath? I would cry. I would go to my dad and complain and he would say, 'Don't be a baby.' This from a man with powder on his balls!"

Two Target workers stopped pushing a cart. "Men's clothes?" Travis asked. They waved at the far end of the store. "Thanks."

"Finally, two nights before the party, I came upon what I thought was a great idea. I called my grandmother and I got her to tell my mother she didn't care if I wore the outfit or not. My mother hung up the phone, smiled, took me by the hand, and walked me into my bedroom. She closed the door, and said, very sweetly, 'Travis, I need you to do this for me. For me.' I said, 'Mom, I can't.' And then she grabbed my wrist and said, just like this..."

Travis stopped mid-aisle, grabbed my wrist and in a hoarse whisper bleated, "'No. It's not that you can't wear short pants. You just won't. Fine. You want to be a man? Next time, try not running to Grandma, you unappreciative little shit...' And then she let go of my wrist and walked out. She left the door open."

As if to demonstrate leaving the door open, Travis released his grip from my arm in a half-wave.

"Uh-huh."

"She was smart, my mother," he went on. "She was smart enough to know that grabbing me and saying what she did the way she did would work. Not calling me unappreciative. She called me that all the time. That was standard for her. As was swearing. But she never swore at me. It was always the two of us and everyone else was shit. Everyone else was the enemy. But now I had gone to Grandma, her mother. I had sought comfort from the enemy. Two days later, when I walked down the stairs in the collarless jacket and short pants, she stood in the front hall and nodded. That's all. She just nodded. I expected more."

He stopped at a large display of socks, but even I knew Target's underage Chinese workers could not produce any combination of color or design striking enough to catch Travis' fancy. And yet he dawdled there long enough to pretend he might find something.

"The party at The Pierre was wonderful. I had never been in a ballroom. I was so transfixed by the chandeliers and the band and all the trays of hors d'oeuvres that I forgot about my outfit. After an hour or so, I ran downstairs to the men's room. The men's room had pay toilets, but I crawled right under. There was nobody there. The toilet seat was high and kind of square, with heavy brown paper that rolled on both sides. I'd never seen a toilet like this. I had a little trouble staying on the seat, but I thought I did a good job. I remember peeing in the toilet, but nothing else. I didn't remember to wipe myself. I probably didn't flush the toilet. I was so excited to get back to the party, I just pulled my short pants up and went running back upstairs.

"I ran back into the ballroom. I wanted to climb up on the stage and watch the drummer. I heard people laughing. One of the head waiters, an old man in a tuxedo, walked up to me and said, 'I zee we've had za little acczeedent' in a French accent. I looked down and my right leg was covered in shit. I had missed the toilet and it had gone into my underwear and was now dripping down my bare leg. I was too stunned to cry. The head waiter said, 'Zees is nothing,' and snapped his fingers and a much younger man dropped his tray and came over. The young waiter took me down two flights to a men's room in the basement. He spoke very softly. He sat me up on the sink and washed off my leg. I didn't cry. I didn't cry until he said, 'Let's see if we got everything' and I pulled down my pants and my underwear looked like the Hershey factory. Then I really started crying. And this man, whose name I can't remember or never knew, was amazing. He never told me to stop crying. He never shushed me. He washed my underwear out in the sink, then he kept handing me wet, soapy paper towels and then wet paper towels and then dry paper towels until I had cleaned myself up. Then he told me to pull my shorts up and go without underpants. For some reason, I stopped crying and started to giggle. I think I said, 'No way.'

"And then, he kicked off his shoes, took off his pants, took off HIS underpants, put his pants back on and threw both pairs of underwear into the trash can. That really made me laugh. The whole thing took no more than five minutes, but I cannot believe no one walked in on us. He took me back upstairs and shook my hand. And then he went back to work. I sat at a table in the corner the rest of the night. One of my parents' friends gave me half a whiskey sour and I fell asleep. I've always been a cheap date. Ah, here we are..."

We were standing in front of men's shorts, size 34. Travis grabbed two pairs. One khaki, one navy blue. He held them up to his waist, then walked silently to the changing room in the back.

Five minutes later, he emerged in the khakis. He threw me the pants he had been wearing, with the belt and wallet still inside.

"Charlie, other than a bathing suit, that was the last time I ever wore a pair of shorts," he said. "but I'm wearing them now, motherfucker!"

He paid the cashier with twenty-nine dollars in bills he fished out of the wallet I was holding. He left the navy pair back in the changing room, along with, as he told me when we were out in the parking lot, his underpants. Did I mention it was the middle of February?

We made it back to McLean just under the forty-five minute limit. So, you tell me, visit or session?

$$\mathcal{E}$$

THE SECOND MEAL WITH Bonnie was worlds tastier and hours longer. We met at an Italian restaurant on Newbury Street, Davio's, where she ate regularly enough to be hugworthy friends with one of the waitresses, a focaccia-warm woman named Betty. "I figure if we were going to talk about eight years ago, we deserved to eat well," Bonnie said.

Betty stuck us in the corner and only came by five seconds before we needed something. And she never rushed us to leave, even as they began to turn the dining room over for supper. I think I might have been more anxious if it hadn't been for Betty. I remember thinking, *If this goes south and I get a drink in my face, I'll stay. I'll stay because Betty is the waitress you want when you have to eat alone.*

Bonnie ordered a glass of Chianti after I declined the offer of a bottle.

"I don't remember if you drink wine or not," she said.

"Not lately."

"That's something people in AA say."

As I laughed, Betty said, "Charlie, you look like an iced tea guy." Just like that. I pointed at her and she took off. What did I tell you?

"I cut way back on the wine years ago," Bonnie said. "Got a little, uh, unladylike for a while there. Speaking of which, nothing happened between us, right?"

"Christ, no!" I cannot tell you what we ate or what Bonnie was wearing. I know the food was great and she didn't have the baseball cap on. Nothing else, which is odd. And it's not as if the non-psychological life allows me never to have to explain such lapses of recall. If I had to explain why I can't remember, it's probably because I've been back to Davio's many times and the toothsome consistency of the menu items and Betty's fetching of them have a way of melding. In the same way when I ended up staying at Bonnie's and stuck my head in her closet every day for two weeks, it coalesced her wardrobe into one giant outfit. We'll get to that, I promise.

"I mean, no," I repeated to her, "Nothing happened between us."

"Good. I mean, I didn't think so, but I used to drink a lot more back then, so I had to make sure." Bonnie Dressler took the deep breath people never take enough. "Okay, then. Before I ask you why you got divorced less than a year after we met in person that one time, or why I never heard from you until your shrink, who I didn't know was your shrink, knocked on my door and mentioned your name, or why my name would come up at all in therapy, before I ask you all that, I probably owe you an explanation for my behavior that day."

"Uh-huh."

Another deep breath. "It got tougher and tougher to appear on your show. I had to care less and less about what was going to come out of my mouth. You know, the blow job stuff. So, after a few months, I'm not sure when, I'd have a couple of glasses of wine before the satellite went up, just enough to make sure I didn't give a shit, but not too much so I would let an inadvertent 'fuck' fly. No one needed to know. That's why I never came down to Washington. I didn't want anyone to see my pre-game ritual.

"I wanted to stop doing the show after three months, but I liked you. And I liked talking to you. Where I went with it is where we ladies sometimes go with it. You know the biggest problem with the women's movement? When all is said and done, it will never be a real movement until women are more driven by the need to lead men rather than the need for men's approval.

"So, I screwed up when I was supposed to come to DC and do the show live and some shit with my ex-husband came up and I had to bail. I can't even recall why I had to come down and be in the studio in the first place. Some Clinton dick nonsense. Still, I felt bad and said I would come down soon, do the show and buy you dinner. It wasn't soon, was it?"

"Five months."

"I thought it was two. Fuck me. The problem was I started with the wine. I didn't want you to see that and I didn't want to quit and have you pissed off at me. See, the approval thing. Finally, I decided to lead. It took, what did you say, five months? That can't be right." She tugged at her fingers to count from March on. "Okay, then. It took five months, but I came up with a plan. And the plan was to come to DC, do the show, give you my notice, quit the show, and then if you were willing, have an affair with you. That was my plan. I didn't want to be one of those gals who poisoned the workplace and then acted the victim. If I was going to not give a shit, better to do it on my own time. So, before I left Boston, I put my wine in a rinsed-out bottle of conditioner. But it wasn't that rinsed out. Yeww. Couldn't choke it down. So, I didn't have anything to drink. Did the show in the studio straight. And felt even more like a fucking fraud.

"It wasn't until we got to The Willard for dinner that I had a drink. I think you ordered a bourbon, took a giant gulp, then let it sit there."

I either said, "That sounds about right." Or thought it. Or was about to say it and nodded vigorously enough to make her stop for a second.

"So, it was all set," Bonnie resumed. "And I had the room upstairs, all paid for. Thank you for that, by the way, it was lovely. I figured after dinner we would adjourn and I would cushion the blow of my giving notice by giving you a little 'let's get this thing started' head. It wouldn't actually count toward the actual affair. Hadn't I been saying the very same thing on your show for the last eight months? Blow job. What's the big deal?

"Then I looked across the table at you and I saw. Well, you're an attractive guy, Charlie. You know that. But terror. I saw terror. I know a lot of cops, and you looked like a cop with two years left on the job whose just trying not to get shot."

"Maybe I should have taken another gulp of bourbon," I said. I have no idea where that crack came from. I have no idea how I could have been that glib when I was still hearing myself being told: *Terror. I saw terror.*

"Nah," she said. "There's not enough booze in the world. Believe me. But I saw you, trying to be willing, and I just could not take that on. Your fear had never figured into my plan. So instead, I gave my notice and made up the story about seeing the guy from CNN for breakfast."

Terror. I saw terror. "I don't remember being frightened."

"Like a kitty."

"I thought I was like a cop."

"Okay," she said, "a crime-fighting kitty."

"If I'd known that, I could have saved myself two years of therapy."

Bonnie lifted her glass of Chianti, still her first glass. "Ah, but then we wouldn't have Travis."

Here was another uncovered tenet of the non-psychological life: Let the other person talk first. I think I stumbled upon this accidentally, in Target with Travis. There is no behavior in listening. Well, there need not be. Once Bonnie volunteered to speak first, it was her account. An account I was unfamiliar with. So, I could just listen. An account that had, oddly, nothing to do with me. And I say oddly until I realize that no other person's account of anything has anything to do with me. What a giant relief. I can just sit there, in the moment, and pay attention. That's all. I'll get my chance to speak, if I want.

Wait a minute. Could it be that the non-psychological life is, when all is said and done, or when all is said and not done... Let me start again. Could it be that the non-psychological life I am striving for—staying in the moment, letting the other person talk first, doing what's in front of you—is just behaving as if one was a psychotherapist? Wow. It sounds profound. It's probably crap. But man, even if it is crap, it would be the perfect crap for Travis' eulogy. If I was doing the eulogy.

"Thanks for telling me all that" was the first thing I said after Bonnie was finished talking and the last thing I specifically remember saying. I guess when I feel vindicated I tend to lose the ability to recount in detail. I should remember that. And Bonnie Dressler so candidly offering up that she wanted to have an affair with me until she saw the fright-etched face across the table from her at The Willard made me feel vindicated to the point of giddiness. I couldn't see my face across the table at Davio's, either, but I can feel when my cheeks jump for joy. Who needs my side of the story when hers was so useful? *I would never have gone through with it.* What a galactic relief. And when I'm relieved, I relax. And when I relax, I entertain. Just ask my mom. So, I locked in for a solid hour of Travis stories and tales from the couch. I told Bonnie her name arose in therapy when Travis asked me to come up with the last woman with whom I had had a "satisfying" relationship. Not a lie. And then he had made me describe the relationship, which I did through an oral anthology of *Memorable Bonnie Dressler Lines.* Again, not a lie. I never mentioned the scene with Jennifer after I came home from The Willard. Why should I, now that I knew *I would never have gone through with it?* Need to know, and now I knew.

Wait. I remember something else I said other than "Thanks for telling me all that." Near the end. Words to the effect of "I guess I must have painted an attractive enough picture for Travis to pursue you after he stopped treating me. For that I apologize, Bonnie." Something like that. No. I didn't say "attractive." I used the word "compelling."

"I thought you were still pissed that I had quit and decided to send me a fruit basket," said Bonnie. "A real fucking fruit basket."

We laughed and did another half hour of "Whatever happened to?" from the cast and crew of *Beltway Today with Rod Richmond,* which left a full two minutes to catch up on the present. I told her I was staying at the Westin indefinitely to keep an eye on Travis and Sy and be of use. Or something even more amorphous. Is amuchmorphous a word? Well, it is now.

Then she asked me if I liked dogs.

"Love them." And I told her the story of trying to cajole the terrier instead of the young couple who came to look at my apartment a few months back.

Bonnie and Mark, Mark Hynes, Mark Hynes the developer, Mark Hynes the developer boyfriend, were going to Italy in March for two weeks. Did I want to stay at her place and take care of her mutt, Yaz?

"Absolutely."

"I live in Cambridge."

22 Sacramento Street 02138. 22 Sacramento Street 02138. 22 Sacramento Street 02138. 22 Sacramento Street 02138... "Oh, right. I vaguely remember that. What's the address?"

"22 Sacramento Street."

"02138," my brain said out loud.

"How do you know my zip code?"

"Uh, I went to Harvard."

"Oh," she said, which in tone sounded a lot like, "Jees. Not another one." But I have to tell you, it was the first time going to Harvard had ever helped me in a practical way. I moved in at the end of the first week of March. Except for the key exchange while Mark Hynes waited outside in the Town Car to the airport, Bonnie and I were never in her house at the same time. Her son Boggs was with the ex-husband, Putzo, so I slept in his room downstairs. The reason I was familiar with the contents of Bonnie's closet is that Yaz slept among her shoes and liked to be summoned personally when it was time for a walk or a meal. That's it. There was nothing lascivious about my stay. Nothing noteworthy, except the way it ended.

I have now discovered that wherever I am lodging for an extended period of time, I take on a few of the characteristics of the person whose room I occupy. When I was staying in my mom's apartment at Windgate Point, I napped constantly, peed even more constantly, hummed when I walked between rooms and jacked up the TV volume for no reason. I may have even mistaken the remote for a phone. All right, I did. And after two weeks sleeping in a seventeen-year-old boy's room, I did something a seventeen year-old boy might do. No, not that. Something else. Something else in addition.

Two days before Bonnie was due to return, I came back to her house from a blur of an afternoon. Two hours trying to work on the Tony Conigliaro book with Sy, a run to Martignetti's for Dennis Duggar, the Dartmouth guy, and my weekly visit with Travis at McLean, where I tried to concentrate on my gin hand as he went into Zagat-level detail about the best card shops in Greenwich Village to get your dick sucked.

It was after five when I walked in the door. I needed to feed and walk Yaz and get my own dinner. Because of the unexpected trip to Martignetti's (Sy had lost a bet with Duggar that Dartmouth did not have indoor plumbing until the late 1950s), I missed lunch and was low-blood-sugar petulant. Yaz was hungry, too. I put out his food and grabbed an old apple out of the refrigerator, the only plausible thing in there to eat. I called the Hong Kong Restaurant in Harvard Square, put in a grandiose order (enough so the woman at the register asked me if I wanted plates and chopsticks for my guests) and figured it would be up by the time Yaz and I got there.

Those of us who try to live the psycho-liberated life do not justify or explain our behavior. There is no behavior. There is no pattern. There is only what is next. And what was next was I took a piss in Boggs' bathroom, finished the apple with my free hand, threw the core down the toilet, flushed and headed out with Yaz and his leash.

Yaz is either twelve or thirteen years old, an age when most dogs retire from the cute business and stop looking for trouble.

He was in no hurry for anything, even a meal, and enviably accepting of his own mortality. Yeah, I said it. I'm envious of a dog. Go tattle on me to Travis. Wait. You can't. *He daid.* Funeral is the day after tomorrow. Bring your own eulogy.

I have no idea where that last outburst came from. And I'm not going to go looking.

A sympathetic blend of German shepherd and pointer, Yaz acted as if he had licked his last face during the 2004 primary campaign, which made him more docile than friendly. Which made him an ideal companion for me. He didn't like to be out walking in March weather longer than ten minutes, but that night, once he realized we were going to the Hong Kong and there was a sparerib bone or two in it for him, he went along like a congressman who gets a dam built in his district in exchange for his name on a bill. Sometimes pork is just pork.

Smart, though. Not educated, but smart. Of the two of us, who do you suppose discovered the flood in Boggs' bathroom? Not the Harvard guy. When we returned from the walk, Yaz went for his post-prandial aperitif cordial from Boggs' toilet and came back quickly, dissatisfied and with sopping feet. I figured out exactly what had happened. I'm quick that way. The apple core down the can. What was I thinking? This was Dartmouth in the fifties?

It took me an hour to clean up and disinfect, and I got a plumber to rush over the next day and de-obstruct everything for $600.

I went back to the Westin a day earlier than planned. I came by the house twice the last day to walk and feed Yaz and not face Bonnie when she returned. If she had been able to see terror across the table at The Willard, she was certainly more than capable of scanning my face for embarrassment. I restocked her refrigerator and dog food supply and left her house keys next to the kitchen phone. If I hadn't done that, I would have never discovered where the plumber left his business card. That card was the only thing I took with me that wasn't mine. And other than a cell phone voice mail thanking me for taking care of Yaz, I heard no more from Bonnie Dressler. Never saw her. Was not invited to the engagement party in June at Davio's. I found out about that from Betty the waitress the last time I dined alone. Not that I expected to be invited. No expectations, remember? Everyone moves on. Even if you don't, if the other person moves on, you, even by doing nothing, have as well. For a while, I was sure I had gotten away with my indiscretion, but last May, while recapping my blind date, when I was telling Polly Trombley about how I reluctantly have to admit how similar I am to my father, she said, "Well, like my sister Bonnie says, 'the apple doesn't fall far from the shitter.'"

$$\mathcal{E}$$

THE MOST MEMORABLE THING about April, and the only thing I've broken my pledge of non-dwelling and never stopped thinking about, happened at quarter of six on the first Wednesday of the month. I parked my leased Impala (the local Avis branch in Waltham let me upgrade after the Kia Rio coughed up a hose) in the Windgate Point visitor lot, walked up to Table 8 in the dining room and said, "Hey Sy, you gonna watch The Boys tonight?"

My father had died the Monday before Thanksgiving, 2004. He had been in Newton-Wellesley Hospital three weeks previous, and as Alison told me over the phone, "I've never brought him home worse than when I brought him in." A volcanic coughing fit had sent him into the hospital. It had begun, apocryphally, just after Johnny Damon's first inning grand slam had given the Red Sox a 6-0 lead in Game Seven of the American League Championship Series. The Boys would hold on to complete the only best-of-seven-comeback-from-0-3-down in baseball history.

The World Series sweep against the Cardinals was so anticlimactic it amounted to paperwork. On the morning of Game Four, I stood in my kitchen naked and tried to distract myself from staring at my unfazed coffee maker. I wrote on the back of a grocery list *I just want it to be over. I want it no longer to be an issue. I no longer want to be described as "long-suffering" when I have long-suffered over so many other things and will continue to suffer over things about which baseball has no answer. I hope that if it happens tonight, I'll just be relieved, like when a bad houseguest leaves. But I would like my dad to see it.*

But Ducky Traub was sitting too far down the line. I called the next morning and said, "Well, The Boys finally did it." And my father, fully versed in the dementia vernacular of a few pocketed phrases that create the illusion of compos mentisness, said, "I think I heard something about that." That was the last time we spoke.

Other than those occasions in session when he trotted out the phrase "Oedipal winner," Travis and I had rarely discussed my father. "Unless you walked in on your parents fucking, the old man is really no help to us," he said. Fine. I could be as disinterested in that subject as any son. Of course, in the clear light of Travis being nuts, you can see how any talk of things Dad might have cut into the time devoted to gestating the Bonnie Dressler Ideal, or reheating and hashing my ex-wife Jennifer. And thanks to our trip to Target, I now knew more about his father than he did about mine. Pere Waldman of the Powdered Balls.

From the first time Sy did the impression of Ducky Traub asking him if he was going to watch the Red Sox, I knew wherever

I was, I would get back to Windgate Point for that first night game and uncork that line. "*You gonna watch The Boys tonight?*"

I didn't have to come far. I had moved back out of the Westin and was in the full-time repair business: Living with my sister Alison, while trying to convince McLean Hospital that I was not a danger to Travis. I don't go where I'm not wanted, but sometimes, I can only identify where I'm not wanted by going there and seeing I've been locked out. And I had been locked out of McLean since late March. Titillating, I know, but first, The Boys.

With the exception of my misreading the schedule the second week and my Polly Trombley-sanctioned blind date in early May, Sy and I watched the first forty-five Red Sox games together from the season opener until just before Memorial Day, when The Boys dropped two of three to the Yankees and he set me free. We ponzied ourselves that it was all research for the Tony C book, that we were chronicling the advances in batting helmet safety technology in the forty years since the beaning. No, that's wrong. That's what we told anyone else from Windgate Point who wanted to watch the game with us, like Dennis Duggar, who I now gave shit to about Dartmouth like I was Sy's publicist ("Is it true your football field lies fallow every six years?"). Took a while, but we shooed them all away nicely.

In truth, by the first week of the season, the Tony C book was deader than its subject. The Conigliaro family refused to cooperate with us. They had collaborated on a 1997 biography and never made the Hollywood money they felt the story merited. When I finally got Tony's brother, Billy, on the phone and told him that I worked in television, he responded as if I had told him I owned a television. The gist of his pre-hang up remarks involved some combination of the phrases "two years ago," "nobody gives a shit," "Bob Costas," "fifteen minutes," "HBO," and "that little fucker."

Sy was not aware there had been an authorized biography. And neither was I. It took a few days for two copies of *Tony C: The Triumph and Tragedy of Tony Conigliaro* to arrive from Amazon. I parked a mile down the road from Windgate Point at the duck-feeding area of the Charles River and sat in the Impala for four hours, just enough time to go cover to cover and raze the walls of my *I Want to Be John Feinstein* Castle in the Sky. *Tony C* was lovingly envisioned, but the prose was dry and perfunctory and ultimately as satisfying as a sleeve of saltines. It was also thorough. Too thorough to be rewrought, even sautéed in the juices of conspiracy.

I am not John Feinstein, but I do own a pen, and that's all you need to see the word "through" in "thorough." We were through.

Sy was undeterred. He read the first four chapters and tossed *Tony C* within ten feet of the wastebasket. "No mention of the rolling pin, Traub. The field is ours!" he shouted. He retrieved the book and continued reading, and when I stopped by two days later, made a point of dramatically placing it under the wobbly leg of a threadbare ottoman. "That's what you do with an alleged piece of research that fails to include Kevin Scappatola," he said. (If you don't remember, and why would you, Kevin Scappatola was either the hospital spokesman or the pharmacist's assistant who sold a hydroculator pad to Jack Hamilton, the Angels' pitcher who beaned Tony.) The day after, he met me at the door of his apartment and handed me his phone. "Traub, before you take off your coat, plug this in, get the number for Lynn English High School and find out the names of every Homecoming King and Queen from 1961-64. Then get cat food."

For someone who was in such a hurry to move out of Windgate Point, I was still turning up there more than the shuttle van that took ambulatory residents to Suffolk Downs or Foxwoods casino. Why? Other than *Get cat food*, I can't help you.

I had embraced the notion of awaiting further instructions. But this might have been the first time I thought I might get my needs met by being available for people. My coat did not come off. I got the number. The school has no homecoming, but calls its royalty Mr. and Miss Lynn English. It took a few exasperated sighs from the school librarian, but she found the names for 1961-64. I let her read all of them, but we had our answer by 1963.

"Nineteen sixty-three...Julie Markakis and Dave Hussey," she said. Julie Markakis was Tony Conigliaro's well-documented high school sweetheart. And now, we had a name. Dave Hussey was the boy Tony C punched, which made Dave Hussey's mom the woman with the rolling pin.

Sy Siegel, who suddenly looked like the only person who had ever been happy to see me, told me to inform the Conigliaro family we were proceeding with or without them. So, there was never a choice. Wait a few days for a call that I never made to be "returned," then report back to Sy the family was now intrigued, but wouldn't commit until we gave them a proposal. That was the last time I lied to him.

The call I did make was to Dave Hussey, who was listed in Nahant, a 3000-person cowlick of a town south of Lynn and Swampscott. I left a message that I was collaborating on a book and needed to speak with him for five minutes. When I hung up my cell phone, Sy had returned to head-shaking disapproval.

"Hey, Balzac. Never use the word 'book.' Use the word 'project.' *I'm working on a project.* A project can be anything. A book can only mean one thing to a guy like that. Intellectuals are coming to equivocate my memory."

"Who thinks like this?" I said.

"Well, not you. That's for sure."

"Do you think he'll call back?"

"If he doesn't, we'll go up there and find the mother ourselves."

"Sy, this happened over forty years ago. The mother could be dead."

"Only if they got to her."

"Who's 'they?'"

"The people who don't want this book to be written," Sy said, "which I'm beginning to believe includes you."

"Don't you mean 'project?'"

Sy smiled. "Traub, do you really want to get into a snotty contest with me?"

From ten to noon Monday, Tuesday, Thursday, and Friday, we took our places to work on the book proposal. I had Wednesday mornings off, when Sy played bridge "with three women who can't hear, and the yelling makes me feel like I'm doing factory work," but once the season started, I was always there by seven to watch The Boys. Saturday and Sunday I came by around one.

Let me just say if I ever meet John Feinstein and ask him about his writing process, I'm confident that other than a table being involved, it will in no way bear any resemblance to one of Sy's and my two-hour sessions. If I recreate one, you'll have them all. Sy would make a face that his coffee had grown cold, pick up the *Times* and say, "Let's see if there's anything here that can help us..."

And then he would begin to read the paper. Out loud. Like an actor reading his sides at an audition. He would start his recitation of an article, clearly and without ideology. He might even get through the lead paragraph before he began a simultaneous skim-reading/edit process that sounded like a cross between scat and tourettes. He would continue until he took issue with some bit of style or syntax or until a reference reminded him of something with which he hadn't amused himself in the last half-century. Or both. Then he would stop, most times in mid-sentence, or mid-noise.

"Here's something..." Sy always began, before launching into transcript.

*A study of Swedish workers has found that smokers take more than a week more annual sick leave than nonsmokers, even after adjusting for smokers' general health and their tendency to take more stressful and physically taxing jobs...*chchchchchchchcheck, chchchchchchchchchchchchchchchcheck, chchchchchchchchch-chchcheckmate...

Using data on 14,272 workers mmmmmmmmmmm, eek!, mmmmmmmmmmm *involved in risky activities.* mmmmmmmmmmmmmmm *smoking* mmmmmmmmm *smokers* zimmyzimmyzimmy *smokers* eek! *and nonsmokers was evident.*

Mmmmmmmmmmmmmmmmmmmmmmmm *7.67 days* mmmm-mmmm *After controlling for other factors* mmmmmmmmm *former smokers* ratatatat, watch that!

Peter Lundborg bupbupbup bupbupAchtungJuden *assistant professor at the Free University of Amsterdam,* (singing) Hey mama, it's Carnivàle time! *not sure why* bipbupbip. *"It may be,"* Dr. *Lundborg said, "that smokers have attitudes or personalities different from those of nonsmokers that may explain the variation."*

"So, in other words, 'Cat Gets Called For Jury Duty.'" That was Sy's way of dismissing an otherwise accurate, well-structured piece as a frivolous and tabloid-type slow-news-day filler. Sometimes, all he would say is, "So, in other words, Traub..." And that would be my cue to pipe up, "Cat Gets Called for Jury Duty." Many mornings, that was my only line.

There were other smug headlines: "Monkey Gets Credit Card;" "Infant Phones Belgium, Speaks to Queen," but Sy was mostly fond of coughing up the cat banner. Which made sense. After three months of hearing me come in and out of the apartment, I finally saw Sy's cat. The feline of *Get cat food* fame. Gonnie (short for Goneril, one of Lear's daughters) was an ample rust-colored yet-to-be-determined breed, who walked into the living room disheveled enough to look as if she was just returning home from a one-night stand. She would stare briefly at us, stagger over to the bowl next to the refrigerator and take a bite or two of food, then brush up against Sy's ankle on the way to her final destination, inside the Smirnoff box atop the Tony Conigliaro papers. And you couldn't move her. You may ask why we didn't set the box on higher ground. You may, if you weren't paying attention. Sy and I, we were not fooling anybody. The only things rustling were the pages of the *Times*.

Dateline Princeton, New Jersey–In 1936 yamyamyamyamyammer yamyamyamyamyammerer yamyamyamyamyamyammmerest *The following year, Stalin's Terror fixed its gaze on Meyerhold and he abandoned the project. Three years later, he was dead by a firing squad.* Rrrrrrrrrrrrrrrrrrrrrrrrrrrip!!!!! Rrrrrrrrrrrrrrrrrripppp!! Rrrrrrrrrrrrrr-sorry...

The mammoth undertaking by Princeton University...

Sy stopped and looked at all four corners of the paper. "Just checking for drool from the writer."

Occasionally, after a line like that, I might press. "You want to go to the premier, Sy? We could be there in five hours."

Sy never stopped turning pages. "Only if they invite the firing squad."

The reading of the paper of record into the record usually lasted an hour and a half, sometimes more if Sy went to the sports section and announced those major leaguers who enjoyed perfect days at bat. It ended when the *Times* came crashing down from his face like a Venetian blind. "Good work, Traub," he always said. "I need to bathe for lunch. See you tonight."

Watching a baseball game with Sy Siegel was a little like two strangers sitting in a room waiting for test results. As an activity, it was constitutionally opposed to the method in which he pursued everything else. In other words, quiet. Look, I am not a chatterer when I watch sports, alone or in company. Never have been. I have a few pet phrases I trot out during the course of a game—"Be good here," "How can that be?," and "Fellas, come on..."—to make sure my voice is working, but I prefer to smugly luxuriate in my own knowledge.

Compared to me, Sy was catatonic. He had two regular utterances. Twice a game, he would ask me, "Do you send the runners here?" and it took me about three weeks to realize the only right answer was "Eh..." His other expression, bubbled up with or without provocation was the all-purpose reaction, "Oh, for Christ sake."

The Zen-leaning like to say the answers come in the silence. Sy and I received our answers in a hurry. The 2007 Red Sox took over first place for good on April 18 and uncharacteristically breezed to the American League East title. They swept the Angels in the division series, and if they can somehow come back from being down three games to one against the Indians (which they are right now, today, mid-October in Montauk) and return to the World Series, I will jump off Tuck Davenport's deck and head directly for Windgate Point, where I will watch the Series in grateful stillness with Sy. If he'll have me.

It didn't wind down gradually with Sy when he let me go, just before Memorial Day. It was abrupt, not bad enough to register as bad, but abrupt. And yet positive. I'll get to it. Besides, when you're no longer looking back, as we of the non-psychological life do not, it takes the shape of just another goodbye. Another goodbye framed in an awkward rub of the back of a hunched Marxist. We of the non-psychological life don't compare goodbyes, either, but compared with how I left things with Travis and McLean Hospital, it was damn smooth.

$\mathcal{E}$

IF YOU COUNT ALL my attempts, I visited Travis seven times at McLean. The first five were all variations on the trip to Target/ Greenwich Village card shop blow-job symposia.

Forty-five minutes in which he stowed whatever filter his mind normally used in a locked box near the admitting desk and galloped unsaddled in his formerly fenced-in past. We might spend a couple minutes on the weather or what he had for dinner, and then I would make the mistake of saying a word like "television." Which would trigger something, something like, "Television...My lasting image of my mother is in bed with the television on and magazines and candy spread out all around her, smeared lipstick and occasionally a tit hanging out. When I would come home with friends after school and she was out of the house, they would beg me to imitate her. So, I would tell them, 'Give me ten minutes, then come into the bedroom.' They'd walk in, and I would have the TV on full blast, the magazines and candy all over the bed. And I would be lying there, naked, barely covered by her comet-green chenille robe, a stocking with a sock stuffed inside taped to my chest like her tit, and my prick tucked between my legs. My friends would walk in and I would slur, in this high-pitched medicated drawl, 'Hi, pumpkin...' First, it was a couple of guys, but by the end, before she caught us, it was up to fifteen kids. I really should have been a performer, Charlie."

Should have been? How would you describe the guy who played the role of my therapist for close to two years? That wasn't a performer? That wasn't a performance? Why didn't I ever get to meet the director, who must have stood in your office before I walked in each week and said to you, "Travis, look at me. Are you there? Good. I need you to, Travis? Travis, I need you to make us believe that you can help this guy. That you can make him recognize his behavior, his issues. There is no room in here for your behavior or your issues. No room. Only him. He is your patient. You need to act as if you understand that responsibility. And just hold on to that for forty-five minutes. You can do this. Remember what you did last week? Just like that. Okay, I'll be looking on in the monitor in the closet..."

Of course, I needed no direction. I went seamlessly from paying customer to paying guest. McLean encouraged patients' having as many visitors from the outside to stir in some reality and counteract the cracker factory stereotype. Since Travis had no family in the area, his wife Muriel came down the third week and had me listed as a family friend. Short list. Me, Polly Trombley, and Brian O'Callahan, the Waltham police officer who had found him naked at the Shell Station and signed the Section 12A.

This is what I know now. At the time, I had no idea about the list. I called ahead to see if there was a protocol about visiting patients. It seemed like a longshot. The receptionist recited a few polite hospital bylaws about how all visitors needed to be approved by the family and I figured well, that's it. Nice try. It would have been nice to see him, but they don't let you just show up, like he was in there getting a chin implant.

"What did you say your name was?" she asked.

"Charles Traub. But forget it."

"Charlie Traub?"

"Yes."

"Here you are," she said. "There are only three names. And you're the only one who has called. When should I tell Mr. Waldman to expect you?"

There was enough circumstantial evidence (hell, the man came to my mother's funeral!) to prove Travis and I were friends, so my presence at McLean was never really questioned by anyone. Other than me. I know what I said about no expectations. I had none. But I do allow wiggle room for hope, and I did hope I might be able to talk with him about what was going on with me. Proving once again, or for the first time, you can be delusional and quaint. I realized the second I saw him shuffle down the corridor and give me an Ellis Island hug that my therapist was gone. Travis was pale, thin, monochromatic and sported a clean upper lip. Moustache shaved. So, you take the belt and shoelaces, but you give the guy a razor? Fine. It's your cracker factory.

And yet that first visit was the only one that technically involved a conversation. We discussed my mom's funeral ("I never told you, Charlie, but you killed!") and the incident at the Shell Station ("The staff here wants to hear something other than, 'I let the day get away from me.'"). He asked me to thank Polly and apologize to Bonnie and said this time every Wednesday worked great for him, as it was in between art therapy and group. We got in four quiet hands of gin, which he won easily. And I'm good. I can play. The only thing he said was when he had gin. As he lay down his cards, he would bark, "Here comes Rusty!"

He shook my hand in the corridor and said, "I appreciate you driving out here, my friend. So, let's make it one-forty."

"One-forty to game? Penny a point?" I asked.

And he laughed. Not the high-pitched squeal of a Streisand sycophant he unleashed after we had gone to Chelsea Piers. But the deep satisfying chuckle of a man. A man who expected me to pay for him clearing forty-five minutes out of his schedule.

"Yeah," he finger saluted. "Penny a point."

I might have said something the next time I saw Travis, except the first thing he said when he greeted me in the library was, "And let's not change things. Keep it at every other visit." I used to send a check twice a month to a post office box at Grand Central Station. Who am I kidding? I might have said something except for the fact that I am a fucking coward. That's harsh. I am not a fucking coward. I am a fucking slave to harmony. And I believe they frown on that kind of confrontation in a locked ward. No more than myself, but they do.

So, I sent the checks to the post office box. I wound up sending two to cover the first four, uh, sessions. After my fifth visit (the trip to Target had gone so well, they let us go back there to get him a cold water humidifier for his room), I showed up the following Wednesday at 1:00 P.M. and was stopped at the front desk by an administrator, a large seventies-dressed woman named Caroline. Can't remember the last name. I think it was a bit involved-sounding, like some town in Eastern Europe. She handed me a $280 check made out to Travis Waldman.

"Is this your personal check, Mr. Traub?"

"Yes it is."

"Mr. Waldman tried to cash it."

"At a bank?"

"No. With us."

As much as I wanted to say, "He tried to cash an out-of-state check at a hospital? He must be nuts!" I opted for, "That's odd. I never gave him that check."

"We know you didn't. Muriel sent it to him."

"Muriel?"

"His wife."

"Oh." And that was the first time I heard the name of Travis' wife. The second was yesterday, Sunday, when she called me in Manhattan and asked me to do his eulogy. Yeah, I'll do the eulogy. Cost you a hundred-forty for forty-five fucking minutes. Cash.

"Why didn't you tell us you were his patient?" Caroline asked.

So far, as I see it, there has been no problem for me with living in the moment. No real jackpots. Except right then, in that moment, with Caroline, when I heard myself say, with great compassion and zero self-awareness, "I haven't been Travis' patient since last October, so I no longer considered myself his patient. I am his friend. And when I found out that I was on the list, cleared by the family to see him, I assumed it wasn't a problem for the hospital. The fact that he wanted me to pay him as if I was still seeing him professionally I chalked up to his delusion. Which, as a visitor and not a doctor, is none of my business. I wasn't happy about writing the checks, but I played along. I didn't want a confrontation. I didn't want to agitate him."

Caroline fingered the pair of reading glasses hanging from the Byzantine knotted lanyard around her neck. Made no doubt by a patient. Or was that a former patient? "I'm sure you can see this is an enormous ethical and boundary problem for us, Mr. Traub."

I wanted to pinch the corner of the lanyard and say, "This is lovely. So, you believe that Travis having absolutely no visitors will help break down the isolation?" But I try not to hold any debate when I know the outcome. And frankly, I really couldn't afford to see Travis, even at the discounted rate. So, I gave her my heartiest harmony-infused, "Of course. I see that now."

I waited two weeks, then tried one more time to visit Travis. Caroline met me in the parking lot in the cold mid-March rain with no umbrella. She knew she wouldn't have to stand there long. Just long enough for me to say, "Look, he came to my mother's funeral, and the next thing I know, he's inside. I was concerned. Not that he wasn't being taken care of. It seemed like the next right thing was for me to be available. And I find I get my needs met by being available to other people." Yeah, I said that. That I would think, even momentarily, that one of the tenets of my non-psychological life would be grokked by someone running a mental hospital should really have entitled me to a free Saturday night stay there.

Caroline put her hand on my shoulder and told me to go home. Wherever that was. At the time, home was another few days on Bonnie Dressler's son's bed. Pre-apple core down the toilet. If I was a guy prone to symbolic gestures, whoo baby, could we have a field day with that. Apple. Toilet. Woman. What a break I am not prone to symbolic gestures. What a break I am just thoughtless. Not all the time. In fact, I can only think of two instances of real thoughtlessness. When I told Jennifer about Bonnie and tossing the apple core down her toilet.

Uh-oh.

ع

WHEN I MADE THAT connection, just now, it was embarrassing. Thank God I'm alone out here. But then again, the fact that it just occurred to me now proves once again that I don't need to dwell on all of this. I settled up with Jennifer. I settled up with Bonnie. I absolutely settled up with my mom. I settled up with my sister, Alison. If there's a pattern of behavior with women, we have discontinued that pattern. Try another store. Everything turned out the way it was supposed to turn out. Otherwise, it would have been different.

Alison was the only one with whom I actively embodied or embraced the phrase "settled up" when I accepted the discounted terms of the Late City Edition of my mom's will. What was left, I guess, was our relationship.

The last time I saw Travis in McLean, I managed to get in a sentence, something to the effect that just about everything in my mother's apartment went to Alison and her family. "Who's Alison?" he says as I'm leaving. "My sister," I say. He bursts out laughing. Can't stop for a few moments. The kind of laugh that makes a hospital aide look up. Finally, Travis high-pitch exhales himself to rest, like he's taxiing to the gate, and he says, "You're incorrigible."

Whether or not Alison's name ever came up in session, whether or not Travis recalled that I introduced her to the audience at the funeral, of which he was a member, none of it matters. The fact is when handed the jumbo stadium seating-sized box of crayons, I have always chosen to draw my sister in black and white. Now, I know people who will only watch black and white movies, who believe there is more depth and nuance in a black and white photograph than there is in color. They could tell you more, but they ain't here. My sister and I have spent the last half-century caring for one another by staying out of each other's way. And as surprised as Travis might have been to find out I had a sister, he wasn't the first. I know that just as I know the first time I met Jonathan, Alison's husband, after they had been married three months, and he shook my hand and his head in unison before uttering, "So, it turns out I was wrong about her being an only child."

Is there such a thing as an arranged childhood? If not, I just made something else up, like I made up the words "hecticity," "uncorroboratable," and "amuchmorphous." I guess you can do that when you're not examining, just observing. We of the non-psychological life are not bound by the lexicon of the inward-looking and their pathologistics. It was an arrangement. As I said before, I was in charge of staging and producing the entertainment of our parents (Essentially the entertaining of Gwen Traub. Whatever trickled down to Ducky he would be fine with.), Alison handled all administrative details. All participants were willing. And it worked as arrangements such as that worked. To the superficial benefit of all.

You know what? I may be incorrigible.

I know you want some big story. There is no big story. There are just numbers and time. Alison is two years younger than me. We haven't seen each other for longer than two weeks since I went away to boarding school in 1968. I was fourteen, she was twelve. After that, between school vacations and post sleepaway camp to Labor Day, figure six weeks a year. And I'm being generous with that figure, because when Alison was sixteen, she spent the summer working on a kibbutz in Israel. Kibbutz Gevim. No idea how I remember the name. I can't remember whether or not I took my Lipitor this morning, but I can remember Kibbutz Gevim.

Alison visited me once early on during my freshman year at Harvard. I took her to the Hong Kong, where she had six spareribs and two tiki bowls and threw up most of the night, to the disgust of my roommates, who I wasn't thrilled with anyway. I looked forward to more of the same, but when I came home for Christmas break, she was packing. She was going back to Israel, back to the kibbutz, and finishing her junior year of high school there. Gwen and Ducky Traub had their empty nest five years ahead of schedule. Junior year became summer became senior year at a school in Tel Aviv living with a family whose daughter she had met on the kibbutz. We were all planning to fly out for her graduation, but she told us not to bother because "It's not like that here." And that kind of thing you only had to tell Gwen Traub once.

Alison returned for two weeks in late August, 1974, just long enough to buy a 1971 Olds Cutlass and load it up for the drive to West Lafayette, Indiana. Apparently, that's where Purdue University was plopped, and apparently that's where you go for an undergraduate degree in agriculture. Jesus, I sound like Sy. Other than the address where Ducky had to send first semester tuition, that was all the information any of us received. What's left to talk about? I'm asking that now. I didn't think to ask that then. "You okay?" / "Yah, you?" / "Yeah." / "Can you believe Mom?" / "Can you believe Dad?" That was it. That was the full outskirts of our dialogue. She was smoking cigarettes, but not drinking anymore. What do you do? I'm asking that now. Back then, I took her to a Red Sox game. We lasted four innings, then some guy with a belly that was not properly zoned for his box seat stood up when Sox manager Darrell Johnson came out from the dugout to remove starter Reggie Cleveland. The belly yelled, "Hey Darrell, what took you so long?" And my sister, Alison Traub, kibbutznik-turned-incoming-Purdue-freshman, screamed, "He was at yah mutha's house!" And we got in our running for the day.

Then it gets hazy. I want to say she stayed a year and a half at Purdue. I know she lived in Berkeley for a while, but I'm not sure whether that was in the pursuit of a degree or a guy. There were a few other schools. I want to say the University of Manitoba. We kept just missing each other. A year after I left Brighton, she went to Brandeis in Waltham. A month after I left Schenectady, she attended a conference at Union College. Three days after I left New Haven, her return flight from Israel was rerouted into Bradley Field in Hartford and she spent two weeks auditing classes at Yale Divinity School.

By then, she must have been thirty-eight, living in Waban thirteen years, married fifteen with children sixteen and fourteen. Don't hold me to that. The only thing I can say for certain is for as long as I have been an adult, my sister has either been on her way to Israel, in Israel, or on her way back. Everything else has seemed ephemeral. I remember calling my mom one night in 1991 when the first Iraq war began its twenty-eight-week smash run on CNN and her answering the phone, sobbing, saying, "How can you call now?" before she hung up. That's how I found out my sister was in Haifa, perilously near where the Iraqi missiles were landing. Except she wasn't. She and the husband (whom she'd met on the kibbutz during stay number seven or nine) and the kids had been back in Waban for a week, but their phone was out. Of course, I didn't find out about this until 2003, when George W. Bush ("They tried to kill my daddy!") tried to become an Oedipal winner by sending the bombers back and I said something to Alison like, "Seeing that night sky over Baghdad must bring back some horrific memories." And she replied, "What are you talking about?"

This is my way of saying we didn't chase after each other.

But regardless of where she was in relation to the tarmac or her curriculum (she eventually graduated from Brandeis, on her third stint there after she had her two children, at twenty-nine, and got her Masters in social work three years later), Alison kept a sentry's eye on our parents. For that, I will always be grateful, although it's a gratitude I tend to display with silent approbation.

When I cleared out my mom's apartment at the end of February, the movers made two stops. A bureau, two lamps, three dozen framed paintings or photos of all sizes and six boxes of books were dropped off at Alison's house, in the nearby village of Waban. The larger remnants—two bedrooms of furniture, kitchen stuff, a couch, three chairs, a desk, a ten-foot by seven-foot wall unit, and two televisions—went into storage in Somerville. Alison and I would each get a key, but Alison would pay for the unit until her two children had hauled off whatever they wanted. She figured it would take two months for her kids to get around to it. Fine. $155,000 in lost inheritance for $205 saved in storage rental costs. Deal.

I grabbed one item for myself. A round glass paperweight my mother had kept next to her bed. It had been in the living room when we were growing up. It was the size of a croquet ball and not as good looking. Clear glass incoherently interrupted by five arrows of orange, which sprang from the flat bottom and opened like flowers, only they weren't. Next to the tip of one of the shoots was the tiniest air bubble, an imperfection forever more compelling than any of the misguided flowers. Or flawers. If only they hadn't been there, it would have made an ideal kid-sized magic crystal ball. Then again, if they hadn't been there, Gwen Traub wouldn't have bought the thing at some dirt road emporium in Belize. So, I'm grateful. How I loved its heft and mostly roundness, and for as long as I had a memory, it is that of me just about to toss the semi-orb to myself, and my mom, from whatever room she was in, anticipatorily growling, "Charlie, don't even!"

The glass paperweight was the entirety of the Gwen Traub Estate that would accompany me on my return to Manhattan, whenever that was going to be. It was sitting on the nightstand at the Westin when Alison called my cell the last week of March. When the phone chirped, I was perched on the edge of the bed, back to paperweight, staring at the in-room coffee maker, trying to hasten the brewing process.

"Where are you?"

"Here."

"Here where?" she asked.

"The Westin."

"The Westin here? In Waltham? Off 128?"

"Yeah."

"I thought you were going back after you turned over Mom's apartment."

"I did, too. But things came up and I had to stay."

"What things?"

"I'll tell you about it some time." The last spoken exchange between us had been in the parking lot of the cemetery, when Alison told me she was done with me and rolled up her window. So, my saying, "I'll tell you about it some time" was just pure flailing. A line that she, the one who had ordered all communication to cease, swatted back.

Long exhale. "Yeah, well," she said, "if you did tell me, that would be a first."

I know I said I await further instructions. But sometimes, the instructions can be vague. Which means I miss them and say things like, "So, what's up?"

"So, what's up?"

"You mean you've been living at the Westin for a month, ten miles away, and I didn't know?"

"Okay, first of all, I haven't been staying here the entire month. I was dog-sitting for a cou..."

"Dog-sitting!!!??!!! Since when do you like dogs?"

"Since all my life," I said.

"Charlie, do you have any idea what a fucked-up conversation this is?"

"I do now."

I heard half a laugh and three-quarters of a sniffle. "Why do I feel I have to keep introducing myself to you? Jesus, what's the point? Look, I was going through the photos and paintings and I found a couple you might want. That's why I was calling. I figured I would send them to you in New York because God knows there's nothing that would ever make you come back here."

And there are other times the instructions scroll in front of my eyes. "How about I come over at one, look through the stuff, and tell you everything?"

"One-thirty is better for me," she said.

"Do you want me to grab us some lunch?"

"I have food here."

"Fine."

"Charlie, do you even know where I live?"

"Have you moved in the last twenty-five years?"

"No."

"Then I'm good."

We spent a good ten minutes in Alison's kitchen that day in March discussing if I ever liked potato salad (I didn't) and if I was sure I had never liked it (quite). I think that conversation was valuable, because it set a humanely low threshold that our memories would ever coincide when we looked through the photos and paintings.

She's funny, my sister. Nobody told me this. Three times, she said, "Okay, let's just recap and make sure we're keeping track of everything you want to take with you. So far, we have the glass paperweight, which you already have, and...that's it."

I did ask for one photo of the two of us. She was probably nine and I was eleven. She is in a ballerina costume and toe shoes after a recital. I am wearing gray flannel pants, a red blazer, and an open white shirt. I have my hands on her shoulders.

"Do you remember that day?" she asked.

I pointed to my blazer and said, "I remember I was showing some houses in the neighborhood and happened to stop by."

"You can't have this. It's my favorite picture of us. I'll make a copy, but you can't have this."

"That's fine."

"So, to sum up, the paperweight, which you already have, a copy of one photo, and nothing else."

"Now you got it."

Alison carefully put everything off to the side and sat up straight. "Okay. Now talk."

"Where do you want me to start?"

"You can tell me about the month since you got rid of the apartment, the three months since Mom died, or 1974 to the present."

This is not a quiz, but remember when I talked about my first session with Travis and how I was worried it would take six months to catch him up on my life and it took forty-some minutes? I was not nearly as economical with Alison. How could I be? Travis was a stranger to whom I only owed the courtesy of information. He just needed to be educated. Alison, who I had unconsciously demoted to stranger over the last thirty-five years, was owed the truth. And nothing snarls time like the truth. It is the black ice-rooted pileup at the side of the road that slows everything down to that which demands a glimpse. The unavertable. I know, I know. I made up another word.

"This may not make any sense," I began. "I'm living here now because it's where I am now. I was trying to write a book with Sy Siegel about Tony Conigliaro, but that looks like nothing and I was visiting my former shrink, who is in McLean Hospital, before they found out I was his former patient and forbade me from seeing him. You may remember him. Travis Waldman? The guy with the bright socks and the moustache who crashed Mom's memorial service and that was why it took me so long to go to the cemetery with you? I apologize for that. It was unavertable. Let me see if I can say this in a way that follows. After I stopped seeing him as a therapist, Travis told me he was having an affair with a woman I had talked about in session. Why, I can't tell you. Ask the fine folks at McLean's. Turns out he made the whole thing up. Well, the affair part. Again, can't help you with why. But I never would have discovered that if Travis hadn't shown up at the funeral home and bragged about it in front of Sy and the woman he brought to drive him, a former student who turned out to be the sister of the woman I had talked about in session. Travis agreed to voluntarily enter McLean for two weeks, but then there was an incident, so now he's there for a while. The way this all jumped off at once, plus the obstacles Windgate Point put in my way for getting rid of Mom's apartment, plus the fact that my only friend was the man who had accidentally killed her made me think I might need to talk to someone. So, I started visiting Travis inside, but it ended up with me just listening. Do we have any coffee?"

Here's where the non-psychological life can bite you in the ass. And by you, I mean me. I was so intent on doing the next thing in front of me and living in the present and looking at the watch on my cellphone (2:17 P.M., March 25, 2007) and if projecting anything, projecting myself at my destination laughing, I had never stopped to synopsize that which had brought me to now, 2:18 P.M., March 25, 2007.

Alison popped up from the kitchen table and fished a nurse's hat-style coffee filter out of a cupboard.

"You're writing a book about Tony Conigliaro?" she said. Of all that I had coughed up, that's what she grabbed.

"Was."

"He was so handsome. He was sooo handsome. When I was fourteen, Joanne Gurson took me to a party at Bob Wolff's house. Remember him? The big sports agent? She used to babysit for his kids. You remember Joanne. She was your age. Well, Tony Conigliaro was there. I guess he was one of Bob Wolff's clients. And I was standing all alone in the corner, hiding behind the drapes, and he saw me, Tony saw me, and winked at me. The next day, I told Joanne and she said during the spring we'd drive out to Logan when the Red Sox came back from the road and meet them when their plane landed, like we'd do with the Bruins. But he got traded like a month later."

"To the Angels. Wait, though. When you were fourteen, you and Joanne used to drive out to Logan and meet the Bruins?"

"We only did it six or seven times. We stood there with a bunch of other girls and screamed. I never asked for an autograph. I was too shy."

"How come I never knew about this?"

She dropped in the third heaping scoop of coffee and flipped the switch on the machine. "How come I never knew you liked dogs?"

So, I told her the story about talking to the Boston terrier when the couple was looking at my apartment, which she loved so much she made me tell it three times, and then about sitting for Bonnie's dog and flushing the core down the toilet. That one, she was not enchanted by.

"Do you plan to tell me about what happened with Bonnie?"

"I can tell you what transpired," I said, "but nothing happened."

"Do you have a law degree I don't know about?"

"*Heh.* No, but she does. Bonnie Dressler. She used to appear on my show in Washington. She's a constitutional law professor. She's from here."

"She works at Simmons, right?"

"Yeah."

"I know her. She spoke at a fundraiser for my old hospital. She used to be on TV here. Channel 2. Pretty."

"Yeah."

"Got a mouth on her."

"Right. Same girl."

"At the fundraiser she used the word 'twat.'"

"Come on. In what context?"

"To describe herself. We had different local celebrities auctioning off items. They introduced her and the reaction was kind of mixed. She gets behind the microphone and the first thing she says, 'Uh-oh. Here's the twat from WGBH...' All the women shrieked and all the men looked at them, like it was a test."

"Yeah. Same girl."

Alison picked up my empty coffee cup and on her way to the sink, hit me on the side of the head with it. Lightly.

"Jesus fucking Christ, Charlie. What, you didn't get pushed around enough by Jennifer? You had to go for Jennifer with red hair and bigger tits?"

"No," I said, and then corrected myself. "I'm not disagreeing with you, I just never thought of Bonnie that way. When I let myself become attracted, I probably looked at her as a departure from Jen, not some shinier floor model. Okay, so I am disagreeing with you. But it doesn't matter. I couldn't go through with it, and I was embarrassed that I thought I could go through with it and then the whole thing, my behavior, my cluelessness, struck me as, uh, comical. So comical, I told Jennifer."

"Who did not share your sense of irony."

"Yes, and those became the grounds for divorce. Irreconcilable ironies."

The only hard data I had left on Alison, and the one thing that enabled me to still think of her as a sister rather than a stranger, was her love of the word "idiot." That she got from our mother, who would toss a word salad and mix it up between "idiot," "nitwit," "moron," "stoop," and the vaguely continental "dumbkopf." I tented my arms and folded my hands in front of my mouth and waited to be called an idiot. And quietly, quiet like all the years we had spoken in only an official capacity to each other, Alison said, "I did the same thing, minus the divorce."

"Hang on," I said.

I jumped up and grabbed my rinsed-out cup from the sink. Alison had turned the coffee maker off, but there was still plenty left in the pot. I once read a magazine piece on Muhammed Ali in which he kept interrupting the interview to bark at whoever he was married to at the time. At one point, this exchange ensued: "Bring me some chicken." / "It's cold." / "Bring it anyway." The coffee was cold. Big deal.

"You're not going to drink that," she said.

"I am. Now, you talk."

She felt the side of my cup and sighed. It was a sigh of resignation and acceptance, not disapproval. A shrink might call that detachment. If there was one around. Thank God it was just us.

"Six, no seven, seven years ago, we had started a new program at the hospital for firemen's wives. A support group kind of thing right after that big fire in Worcester. We did it for a little over a year, and then 9/11 happened and everything got reprioritized. The group met twice a month, and after the first month, the hospital wanted me to get some publicity for it. I knew an editor at the *Globe* and they ran a blurb, nothing, but I was listed as the contact and I get an email from this guy who writes a regular column for the *Improper Bostonian*. Do you know this magazine? They started it a few years ago. It's a big glossy thing that comes out every two weeks, mostly arts and lifestyle pieces, but people read it. It's like the *Phoenix*, but much slicker.

"The first email says 'I'm Alex So and So, I'm interested in possibly doing a column about your group.' I know this guy. He's the guy in that magazine everyone reads. I tell him I'm a big admirer of his. He makes some self-effacing remark, and we go back and forth with the where'd you grow up, oh, do you know so and so? Turns out we're the same age and would have been in the same class at Brandeis if I had gone there on time. And he asks how I wound up at New England Baptist, so that's a whole thing, you know, 'Ever met any of the Celtics?' And then all the places he's written for and how the *Globe* is still an Irish Mafia and then I mention the kibbutz and we went into a whole spirited thing about Israel. That went on for a few days. Just an incredibly stimulating conversation. I couldn't remember the last time I had been involved in one of those. He's not Jewish, so he needed to be straightened out on a few things. But he raised some good points. I'm not an email person out of the office, but I started checking for new messages all the time. The kids were long gone and Jonathan was in the middle of this power play at his job where he had to work these insane hours. He'd come home at ten and that's all we'd talk about until one in the morning, when I'd finally say, 'Sweetie, we have to be up in five hours. Let's get some sleep.' But don't think when 6:00 A.M. came, the first thing I did, before I got in the shower, was check my email.

"I think we were writing each other about ten days when I asked him, 'Alex, so what about it, are you going to do the column? Or is this online dating?' He gives me an 'lol,' then asks if he could come and observe the group. I tell him that would be too intrusive since it was all women, that I was thinking more along the lines of offering the women the chance to talk to him individually and maybe a couple of other social workers or therapists to give insight into the benefits. He writes back, 'Hmm. That's a little press-releasey for what I do.' I say I see his point and ask if I should apologize for wasting his time. He says not at all and goes into a whole thing about a longer feature he's trying to put together for, of all places, the *Globe*. It deals with the scenario that happens after a fatal fire, when firehouses send men from the house to console women who have lost their husbands and check in regularly and help out. And what starts innocently ends up with the two having an affair and the fireman leaving his family. I didn't even know about this. But it's more than a little common.

"Again, it was a lively exchange, but I was beginning to feel a little taken advantage of. Like he was only interested in my group for who might be getting laid. And I wrote, 'I feel a little worked here, Alex.' He comes right back with, 'Maybe I can repay you for your time with dinner.' That's when it dawned on me that with all the emails and all the banter, I had never told him I was married. And I can tell you all day that I had approached him as business so that was not relevant, but I knew when I saw 'dinner,'" and felt—what? cold?—that I had created a lot of this. Not all, but a lot. So, I wrote back and said while I was flattered by the offer, my husband wouldn't be and good luck with the consoling the widows piece."

I think I held up my hands and rotated the wrists, like "Is this anything impeachable?"

"Wait," Alison continued. "So, that was it. The last thing I wrote. I was a little embarrassed, but I felt like I hadn't done anything wrong. It's over, right?

"Three years later, 2003, I get an email from Alex. He's attached the affairs with firemen's widows feature, which ran in some national magazine. I want to say *New York Magazine*. Of course, after 9/11, he had all the examples he needed. Now that I think of it, that's probably where Denis Leary got the idea for *Rescue Me*. Have you seen that show? No? Oh, you have to.

"The body of the email says, 'Thought you'd want to see how this turned out. Hope you're well.' And the subject line is still 'RE: I'm Alex So and So and I am interested in possibly...' from three years before. I guess that's how he saved my email address."

She inhaled for what seemed like the first time since she had made the coffee.

"Take your time," I said. I remember this because I'm pretty sure I've never said that to anyone my entire life.

Exhale. "The piece on the widows was long. I started it at work, but it got busy. I got home, called it back up on our computer here and was reading after dinner. I was trying to finish it before *American Idol* came on, but I didn't."

"That may be the most humiliating part of the story," I said.

"Shut up. Jonathan had been laid off and was out of work at the time, so he was home all the time and spent his days cooking, cleaning up, and sending out his résumés or following through with headhunters on the computer. I'm watching *Idol* and it's almost over and he walks in the living room with a stack of paper and throws it down in front of me. And he's crying. I think he lost out on a job. 'Look at this,' he says, and fans out the papers."

I made some noise. "Yewwwww... Emails?"

"Yeah. The whole two-week chain from three years before. At first I was defensive and said I had nothing to apologize for, and, like you, nothing happened. BUT NOTHING HAPPENED! Which you should never say, especially when nothing happened. And then Jonathan said something, it was hard to make out, but something like, 'It's the intimacy that hurts.' And then I tried coming from the angle that maybe it wouldn't have bothered

234 • Bill Scheft

him so much if he wasn't out of work... Yeah, I see how you're looking at me. I got that times a thousand from him. And that's how the first night ended.

"I tried again the next night, a full apology, but Jonathan asked me why and all I could do was give the history of the emails. We took the next night off, then he asked me again, 'Why?' and I realized he wasn't asking why it had started but why my responses got longer and longer. And I said, 'I guess because I don't think I'm enough.' That's when Jonathan got angry, which he never does, and said, 'So, what the fuck am I supposed to do? Sit here and wait until your self-esteem grows back?' How about that? 'What the fuck am I supposed to do? Sit here and wait until your self-esteem grows back?' Said the mathematician to the social worker. We were in counseling two days later."

"How long were you in counseling?"

"Not long. Three months. It was a 'bad moment.' That's what she said. Not a pattern, but a product of the other stuff. You know—kids out of the house, husband out of work, the comfort of non-communication—that other stuff. Pretty standard. So, we dealt with all that. And I hate people who say this, but we worked at it."

"I like the comfort of non-communication," I said.

"Good line, huh?"

"It may be. But I'm saying I like the comfort of non-communication."

"Hey, who at this table doesn't?"

"My old shrink, Travis, used to say, 'A good marriage needs resiliency from inevitable conflict. Anything else is fantasy.'"

"The guy locked up in McLean Hospital said that?"

"Yeah. He used to also say, 'Charlie, it's a miracle you're not more fucked up.'"

"The guy in McLean."

"Same guy."

And then Alison told me to go get my shit at the Westin and stay with them. Just like that. "Go get your shit." I asked if she wanted to clear it with Jonathan, but she said it would be funnier if I was sitting there when he came home. So, no. I explained that I had no idea how long I'd be staying, words to the effect of, "Are you sure you want to do this? Because, as your brother, I would advise against it." I don't think I was that clever. I was stunned at the invitation. I'm pretty sure living the non-psychological life and having no expectations drastically reduces the odds of getting blindsided to just above zero. But I never saw this coming. So, I said, "Wow."

"Wow." And then, like a farmhand, "Is there anything I can do to earn my keep?"

Alison smiled. Up until then, she had looked so much like Mom. But Sy was right. They looked nothing alike. Gwen Traub knew how to laugh. Smile? Sorry. Never got the paperwork.

"You can do three things," she said. "Jonathan and I can't get down on our knees, so I need you to put Vaseline on all the bedframe wheels."

"I won't ask why, but sure."

"Join us for Seder dinner April third. It's a Tuesday."

The Red Sox were off that night. "Absolutely," I said. "That's two things. What's the third?"

"And just," another smile, "just be available."

That was probably where I came up with the idea of being available.

I stayed about two months, until Sy let me go. I had a couple of weeks alone in the house in late April/early May, when they went to Israel and I went on my blind date. No toilets were harmed.

As for earning my keep, it took three hours and twenty minutes to take care of my first two responsibilities, and the other nine weeks to be available. Turns out applying a layer of Vaseline to bedframe wheels is the most effective defense against bedbugs, which Alison didn't have, but which a hospital colleague had checked in her luggage and brought back from Florida to her home in Winchester, eight miles away. When I finished greasing, I came up with a line that was much too clever and way too Jewish for me. "Just call us the *Vantz* Trap Family," I said.

I summoned nothing that remarkable during the Seder, my first in forty years. The haggadah-directed service was longer than anyone but me remembered and now included opportunities for rebuttal. The food was mostly bland but heavily spiced with over-talking. And there was just enough sugar in the wine and the dessert to vault us all through off-key renditions of the songs. Mostly, I sat quietly and tried to do that thing where I am just there and not asking why or if it's enough. And awaiting further instructions, which during a Seder, there is an overabundance of, from "pass the haroses" to "you read this paragraph as Moses, Charlie."

My great niece Jillian said that to me. Don't ask me anyone else's name. We were thirteen. Alison, Jonathan, their kids (Victoria and Jack), their spouses (forget it), their three kids (Jillian, the other one, and the one from Jack's wife's previous marriage), Jonathan's mother, Libby, and Victoria's husband's parents (can't help you), which mercifully knocked me down to the fourth oldest person there. The Seder table was set for fourteen, but Sy backed out at the last minute. "I will not participate in mock heroism," was his version of sending regrets.

As much as I appreciated and was shocked by Alison's invitation, I was relieved not to have to unleash Sy on strangers.

But Jonathan, whose downshifted mutterings I had come to enjoy in the short time I had shared a roof with him, was disappointed. As he was loading meat dishes into the dishwasher after the Seder, Jonathan said, "I was so looking forward to your friend Sy meeting my mother tonight." Then, downshift to mutter, "Maybe, eventually, he could have bumped her off, too."

Alison and I never had a big discussion about Sy. Or the big discussion. I told her a few stories and the whole vomit clean-up workers' rights half-court press that hastened my exit from Windgate Point. But mostly, the exchanges consisted of her looking up from the *Globe* or looking at me during a commercial and saying, "And what is it you like about him?" And I would say, "Well, he's someone who's fond of me. And that's a short list. But I like him because I get to see the way I think he treated Mom." See, there? That's me being available. After the third or fourth one of those exchanges, Alison stopped asking, and we moved on to making jokes about him as a murderer. Which, as you can see, Jonathan may have started. Fond jokes. Jokes like, "You following the Phil Spector trial? Thank God Sy wasn't implicated."

Alison and Jonathan were not Orthodox Jews, but they supped from the parts of the faith that most appealed to them (my sister was not going to be married to anyone whose first waking thought was to bow his head and thank God he wasn't a woman). They observed the Sabbath quite stringently. From sundown to sundown, the house was bathed in a studious quiet that I'm sure I would have benefited greatly from. But the Red Sox played Friday night and most Saturday afternoons and I answered to a Power greater than myself. Sy Siegel. Marxist, baseball fan, collaborator, person of interest in his girlfriend's death.

"When did you find out about Mom and Sy?" I asked Alison one night.

"I knew him from the place. Mom and Dad and Sy were all friends. He was this eccentric they were charmed by. Then Dad went out to lunch, you know, demented—and Sy and Mom would eat together in the dining room a couple of times a week. After Dad died, he was very protective of her. It was kind of sweet. Whenever I came over and he was there, he'd jump up and say, 'I'll come back when the heat dies down.' Mom and I had a big fight when he moved all his boxes into Dad's bedroom, but that was more my shit. It was her apartment. I still hadn't put it together until I called one night around eight and said, 'Hi Mom, what are you doing?' 'Well' (*perfect impression*), she said, 'I was just about to take my clothes off...'"

Okay then.

That line, "I was just about to take my clothes off..." which I have thought of more than twice, may be the single greatest test of living the non-psychological life. Here's what I do when it knocks on my mind's door. I breathe in. I breathe out. I laugh. I look at the clock on my cell phone. I rotate my shoulders. I look at the clock on my cell phone again. *2:12 P.M. October 14, 2007.*

Alison and Jonathan have a good marriage. Not that I would know. They vie a bit. Jonathan will at times suspend what might look to the world as if he's on a silent retreat and begin to carry on an animated discourse with either a person or an object in the room, and Alison will wait for an opening and say something like, "Jonathan, you're on the verge of being relevant." No, not something like, exactly like that. And they'll bicker for a while, like two hockey fighters who just tug at each other's sweaters until they get tired and allow the referees to separate them. Nothing is ever resolved, which means that the same topic and sweater-tugging can ensue ten days later. I always had two thoughts as I watched this. Thought One: *A good marriage needs resiliency from inevitable conflict. Anything else is fantasy.* Thought Two: *They're acting like I used to act.* By that I mean dwelling in the past. I don't mean the resiliency from inevitable conflict. Jennifer and I did not have that. We just had the one goodbye scene.

I know what you're thinking. Isn't that last musing about you and Jennifer dwelling in the past? Not if I'm doing it to provide context. That's the other aspect of the non-psychological life I've discovered. Occasionally, you must acknowledge that which you are no longer. Even celebrate. Okay, acknowledge.

While we're on resiliency from inevitable conflict, I should mention Alison and Jonathan kept a kosher home. This was a relatively recent development. Maybe in the last ten years. I never recall them making this transition, and if that surprises anyone, you haven't been paying attention. In the world of awaiting further instructions, a kosher home is The Hague. I tried. I did my best. I asked where things went a couple of times if I had to, and like some *treyf* ex-con, I mixed my meat and cheese on the outside.

Listen to me. *Vantz. Treyf.* I know the words and yet, what kind of Jew am I? No idea. I think I've led a pretty charmed life in terms of never having to deal with this question. I did the minimum as a kid. Temple twice a year. Learning just enough Hebrew while my tutor, sixty-year-old Abe Schindler, sat ten feet away on the toilet with the door open and told me to keep reading. My bar mitzvah was a lot like the life that would follow. Few friends in attendance, nobody really understanding what was said, nobody there who could help me, and everyone else winding up making more money.

The only time I ever recall being targeted as a Jew was an accident. It was my last year in New Haven, 1994-95, shortly after the introduction of inter-office email at WTNH, Channel 8, where I was the coordinating producer of the 6:00 P.M. news. I still made coffee, good coffee, but it was usually just before I had to rush out with my camera crew and some on-air talent to cover a fire or somebody at Yale getting their feelings hurt.

My boss at WTNH was Kal Davidson. Smart man. Gentle guy. Well, gentle by the time I met him. He had spent the better part of three decades in local news, running and gunning on the road suffused by alcohol and pills. One of his colleagues at the station in Oakland had nicknamed Kal "Raider Game" because every Sunday he was blacked out at home. There were three stories (that he remembered) of him taking off all his clothes and diving into hotel fountains. The first time, just before plunging, he claimed to be the Dalai Lama. The second time, Jesus Christ, the third, Sean Connery. Which was a bit of a stretch because he was just north of three hundred pounds.

Fortunately, around the time of the Sean Connery baptism, Kal was working at KSTP, the ABC affiliate in St. Paul, Minnesota, and they sent him up forty miles to Center City and the famous treatment center at Hazelden, where he got sober, and (at least the last time I heard) stayed sober. When I came to work for him he hadn't had a drink or a pill in nine years. Kal Davidson employed a combination of twenty percent Alcoholics Anonymous and one hundred twenty percent Protestant Church. He was the first person I ever heard use the phrase "faith-based initiatives." Long before it came out of the oil-anointed head of John Ashcroft.

I found Kal's devoutness unobtrusive and, yes, charming. If anyone in the newsroom said "fuck," which happened with the regularity of a sniffle, you'd get a little *shhhhh*. First from him, then it caught on. And if there was ever some kind of conflict with stories, budget, management, or personalities, he would invariably slip into his office and read a few pages of scripture before emerging with his decision. And I don't remember it ever being the wrong decision. I remember disagreeing with him a few times and he would get all fat-guy twinkly and shift his belly and say, "Charles, you are going to be great when you get your own shop." Such, I gather, is the charity of those who humbly accept Jesus Christ as their Lord and Savior. The real Jesus, not the guy who makes the staff at the Hyatt Regency Dallas bring out the mops and towels.

With a last name like Traub, people tend to assume you're German, especially if you're not letting the occasional *vantz* and *treyf* fly out of your *punim*. I did not feel I hid my Jewness. I just made sure not to be around when the type of people who ask came around.

Okay, so inter-office email. One night, just after we aired, I came out from the editing bay. I had been working on some three-part series on charter schools, which was a little more meaty than my usual fare. The edit was involved and needed some B-roll reshoots, which were scheduled for the following morning. I came back to my desk to check my email, which I had had all of two months and was already captivated by. Come on. Immediate communication without interpersonal confrontation? Where do I sign up and begin to not commit?

There was one message in my inbox from Kal.

TO: Traub, Charles

FROM: Davidson, Kalvin

SUBJECT: Tomorrow AM

Woman in Meriden has grilled cheese sandwich with image of Virgin Mary. Ashley's crew already at Civic Center. Is this a conflict for you people? KD

I responded thoughtfully.

TO: Davidson, Kalvin

FROM: Traub, Charles

SUBJECT: RE: Tomorrow AM

What the fuck do you mean "you people?"

KAL DAVIDSON STOPPED BY my cubicle to say "Shhhh...," followed by "Your people. I meant *your* people. Your remote crew. But now I know, so thanks."

Until I bunked with my sister and her husband, that story and its coda, *But now I know. So thanks,* was the entire text of my adult history as a Jew. Otherwise, it never came up in my work or in my marriage, and if it did, I was in another room. During my two months in Waban, though, it became unavoidable. I don't mean unavoidable as in not answering the phone Saturday morning or putting the correct flatware in the correct sink. I mean unavoidable as in me in my own way. And even though between hers and Jonathan's schedules and my shuttling to Sy's for book sessions and Red Sox watching, we only saw each other over 8:00 A.M. coffee and whatever was on TV that night at 10:30, I was around it and it was around me.

Maybe that's what Alison had meant by telling me to just be available. Allow for the fact you're Jewish, and the possibility that it might be okay. That just occurred to me, sitting here in Montauk 2:54 P.M. *October 14, 2007.* Hah! How about that? I should call her. Son of a bitch. But now I know, so thanks.

ع

AS I MENTIONED, I waited until Alison and Jonathan went back to Israel before I went out on my blind date. Polly had called to tell me Travis had left McLean, was back in New York and "he's all yours." She was, like Alison, stunned I was still in the area.

"You never took me up on the opportunity to fix you up with one of my friends."

"I am now," I said. Come on. Is that being available and living in the moment, or when?

Here I come with a blanket statement. Arranging blind dates is all about the fixer, never about those fixed. You need to be fond of the person arranging the date the way you like the guy who sets the spread on the big game. Years ago, I saw Donald Trump on the *Late Show With David Letterman*. Dave, always looking to slip in a jab on Trump, says, "How's your ex-wife, Marla Maples, doing?" Trump said, "She's terrific. Would you like to go out with her?" Then pulls out a pen and starts writing down a number on Dave's sheet of questions. That? That's what you don't want.

While we were living in New Haven, Jennifer set up one of my coworkers from the station and a woman she met in Kokomo, Indiana, while trying to set up a fundraising phone bank for the Ryan White Foundation. The names are not germane, other than Ryan White. Six months later, the two of them were married. "Well, I'm never fucking doing that again," she said. It was the only time I had ever seen Jennifer emotionally wobbled. Until I coughed up the Bonnie Dressler fuse.

This is a long way to go to tell you something you already know. That I was fond of the fixer. Did I offer to go on the date to get Polly's approval? If I was the kind of person who still thought about those things, sure. Absolutely. But again, what a break I don't think that way anymore.

The only information Polly gave me about my date was her name (Justine) and that she was frustrated after running an un-nibbled personal ad in *Harvard Magazine*.

Yeah, you heard me. *Harvard Magazine*, the official alumni magazine of the world's most mostiest, has personal ads! If you are eating, or have just finished eating, I apologize. How was I supposed to know?

You don't have to have attended Harvard to run a personal ad in their magazine. Your money is as good as anyone else's, even though it isn't. But if you are trying to land the type of guy or gal who reads *Harvard Magazine*, I would imagine you'd need to step up your profile. I had never read a personal ad except by mistake, so you tell me. Do they usually contain lines like this? "Heroes: Mies van der Rohe, Giorgio Morandi, Ian McKellen as Richard III and Bill Belichick." Or this? "Great cook, great conversationalist, but not both at once unless you don't mind Grey Goose in your coq au vin." Or this? "Adores trekking Nepal and dark chocolate. Allergic to attitude." I know what "seeks slim DWF" means, but what is "must be verbal" code for?

I went through three back issues trying to find what might be Justine's ad, but the age range skewed too high and my mind kept whiplashing from the juxtapositions of Prado with "Big Papi" Ortiz and chamber music with Texas Hold 'em.

Not surprisingly, the ads ran four-to-one women seeking men. The eternal seller's market. But...Jewish women outnumbered their non-Chosen aspirants two to one, easy. I never asked Polly if this was the case here.

I have been on three blind dates. Actually, two blind dates and a karate lesson from a complete stranger when I was expecting Uma Thurman to show up. Seriously. This is now three years ago. I get a call on a Friday at the office, frantic, from a woman I've never met who works for a prominent female anchor. Another complete stranger, she asks me if I know any comedy writers. I know one guy. The woman says, "Uma Thurman is our friend.

She is receiving an award tomorrow night in L.A. She's getting on a plane in three hours. She needs twenty jokes about *Kill Bill.*" Before I can say, "So, in like an hour?" she gives me the fax number and adds, "Now, Uma can't pay him, but she's willing to give him a free karate lesson."

I tell her I'll call the guy I know, who I barely know. We had met at the 2000 Hillary Clinton birthday party/Senate fundraiser I told you about. He was writing material for the host, Nathan Lane, and they had me backhand a line to the teleprompter that wasn't in the vetted script about how Hillary was carried for nine months in her mother's womb, then stayed an additional three to establish residency.

Let's all let that sit for a second.

So, I call the guy, the writer (again, can't help you with the name) and he's home. He laughs, says no problem. Turns out he's already writing for the same awards show. I do his now four-year-old Hillary womb line back to him and he says, "I wrote that? Wow..." then passes on the karate lesson. I call the stranger in the female anchor's office back and tell her it's done and I'm taking the karate lesson.

Two months later, I'm in Uma Thurman's private gym on the West Side and a four-foot, eight-inch college student named Sharmila walks in, bows, says, "Uma not here," then cuts my legs out for a good hour.

So, we'll count that.

The two conventional blind dates, the ones that had my full cooperation, fell a quarter-century apart. My junior year at Harvard, my roommate Tuck Davenport asked me if I wouldn't mind going out with a friend of the girl he had started seeing from Wheaton, an all-women's college an hour away in Norton, Massachusetts. The friend, Mary Ann, had family in Arlington, the next town over from Cambridge, so she was coming in anyway. Said she was cute, maybe a little heavy, he couldn't remember. Said he would consider it a favor. Threw in the use of his car. The usual barter banter between roommates. I would suspend my Saturday night tradition of getting drunk alone and passing out in front of reruns of *The Rifleman* to help him out. Even back then, a child who had neither known nor tasted the fruits of the non-psychological life, I was eligible to do that which was in front of me. And, I won't lie to you, the car helped.

I'm sure there are several books entitled *How to Pick Up Girls*, but the one I bought the summer before I entered Harvard had a chapter near the end emblazoned "The All-Time Surest Most Foolproof Way to Pick Up Girls." I read that first, back to front, like any Hebrew scholar. The author's unpatented three-step method: Step One: Buy the book *How to Pick Up Guys*. Step Two: Read the chapter "Where to Go to Find Guys." Step Three: Go there. I was eighteen and hadn't been to school with women since second grade. I never found the book *How to Pick Up Guys* because I never figured out a breezy enough way to ask whoever was behind the register at the bookstore if they had the book *How to Pick Up Guys*. Thwarted, I came up with my own three-step method: Step One: Buy a bottle. Step Two: Turn on television. Step Three: Go there. I am painting that sad picture now because it is much more intriguing than what would be on my undergraduate social transcript: Four years, twenty-four first dates, eleven second dates, four third dates, two fourth dates, one broken heart, one "What was I thinking?"

Shit, I was nothing but available.

Mary Ann and I agreed to meet at the Nini's Corner, a giant newsstand across from the Harvard Square subway station. I think Ali McGraw ran past it as a Radcliffe coed in *Goodbye,*

Columbus, but not *Love Story.* She said she'd be wearing a blue jean jacket and a peasant blouse. I wish I had said something like, "So will I" or "I haven't picked out my wardrobe, but I'll be the guy looking for the girl in the jean jacket and peasant blouse." But I probably said, "Uh, okay."

Tuck had driven down to Wheaton in his parents' Mercedes 480, so I had the keys to his 1972 burnt orange Mercury Cougar. You know, just in case. In case of what, I couldn't tell you back then.

I made the decision not to drink on the date. On the date proper. I had two beers before we met at Nini's Corner. She was as described. A little heavy. Jean jacket, peasant blouse. Short brown hair. I won't say she was pretty and I won't say she wasn't, because I know what I look like. But I will say this. When Mary Ann saw me, she smiled, and if you were ever around Cambridge in the 1970s, you know that smiles were in short supply among Radcliffe women. Forget gas rationing and odd-and-even days. This was the real embargo. So, tremendous start. I have forgotten ninety percent of the people in my life, but staring out at the memoryless ocean here in Montauk thirty years later, I can see Mary Ann whatshername smiling at me. Sadly, when she reached her limit of three, she had to throw the rest back.

We went around the corner down Brattle Street to Buddy's Sirloin Pit, a wonderfully reasonable cafeteria-style steak place way way before Ponderosa and Sizzler turned the concept into something more trough-worthy. Mary Ann wasn't hungry, but said she'd watch me eat. I suggested she get a salad and dessert and got my second smile.

The front door of Buddy's is just past a mammoth picture window, where you can see an ex-con grilling what might be your steak. You make your order and grab your tray and head down the line. There's an ex-con pouring drinks. There's one handing out desserts. There's one with a paintbrush lathering butter on the baked potatoes. And there's a guy serving salad. I'm not trying to insult you. I know you've been to a cafeteria. I just need to set this up. The ex-con serving the salad just says, "Salad?... Salad?... Salad?... ...Salad?" and you say yes and choose your dressing. In the 1970s, before Reagan deregulated the industry, there were only three kinds of salad dressing available to the dining-out public. French, Russian, and Italian. I turn to Mary Ann and asked what kind of dressing she wanted. Roquefort, she said, followed by the third smile.

Here now is a reenactment:

EX-CON: *Salad?... Salad?... Salad?... Salad?*

ME: *Yeah, two. One with Italian, one with, you got Roquefort?*

EX-CON: *Roquefort?*

ME: *Yeah, Roquefort.*

EX-CON: *You want Roquefort, YOU GO TO THE FUCKING RITZ-CARLTON!!!!*

OTHER CONS: *Blinky! Blinky!! Cool it, man!!! Be cool!! Blinky, he didn't mean it! He meant French! French!!! You need to calm the hell down!*

MANAGER: *Is there a problem?*

OTHER CONS: *No, we cool.*

MANAGER: *Sir?*

ME: *French*

MANAGER: *Okay, let's go. Back to work. Wait on the trade.*

(*moments of awkward silence later*)

BLINKY: *Salad?...Salad?...Salad?...Salad?*

ع

THERE WAS A MOVIE afterward where I laughed and she didn't. I want to say *Freebie and the Bean* with Alan Arkin and James

Caan, but I may have seen that a year later on an early date with Jennifer and confused her not laughing at the film with Mary Ann not laughing. When I suggested going to a party at Winthrop House after the movie, she again deferred to watching me drink. I was about to tell Mary Ann I wasn't drinking that night when she said, "Well Charlie, we tried, didn't we?"

I grabbed Tuck's burnt orange Cougar and had her just down the block from her house in Arlington Heights before ten. We made out in the front seat as if she had ditched me and was trying to get lucky with my driver. That stopped when someone started wildly flicking the front light on the house next door.

My dream of easily making it back in time for cocktails and *The Rifleman* was dashed when I got lost on the way back to Cambridge. Six months before, I had been fitted for glasses, which I needed to read lecture hall blackboards and if I had shitty seats for a night game at Fenway. Which means I never remembered to take them with me. I had no idea they would have come in handy trying to decipher street signs in Arlington after ten. The third time I swerved left at fifteen mph and stuck my head out the window to see an ivy-covered pole that might say Route 1A, a cop pulled me over. He thought I was drunk, but he was an hour early. I told him I had left my glasses at school. You know, Harvard. I showed him my license, which had expired two weeks prior, and instead of a registration, reached into Tuck's glove compartment and handed him a speeding ticket. We shared the laugh that Mary Ann and I had not, but he said the best he could do was let me pull the car over to the side of the road, keep the keys, and he would drive me to Mass Ave, where I would find my way back to school and "your buddy on the ticket could come get his Coogah." By the time I had slept off my *Rifleman* load, taken the bus out to Arlington and driven the car back, it was Sunday afternoon and when I returned to our suite, Tuck had been back a half-hour. He smiled at me, and I never corrected him.

There is no entertaining tale about my second blind date, which occurred somewhere during 2000 after Jennifer and I had been divorced two years. Nor is it an uncommon tale. It happens, as I now know from other fellows with whom I've shared this story, with the frequency of credit card fraud. Guy gets number. Guy calls woman. Woman answers. They agree to meet in restaurant bar on East Side that Friday. Guy waits in bar. After a half-hour, guy calls woman. Woman answers. Woman is at another bar downtown near work. Guy and woman have discussion about the semantics of "that Friday," "next Friday," and "this Friday." Woman apologizes and says, "Why don't you come down here? I'll be at the bar." Guy has trouble getting cab. Guy shows up. There is one woman at the bar, sharing a drink with the bartender. Guy leaves. Guy gets home. With his jacket still on, guy calls cable company, gets Cinemax.

Remember, I am alone because it's better this way. Remember what Travis Waldman said, "You're a bachelor. You're a fucking bachelor. And everyone needs to grow up and accept that." And if you cannot accept the word of a therapist who pretended to have sex with a woman who I was too frightened to have sex with, who wound up confiding the secrets of his childhood to me while in the cracker factory before resuming his fraudulent practice and marriage until he died by hospital hijinx, then maybe you are not ready for the non-psychological life and all of this has been throat-clearing.

Nevertheless, I went on the date.

Here is a list of the four things I did well. I let Justine pick the place to meet for coffee. The thinking was if coffee went well we would move on to dinner. Not my thinking, but apparently that is the new millennium date construct. Fine. Await further instructions. I told her she looked great. And she did. I asked her, "Who do they tell you you look like?" And she said she got a lot of Susan Sarandon and Stockard Channing. Which she deserved. (Someone should have thought to throw in the smoky 50s-60s actress Janice Rule, which if you've seen *The Swimmer* is a giant compliment. But it wasn't going to be me. That's something a retired hairdresser might say.) And just after we ordered, I said, "So, tell me your story," which she was absolutely charmed by. Even I noticed that. I'm telling you, I had no idea I could be this smooth. And there's a reason for that. I ain't this smooth. I ain't smooth. Not at all. Or, should I say, being one who lives in the moment, I am not smooth right now.

We ended up ordering a second coffee and some cheese and fruit. Calm down. The date was a mistake. Not a misfire, like Mary Ann saying, "Well Charlie, we tried, didn't we?" I would have killed for that. Mistake. Actually, a series of mistakes. In less than a third of an evening, one attractive, bright woman, just by her presence, just by her Janice Rule of Order, unknowingly dismantled the no longer examined life I had built underbaked brick by unbaked brick.

She'd worked in public radio. She had traveled the world. She'd been married. Her kids were grown. She had her own money. She'd bracelet-jingle touch your elbow to make a point. She probably had a great laugh. I can't remember. More likely I never said anything that might have winched a laugh onto dry land. The truth, or what's left of it, is that they have not invented the instrument that could measure the level of how much I didn't want to be there when she stopped talking. I had no satisfactory answers to the questions that were or were not coming. "How do you know Polly? How do you know Bonnie? Have you ever been married? Why no kids? What are you doing in Boston? What are you doing?"

Did you know Janice Rule essentially left acting in the early seventies, went back to school for ten years and became a psychoanalyst in New York? Of course not. Why should you? You didn't know who the fuck she was until the retired hairdresser told you fifteen seconds ago.

If only someone, anyone, had summoned the presence of mind to come forward and tell me that on a date with a stranger one of the topics of conversation might be...me. And not just me, but the me that existed before the date with the stranger. But who would have thought to do that? Who would have thought I needed a heads-up? "Psst, Charlie. Have some material ready." Who, other than me, knew I was trying to move through each day without reflection? Without expectation? Living in the moment. Okay, you. But what do you know, other than what I've told you?

Never occurred to me until the instant I sat down on one of the café's least forgiving wooden-seat/wire-backed chairs. Living in the moment, and at that moment, it was "Uh-oh." Or, to be more precise, "Uh-oh. I'm the only one at the table living the non-psychological life."

I hung in there. I nodded. I smiled. I served up a variety of "Is that right?," "Are you kidding?," "Well, sure...," "Yeah, that sounds about right...," that outnumbered the selections on the cheese tray.

After a solid forty minutes, Justine snapped a slice of apple in her teeth and said, "Okay. Now you."

"Now me what?"

"Tell me your story."

"Why spoil the evening?"

"How do you know Polly?"

"Friend of a friend."

"And you know Bonnie?"

"Bonnie?"

"Her sister."

"Right."

"Charlie, I feel as if you are stalling."

Onethousandone, onethousandtwo, onethou—"No,"—*sand three, onethousa*—"not at all. I didn't know Bonnie was Polly's sister until after I had met her, through a guy we both knew."

"Sy Siegel."

"Right. So, you know the whole story."

Justine gave half a squint and used a strawberry to point at me. "Polly said you were cute, but a little, uh, lost. I'm sorry, what am I saying? Didn't you meet at your mom's funeral?"

Remember the fake throat catch I used to do with Sy to ever so emotionally blackmail the people at Windgate Point to sign the petition? Remember how it turned out not to be fake? It was back. Not right back. It actually started as a titter.

(Heh heh...) "Well, now we're all *(throat catch)* caught up."

In one move, Justine waved for the check and burst out laughing. That's how I know she had a good laugh. I looked off to the side because I could hear my eyes preparing to well up like a toilet with an unjiggled handle. Her laugh throttled back to a giggle and I desperately wanted to join her, or at least say something. But...let's say you're me. Living in the moment. In that moment, how could you have done anything, other than almost look at her?

"Jesus," she said. "You're not kidding."

Here's what I finally came up with. "So, dinner?"

She slumped in her chair, pushed her arms through her jacket, then fanned out four tens on the table. That's how I know she had her own money.

"Charlie, there's a date in there somewhere. But not tonight. You're smart. You know we want you to listen to us, but if I'm finished telling my story, as you put it so well, and you aren't willing to start, if only one of us shows up and participates, then this isn't meeting for coffee. This isn't a blind date. It's, it's a blind therapy session. And, I don't know about you, but I've already spent enough time in therapy."

There it was. All teed up for me. The chance to say, "Hey funny thing. I've spent enough time in the tank as well. Now I'm living the life between sessions. What does that entail? Well, let me tell you, because I think I'm really onto something..." But there, in that instant, the only thing I was onto was that all of this, this non-psychological life, goes threadbare in a hurry when you unwillingly add another person, another voice.

The bad news is I may be almost completely full of shit. May be. Sure, it's a setback. In my defense, though, the date clearly proved that I am alone because it is better this way. Which would have been the truthful thing to say to her. Which would have been the not-completely not-full-of-shit thing to say.

But, after another throat catch, this is what I decided on.

(*Throat catch*) "You know, you're great."

"You know," Justine said, "I'm getting fucking tired of hearing that." She got up and told me to settle the check while she went to the ladies' room. It took a good ten minutes before I realized she meant the ladies' room in her home. I wasn't embarrassed, because why? Because we've gone over this. When you do what's in front of you, there is no regret.

And I know there is supposed to be no reflection, but now that I rerun the evening, Justine offering Polly Trombley's description of me as "cute, but a little lost?" God help me, I love it.

$\mathcal{E}$

THE DATE ENDED SO early, I could have easily made it back to Windgate Point in time to watch the last five innings of The Boys with Sy, but I didn't want to show up in a coat and tie with my hair reasonably combed and deal with an hour and a half of Sy finding different ways to ask me what time I was due in court. He might have gotten around to giving me shit the next day, but that would have meant talking about me, which neither of us was fond of. And it might have happened the day after that, except I got a call from Dave Hussey, whose mother had allegedly hit Tony Conigliaro in the head with a rolling pin.

My cell phone yipped as I was driving over to Windgate. I was sure it was Sy telling me to get cat food. Dave Hussey apologized for taking so long to get back to me. He and his wife spend their winters in Florida catching blue crab after the lobster season has ended in Nahant. They usually didn't return North until after Memorial Day, but they had a wake in Swampscott.

"Are you sure you have the right guy?" he said.

"Well, I'm researching a book, a project, about Tony Conigliaro, and I believe you may have had an altercation with him about forty-four years ago."

He made a laugh seem like a cough. "How did you find me?"

I pulled into a Mobil station. "Believe me, it was nothing exciting. A couple of phone calls. Look, I've read a few different accounts of the incident, but not your version."

Dave Hussey, the right Dave Hussey, did not cough. "Well, I never told anybody. It was just a fight between high school kids.

Long time ago. But Tony's been gone a while now, so if you want, I'll tell you what happened."

"Can I call you back in ten minutes from a better phone?"

"Can we make it three hours?" he said. "I'm on my way to pick up my buddy and go to anger management."

I made Sy promise if I put Dave Hussey on speaker, he could not interrupt. If he had any questions, he could ask them on the follow-up phone call. He muttered something about my conditions being the same as those offered by Pol Pot, but he agreed. Other than slamming the door to the bathroom five minutes in, he behaved.

Around two, I made the call. I hadn't written so much so fast over the phone since Robert Kennedy, Jr., gave me ten minutes of chapter and verse on voter fraud after the 2004 election. I know I got all of it because when I called Dave the next day and read my transcript back to him, he said, "Wow. That sounds exactly like me."

This is kind of funny. Every week when I'm up North, I go to the VA Hospital in Wrenthfield for anger management. I'm disabled from Vietnam. I got diabetes from Agent Orange and a few other things. It's a bunch of Vietnam vets, sixty-seventy of us. We sit in two big circles. Sometimes it's the first time in forty years these guys have opened up. It helps. It helps an awful lot of guys. I just started going last June. It's been a huge help. It's helped me with my anger. Not that I have much anger. You bite your lip and you climb up the ladder and you just go so far and then you back off and think about things.

I served in the infantry in Vietnam. Got drafted out of college at twenty-four. I flunked out of Arizona and lost my football scholarship. Elmo got me into Parsons College, which they used to call Flunk Out U.

The saying back then was "Everybody owes Uncle Sam two years." I trained for a year, nineteen sixty-eight, then went to Vietnam and was assigned to the infantry. I ended up an infantry grunt in the jungle. Northwest of Saigon by the Cambodian border, right by what they call the Parrot's Beak. I was there nineteen sixty-nine-/seventy. Platoon sergeant. First Air Cavalry. We worked off the LZ. LZs were landing zones. Where they put the artillery, one-oh-fives and one-fifty-fives. We'd do sierra tangos trying to find the enemy.

I grew up here in Nahant on Cemetery Hill. There were three of us, and we'd play war games. We wound up at different schools. One guy was EJ Breen, who went to St. John's Prep and became hockey captain at BC. EJ would jump off the rocks on Cemetery Hill. He was fearless. He became a pilot in the Navy. He served two terms in Vietnam, then went to work for Eastern Airlines. Me, I hate planes and fast things. He was a hero, EJ. I was a draft resister.

EJ had a tough time coming home. He dropped napalm. He had trouble sleeping. He's the one who told me about this thing at the VA. They have different classes up there. It's a drive, but it's worth it. Amazing. The other kid was Peter Devens, who was five years younger than us. Good hockey player, good student. He wound up at Tabor Academy. He also served in Vietnam. Now, he stands in his living room and he knows none of us. We're trying to get him to go to the VA. He won't do it.

This is why it's funny. This morning, EJ and I, we're driving on the way to anger management class. EJ says, "Every time I go to anger management I get mad." You should call EJ. He'll tell you some stories. We're just shooting the shit, and I said to EJ, "Did I ever tell you that Tony C story?"

"No," he says. I know him my whole life and never told him the story. Like I said to you, I had never told anyone. So, I start. "Julie Markakis, you ever hear of her?" He takes out his cell phone and dials her number. She was a stewardess with him at Eastern! We said hello. I hadn't talked to her since we were in high school.

Julie Markakis was Tony's girl. The fight happened in the spring of my senior year. I was getting close to graduating. There's a circular driveway in front of Lynn English High School. Julie and I were standing in the driveway talking. Tony C pulls up in his Corvette with another guy. I think it was Julie's brother. I'll never forget that. He had a Corvette. Well, he almost hit me with his car.

I think he had heard that I was dating Julie. But it wasn't like that. I was Mr. Lynn English. She was Miss Lynn English. That's all. We were supposed to go to a dance together. I was very shy. I never dated. It was a different time back then. You, you're young, you don't know. But back then, we weren't sexually active.

I knew Tony. I had played football against him. He went to St. Mary's. Now, he was with the Red Sox. I thought he was already in the big leagues, but you say he wasn't. Anyway, he was doing really well, and I think back then a lot of us were jealous of him. He had an attitude. He had the Corvette.

So, he almost hits me with his car. As Julie was waiting for her brother to get into the back, I came around to the driver's side and told Tony to go fuck himself. They drove off and I figured that was it.

I took the bus home. I live where I live now. My great-great-grandfather built this house. 1903, 1908. I was in the room next to the porch. I hadn't been home long. Someone knocked on the door. I answered it and all I saw was the fist. He hit me with a punch at the side of the head. I never went down. I think I was bleeding. I know there was blood everywhere.

I played hockey. I was captain of the football and hockey teams at English. I wasn't a great athlete, but I was tough. After he hit me, he was screaming bloody murder. Running around holding his hand screaming, "You've ruined my career, you've ruined my fucking career." Both doors of the Corvette were open. The car was still running. Julie's brother was standing there with his arms crossed. We tussled around on the porch for a while. My mom heard the screaming and came out. Here I asked my only question: "Is it true about the rolling pin?"

Ha-ha! Yes. My mother was baking in the kitchen, she came out in the apron with the flour all over her when she heard the screaming. She was hitting his back, because he was on top of me.

Finally, he got off me and left. My mother said, "We're gonna sue that bastard." The next day or the day after, I'm pretty sure, the Red Sox ownership called this house. I got on the phone and said, "We're all Irish here. We were brought up not to sue. It's over as far as I'm concerned. It was as much my fault as it was his and I'll never tell anyone." So, when people over the years ask me, "Did you get in a fight with Tony C?" I say,

"No." And I never told anybody about it. Until this morning, when I told EJ. And now you.

ع

I WAS ABOUT FIVE seconds behind writing my notes, so Dave Hussey had to say "Hello?" a couple of times before I was able to speak. He gave me EJ Breen's number and told me I could get Julie Markarkis' number from him if I wanted to talk to her. He said his wife had worked as a waitress at Tony C's, Tony Conigliaro's nightclub in Nahant and she had a few stories.

"Your great-great-grandfather built that house?"

"Shit, yeah," said Dave. "I'm standing on the porch where it happened. You should come up and visit. We'll show you around. Judi and I are retired now. We just do the crabbing to pay our way in Florida. We catch these big male blue crabs. We get twenty-five to thirty bucks a dozen. Sell them right out of the house. We make ants and birds out of coconuts and sell them to tourists. People drive by our shack in Florida, they see the traps and the ants and the birds out front think they're in Gloucester."

"I'd like to come see the house. Can I bring my friend, my colleague, Sy?"

"Absolutely. Let me know so Judi can get some lobsters."

All I had done was leave a message on a sixty-year-old retired lobsterman's machine.

Sy came out of the bathroom and I shook four pages of legal pad in his face. He patted my shoulder and shuffled toward the kitchen. This would have been a great time for me to be available. It really would have, had I noticed. But I talked longer than I had since he'd known me. I read my notes, stopping to fill in Dave Hussey's words as they came back to me. Sy was making a pot of tea on the stove and was turned away from me when I told him about the rolling pin. I had never seen him make tea. This occurs to me now 3:46 P.M. *October 14, 2007.*

Here, at long last, I have stumbled onto a regret. I regret I wasn't more diplomatic. We of the non-psychological life do not need to choose our words carefully. They come to us as they should. Or as they're supposed to. Or, in this case, as they didn't.

"Sy, son of a bitch, we got confirmation on the rolling pin," I said. "But we may be out of business. The mother hit Tony C on the back. Not the head."

"Charlie," he said. "I'm going to take a nap. Come by tonight and we'll watch The Boys." Sy had never called me anything but Traub or Traub scion. That I noticed.

"You okay?"

"I'm eighty-one. This is okay for eighty-one."

The next week was, well, I'd rather not think about the next week. Twice, Phyllis Soriano knocked on Sy's door and told us to keep it down. And there were three other calls from the front desk. We were quiet at night while we watched The Boys, but our day sessions had turned hissy. My idea was to go up to Nahant and interview Dave and his wife, see the house, call Julie Markakis and whoever else and instead of a book, write a long piece about this incident with Tony Conigliaro that no one knows about. And sell it to the *Sunday Globe* magazine or *The Improper Bostonian*. Can there be anything more improper than Tony C getting hit with a rolling pin? We'd run through the later tragedies to set the context, but this was the meat. And more important, we wouldn't be two unspoken Gwen Traub mourners living out of a Smirnoff box. We'd be Sy Siegel and Charles Traub. Published, perhaps.

I tried eight ways to reframe my point, but Sy kept alternating between two semi-nuanced, semi-rhetorical responses. It was either, "What kind of man takes great pains to point out that he was offered money but never took anything?" or "What kind of man defends the word of a man he just met over a man who in nineteen sixty-one lay down in front of the lieutenant governor's car?"

"Sy—"

"ANSWER THE QUESTION!!!!"

That's when the phone would ring, or Phyllis Soriano would knock.

The Boys swept a day-night doubleheader from Detroit on a Thursday and got rained out the following night. As I left, I asked Sy, quietly, "You want to take a ride up there next week and see how full of shit it all is?"

"Try and stop me."

We got lucky with the weather. Mid-May auditioning for the part of a day in late June. We were making good time when I made the wrong turn on Route 1A and started going south instead of north on the Lynnway, an unfortunate section of 1A, an eyesore of a strip that still seemed to be waiting for renewal funding from the Eisenhower administration. It can be confusing because the Lynnway looks the same on both sides, and I'm sure some high school punks had turned a sign around. Or I was excited about seeing Dave Hussey's porch.

"Hey, Prince Henry, you want to keep the ocean on your right."

"Well aware, Sy. Just looking for a place to turn."

He laughed and said, "When you find one, do me a favor, kid. Make the left, then take it down as close to the water as you can."

He must have called me "kid" before. Must have, because the word came out of his perpetually wary puss like it had a timeshare in there. I just couldn't remember, and I was too busy trying to find a legal left turn to look back over the last eight months since we had met. But I am positive Sy Siegel had never used the phrase "do me a favor" with me. That got my attention. And we had time. We weren't due on the porch for another hour.

Never heard "do me a favor" from him. And twenty minutes later, I heard it again.

The left I took grabbed a little road that went a half-mile past two-bedroom cottages of people too honest to call their homes beachfront property. I nudged the Impala to six feet from where Broad Sound smacked its lips against whatever the name of this dead end was.

Sy was more hunched than usual with the passenger-side door open, until I noticed he was taking off his shoes and socks. The tide was low, so there was a bit of dance floor, well-encrusted with shells, rocks, beach glass, and the requisite shelf of convenience store detritus.

He paced slowly, feet unperturbed by the jagged beneath. He stayed in the fifty degree stoop for a while, picking up a couple of shells and tossing them sideways, like he was he helping a periwinkle look for his contact lens. And then he stood up to his full ten-past-noon bearing, rolled his shoulders back, and started talking to the water. I made it up behind him in time to hear.

"We rented a tiny tiny place in July on Nantasket once. Half of one of these shacks," he began. "My father worked at a tannery in Brockton, about twelve miles away. That's where I grew up until I didn't. I was six. My mother loved to get me and my brother and sisters fed and in bed before he got home. Traub, if I told you how early, you wouldn't believe me. But in July, out here, we got to stay up till, Christ, seven-thirty. When my father got out to the shack, never before seven, we would follow him down to the water. One of my sisters carrying a towel, the other with a robe. My older brother Nate held his cigarettes. Nobody said anything on the way down. Just watch. He worked a twelve-hour shift, and he looked like the dog's dinner. There, on the beach, my dad would strip down to his underwear, walk out as far as he had to until the water was waist-high, then drop down, dunking himself. And he would stay down. My sisters would count the seconds. A hundred was nothing. That's where I learned to count. He'd do that a few times, then he would walk in to the edge of where the tide went out, where the bottom was muddy, and bend over, looking for razor clams. When he would find one, he'd dig it out, wash it off, and rip the meat from the shell and eat it right in front of us. My sisters would scream and giggle and my father would say, 'Don't tell your muhthah.' And then they'd bring him the towel, the robe and the cigarettes and we'd all walk back. My sisters and Nate would be yammering all the way up, but my father never said anything other than 'Don't tell your muhthah.' Not a goddamn word."

I was all set to ask Sy, "What do you mean 'that's where I grew up until I didn't,'" when a rogue wavelet broke formation and encircled my sneakers. As I backpedaled, I heard the end of a whimper. Sy turned around, hands over the spreading puddle in his crotch.

"Traub, do me a favor."

I called Dave Hussey from the car, mumbled something vague except for the word "exterminator" and asked if tomorrow would be okay. He was fine with it. "Don't even think about it, Charlie," he said. "Just gives me an excuse to eat fresh lobstah two days in a row." When I told him I'd probably be alone, he said we'd flip for the extra lobster.

Thanks to the car heater, Sy's pants were virtually dry by the time we were back on Rte 128. I took the exit before Windgate Point, Rte 117, and headed for the Dairy Joy, a family-owned ice cream/hot dog/burger/fried clams stand that always had a minimum ten-deep on line at three in the afternoon or twenty-two on the thermometer. Never said anything. Never asked. As I curled around on the off-ramp (we were still two miles away from Dairy Joy), Sy spoke for the first time since he thanked me for wiping off his feet with his socks and putting on his shoes after we left the water. "I'll take a dog with relish. And I'll have three of your clams."

"How did you know where I was going?"

"Because you're your father's kid. And when he could still drive, he never made it past this exit." He wasn't wrong. Ducky Traub had shown me the way to Dairy Joy the first time I visited after they moved to Windgate Point. In the last few months, I had detoured over from Sy's apartment or the Westin or Alison's place in Waban too many times to count. *The apple doesn't fall far from the shitter.*

"I wasn't planning on getting clams," I said.

"I'll let you know when I'm turning all the major decisions over to you, Traub." That's how I knew I'd be driving to Nahant alone the next day.

ع

THE PORCH LOOKED MORE modern than something built just after the Wright Brothers. It was thick and sturdy, but small. Too small, it seemed, for a fight between two well-built athletes and a woman with a rolling pin. I spent maybe five minutes standing on the porch with Dave and his wife Judi, who reiterated that Dave's mother had wanted to sue, then told a story about the closest she had come to a settlement.

"I was working at Tony C's nightclub one night when Coey, David's mother, showed up," Judi said. "Teresa Conigliaro, who could drink, is at the bar. So could Coey. Teresa sees Coey and says, 'Oh, you're Mrs. Fuzzy.' Just like that. She kept calling her that. 'Hi, Mrs. Fuzzy.' Coey walks back out and steals the flag from the flagpole in front of the nightclub and drives off to the Thompson Club, another bar. They call the cops and the cops just drive over to the Thompson Club, and grab the flag out of the backseat of her car and return it. Everybody knows everybody here. They used to have a lot of fights in the parking lot at Tony C's and the cops would come and the Chief of Police would wait at the end of the street. If you were from Nahant, they'd let you go."

I now knew how to pronounce Dave Hussey's last name. He said very little while we stood on the porch. "This is it. This is where it happened. Tony knocked on the door, I answered it, then bang. See where you parked your car? That's where the Corvette was." Done.

That was the next to last time Tony Conigliaro's name came up. Later in the day, I got the tour of Nahant and saw the nightclub and the house Tony bought for his parents, where he passed away at forty-five.

"The last time I saw him was nineteen ninety, just before he died," Dave said. "He was living here, and his brother Richie was pushing him around on the street in a wheelchair and he had one hand that kind of waved. Really sad. I said, 'Hey, Tony C' And Richie said, 'He doesn't recognize anybody, Huzz.'"

What if I told you all of this was anticlimactic? What if I told you the porch was the eighth most memorable thing I saw that day? If you didn't believe me, I wouldn't blame you, because as my blind date proved, I may be almost completely full of shit. But while I tried to make the trip to a retired lobsterman's house with no expectations other than the too, too sweet flesh of a local two-pounder, I was pretty confident I'd leave with enough background to excavate this earliest crossed star of Tony Conigliaro.

Didn't happen.

All that happened was the beginning of everything else.

Behind the 1903 house with the too-small porch sits an 11x7 now-enclosed shed, also built by Dave Hussey's great-great-grandfather, Bunker Webster. "Where we are right now, this was the garage," he said. "Bunker Webster had the first car in Nahant. A Model A." A black and white woodpecker staccatoed a tree next to the shed like he wanted us to move it along. "That guy's been here forever," said Dave. Judi came down three times to refresh our coffee, each time smiling and saying, "He never talks." The haddock chowder she made could sit, and the lobsters took no time once the water boiled. We wouldn't eat till 2:30, "like rich people."

There was just enough room for two easy chairs, a lamp, a television and a space heater. You're lucky I noticed even that, because I spent well over two hours with my head bobbing between the retired lobsterman, his photo albums, and my legal pad, occasionally gasping, "Hang on," as I struggled to write notes fast enough to keep pace with the gentle torrent of recollections from Dave Hussey, a hemisphere away from Tony C's fist.

It's nobody's fault, but I am the wrong age. My education about Vietnam was provided by David Halberstam, Oliver Stone, and whatever pissed off guy I had the misfortune of sitting next to at a bar too late at night too far from home. Or maybe I just never paid attention. Yeah, let's go with that.

Dave took out the first of four photo albums and, again I cannot tell you why, for the first time in my photo album–viewing career, the goal was not to get through the photo albums. So, I must have decided to let Dave put each one in my lap and do the flipping. On his time. And I know you're waiting for me to say I was being available to someone else's needs, but we know now I am almost completely full of shit. What I was doing was paying attention.

Four books, hundreds of photos. Not one sad shot. This was what he sent home. Guys smiling, waving. Shirts off. Lumber and shovels and cement. They might as well have been building a rec center somewhere in Florida.

Every so often I would point to a photo when I wanted more information. "These things?" he'd start. "These are the bikes the South Vietnamese reinforced with bamboo so they could get down the Ho Chi Minh Trail. We used to get pissed off about the South Vietnamese soldiers, how they would hide and how lazy they were, but my buddy EJ, who I told you about, made a good point in anger management class one day. He said they were there forever. You can't blame them for backing out of a fight once in a while. We'd been there a year.

"These? These are the old rifles we took off them. You were allowed to bring one home. My captain would say, 'Hussey, of all people, don't you bring a gun home.' I guess I was angry.

"This guy? Hah! This is when I was supply sergeant and had a pet monkey. Hah! Look at him. He kept the rats away. I traded some C-rations for him. I named him CW after C. W. Moss in *Bonnie and Clyde*."

It was the only time I held the page of the album down. I told him the monkey looked exactly like Michael J. Pollard.

"Was that the actor's name? For God's sake... You know that imprinting? He thought I was his father. We taught him how to play with himself and smoke pot and drink with us. I used to bring him over to the other LZ where they had a female monkey so he could get laid. One time, the female monkey bit me and the doctor said if she stayed alive for nine days I'd be fine. So, I would come over every day to the LZ and the guys would hide her and say she died."

The monkey bite was by far the most ephemeral thing he came home with.

"I told you about the diabetes, but I also have H. pylori," Dave went on. "I got it from drinking the water in Vietnam.

We used to drink water out of bomb craters. I also have Phước VĩnhFlu. I didn't know it. The bacteria lay dormant in the mucus membrane. All of a sudden, fifteen years after I got back from Vietnam, I'm suffering. Migraines, joint aches, vomiting. I was taking Tums all day. Nothing worked. I went to the VA. They put me on twenty pills a day for thirty days, I was cured.

"You know, Charlie, thirty-three percent of the population has H. pylori. The pharmaceutical companies don't want people to be cured. They want to keep selling the medicine. The doc at the VA asked me, 'Do you drink?' And I said, 'Like you eat ice cream.' And he said, 'Stop.' So, I stopped. Twenty-one years ago. And that's when I really got better."

"AA?"

"Nah. I just did it. I'll tell you something, though. A lot of the guys in the anger management class say it's a lot like AA."

There's a move I do from years working in television news that I need to stop doing. It's asking a question as if someone else has asked you to ask the question. You've heard it a million times. "Senator, there are some people who say you have a small dick. Why would they say that?" This device has as much to do with being a journalist as clear nail polish. It is slick and transparent and usually comes with requisite cutaway shot of the interviewer looking concerned. Why I did it here, with someone this engaging, this forthcoming, I cannot tell you, but the question must have been so critical for me I was afraid to be associated with it.

"Dave, when people hear all this, they must wonder, 'What made him suddenly go to the anger management class at the age of sixty?'"

He picked up something off the small table next to his chair and handed it to me. It was maybe four inches long, bleached white and looked like the beginning of a model he was building.

"What do you see?"

I didn't hesitate. "It looks like the crucifixion."

"Ha! That's right. You got it right away!" He was delighted. "That's the backbone of a catfish. I pull it out, then lay it out in the sun so the ants can eat all the meat away. When I get enough together, I sell them to a guy in California for five dollars apiece and God knows what he sells them for."

I am no therapist, other than my own, but this guy, with his *How'd you find me?* glee, his happy monkey photos and Jesus catfish spines and chowder-making wife, this was the last guy who needed anger management. Dave Hussey cleared his throat and proved why I am no therapist.

"Vietnam vets are loaded with diabetes," he said. "That's from the Agent Orange. They dropped it straight into the jungle. Full strength. Normally, when it's used as an exfoliant, you dilute it four to one. So, they'd fill these giant barrels with the stuff, put it on ships, eight hundred-to-nine hundred guys per ship. Now, ninety percent of the Navy guys have diabetes. But they can't collect for Agent Orange because you have to have boots on the ground. They have a saying in the VA. The three Ds: Delay, Deny, hope they Die.

"The diabetes from Agent Orange affects your vision. Six months ago, I got cataract surgery. It's a miracle. But six-seven-eight months before that, I was at the VA in Florida getting my eyes checked. This little oriental girl doctor comes in to talk with me. She's telling me, 'Mr. Hussey, it's a five-minute operation.' But I don't hear her.

"When we were doing sierra tangos in the jungle, we'd throw gas grenades into spider holes to force people out. They lived there. One day, out comes this old man and his daughter. My leader, Captain Collins, he was a maniac. The little girl spat at him. He cut her head off right in front of me. She was dead before she hit the ground. So now, I'm looking at this little girl at the VA who's telling me, 'Mr. Hussey, it's a five-minute operation,' and I kept seeing her head fall off. I ran out of the office and down the hall and I said, 'I think I need some help.' I tell them what was happening and they said, 'You have PTSD.' It took a year to get PTSD disability. The three Ds. When we came back North, I called EJ and told him about the thing with the girl doctor. I knew he was going to the anger management class in Wrenthfield, so he took me. That was last June. I'm telling you, you really need to talk to him.

"It's every Wednesday morning, ten to noon. Three guys lead the group. Two psychiatrists and another guy who is a therapist, but was there. He's one of us. I love this guy. We sit in two big circles, there's like eighty of us. Last week, this black guy is the first one to talk. He says, 'I got asshole cancer. They hurt me. I tried to strangle my wife last night.' And all three of the leaders say, 'That's a little too much to start with.' I really look forward to going."

I had to eat the haddock chowder with my left hand because my right was so cramped from writing. Small sacrifice. The lobsters didn't need a nutcracker. Mercifully, Dave and Judi talked about how they met and their non-fishing careers, so I had lunch off. Judi gave me six ginger cookies and a lobster to take back to Sy. She was planning to send along some chowder, but I got very accomplished with the left hand.

The Lynnway going back was bumper to bumper, so I called EJ Breen. I introduced myself, and asked if when I hung up he would call back and leave Julie Markakis's phone number. I told him I was in traffic and begged him not to say anything interesting and made an appointment to talk over the weekend.

He almost obliged. He said two things about the VA anger management class which forced me to pull into a Midas lot and jot them down: "I tell you truthfully, if I miss a Wednesday, I start looking over my shoulder and sliding back to where I was two/three years ago." And: "One thing about PTSD. You don't give a shit about anything."

$$\mathscr{C}$$

THE NEXT THREE NIGHTS, I barely slept. This is one of the rewards of the non-psychological life that I have not mentioned. You go right to sleep, and you stay down. When you don't dwell and you do the next thing in front of you and the next thing in front of you is a pillow...hey, who can explain? Who needs to explain? I didn't mention it because it hadn't occurred to me, which is another benefit that I might have touched on. Things don't occur to you. No wonder you sleep.

But for three nights maybe I got an hour or two in. Maybe. And you can only keep saying, "Okay, this is me not sleeping..." so many times before another voice that sounds like you says, "Shut the fuck up. This isn't working. You're guilty." Come to think of it, there was a lot of "Shut the fuck up." Back and forth. Said and unsaid. Sympathetic and accusatory. It was almost rhythmic, chants people who want to be Buddhist do. People who aren't lucky enough to have harnessed the ability to shrink thyself.

I had been waiting for Sy to ask about the trip to Nahant, or Dave Hussey, or the rolling pin, or anything. He never did. Never even ate the lobster I brought back in case he might ask, "How was the lobster?" His cat, Goneril, polished that off, and did it, like I have to tell you, without so much as a thank you.

So, for three days, I showed up bleary-eyed for the morning session, and Sy would say, "You look like you woke up on the wrong side of the Bronx," then read the *Times*. To himself. You heard me. To himself.

I'd leave and come back later for the Red Sox game. We'd do our lines. I'd say "Fellas, come on..." He'd say, "Do you send the runners?" Both of us with the energy of the cast at a lighting cue rehearsal of *Sleuth*. The only ad lib was the second day, when Sy emerged from the bathroom, found Goneril in his chair and shooed him off by saying, "Your coup is scheduled for the middle of next month."

The Boys split a day-night doubleheader with Atlanta on Saturday. Rather than stretch the awkwardness out ten hours, my plan was to go back to Alison's between games and call EJ Breen, then return for the 8:00 start. But Mike Lowell, the Red Sox third basemen, had a monster game in the opener, driving in five runs, and as I came out of the john to say goodbye, Sy addressed me for the first time since *hello*. "If Lowell had any insouciance, he'd take off his jersey, and have a clubhouse boy walk it up to the owner's box with a note, 'Now you can retire this number.'"

Mike Lowell wears number twenty-five. Same as Tony Conigliaro. I figured that was all the opening I would ever get, so I kept my coat on, sat down and went through the entire day in Nahant. Maybe that's why I hadn't slept. I was excited. And I was alone in my excitement. Sy sat impassively, although he loved the story about Dave Hussey's mother stealing the flag. He asked me if I got her phone number for him. When I told him she was dead, he chuckled and said, "Well, now I'm especially thankful I didn't go."

If I was someone who got the wind knocked out of me by remarks like that, as I used to be, I wouldn't have been able to stand in front of the TV and finger-point out all the shit that I was no longer going to take from Sy. Not that I stood in front of the TV and let loose, but I felt able to do so. And that's the important thing, isn't it? That's the important thing when you're almost completely full of shit.

Almost.

I did stand up. And I did say something. I said, "Nevertheless..." And I said it loud enough for me to hear it.

"NEVERTHELESS, I went and now you know... And now, I'm going back to Alison's to make a call."

"You're calling the girl, aren't you, Traub." Sy said.

"What girl?"

"Tony C's girl. Julie with the Greek name."

"Markakis? Nah. I'm not up to that yet. I'm calling Hussey's pal, EJ. I cannot stop thinking about those Vietnam vets sitting in the circle. Maybe there is something there." I told him I'd be back for the second game.

"Come by tomorrow," he said. "I forgot about the doubleheader and made plans tonight."

You heard him. *Plans.*

"New resident," he went on. "Another Greek girl. Five forty-five seating in the dining room, then they're showing *Advise & Consent* on Turner Classic Movies at eight."

"Wow."

"Settle down. Are you familiar with Lawrence College in Appleton, Wisconsin, Traub?"

"No."

"Well, that's what we're dealing with here."

Whatever made me unable to sleep the first two nights (and I may have mentioned guilt and excitement, but that was just to

move it along) was joined by another ally the third night. Anger.
That I know. Recounting the phone call with EJ Breen, which
was exhilarating and, as it turns out, life-changing, is better left
for another time, when I am not as inarticulate as I am now,
staring out at the ocean in Montauk, just recalling that third
night of awakedness. This is why I don't look back. This is why
I don't dwell. This is why I don't try to coalesce action with
feeling. This is why I don't bother. This is why I'm not doing
Travis' eulogy the day after tomorrow. You thought I forgot
about that. Maybe you forgot.

Thrashing around in bed that last night, all I could think
was, *That prick. He's got a girl now?* That, and the onrushing
notion that for all my self-propelled narrative about availability
and needs and all the next things in front of me, I had come
through nothing and taken care of less. Why couldn't I get me a
case of that PTSD and not give a shit about anything?

Or maybe I was just really really tired. Can't help you. Fuck, I
don't know if I've helped you yet. All I know is the sun came up,
and I listened to Alison and Jonathan fight in the kitchen over
who was going to take the car in to be serviced Tuesday morning,
before I went to the top of the stairs and screamed, "I WILL!"

It was my first anxious drive to Windgate Point since my mom
had died. I tried looking at the clock on my cellphone (*12:48
P.M., Sunday, May 20, 2007*) and imagine myself laughing at my
destination. Didn't work. Didn't work until I showed up at Sy's
just before one and walked into an empty apartment. I had misread
the schedule again. The game did not start at 1:30, but 4:30. Then
I laughed. I laughed hard enough to fall asleep in a chair.

Sy walked in around three, wearing a coat and tie. I would
have done the "How'd it go in court?" line on him, except he was
followed by Desiree, who was carrying a large gift-wrapped box
with a giant bow on top.

"*Aquí por favor. Gracias.* Desiree, be sure to *diga* Enid and *la cucina trabajanes* that we are working on *los pensiones.* Again, my deepest *gracias.*"

Desiree made a point of thanking Sy in perfectly imitated unaccented English.

"You remember, Traub, don't you?" Sy said. "He was helpful for an hour and a half a few months ago."

Desiree winked at me, then left. I know I mentioned that I get to go through life regret-free, but in that moment, I let myself realize all the wreckage I could have undone had I been able to wink at people when needed. It left me light-headed, a perfect set-up for Sy.

"Traub, I know you're wondering about the coat and tie."

"Actually, I was wondering about the box. Must have gone well with the gal from Lawrence College you ditched me for."

Hadn't meant to make him laugh, but I did. He shuffled over, smile-first, and looked me directly in the chest. The hunch was still there, impervious to good grooming. I could see he was clean-shaven. Son of a bitch.

"The box is for you. The coat and tie is what I wore to the card room today. I gave a bridge lesson to Maureen, the gal from Lawrence College, as you so derisively sniffed. She worked at the Milwaukee local of SEIU for thirty years. The service employees union, Traub. Why wouldn't she help set up the pension here once I soften her with some bidding strategy?"

"You're back in the game."

"So are you. Open it."

At first, I didn't have to. Just feeling the familiar weight and dimensions when I swung the box around on the kitchen table to get at the ribbon, I knew what it was.

"You're giving me the Tony C files?"

"I'm loaning them to you. I'm giving you what's under the bow."

There was a white No. 10 envelope with a rubber band around it, which separated two small jagged bulges. I picked it up clumsily and two silver pins fell out.

"Navy?"

"Lieutenant's bars," said Sy.

"Your lieutenant's bars?" He nodded. "I don't get it."

"Why start now? Traub, Good Christ, you've invented Viagra and I'm still making hydraulic penal implants."

"Sy, I'm begging you," I said. "Can we have one exchange where you actually tell me what you mean? That could be your gift to me."

He had stood long enough. He turned to shoo the cat that wasn't in his chair before sitting down.

"You need to pursue the Vietnam vets at anger management. You said you think there might be something there. Something? It's a goddamn book! It may be your goddamn book, antipode this interregnum of scholarship we've enjoyed. You want to call some woman to find out what she may have heard about what happened on a porch to a dead ballplayer who wouldn't marry her? Maybe you do. But do it after you take care of Hussey and those men sitting in the circle. That is what is next. That is why you get the bars."

"Hate the war, love the warrior. Right?" I said.

"Oh, for God's sake, did a bumper sticker salesman just show up?"

I did that TV news move I hate. "Sy, some people would think that sounds like you're letting me go."

"Here endeth the lesson, Traub."

I recovered. "I always said I would stay until we were finished, or until you used a cliché."

We negotiated a five-day extension, but I just came by to watch The Boys. The fact that they dropped two of three to the Yankees at home was enough to chase me out of town, and when I got back to Manhattan, the Sox dropped another series at Yankee Stadium. But that was the last time it was sweaty for The Boys. Until now, down three games to one to the Indians in the ALCS. 5:08 P.M. *October 14, 2007*, and me trying to picture myself smiling at their destination.

I told Sy I was leaving that Thursday night, but I lied for the last time. I woke up at 4:00 A.M. Friday, drove to Windgate Point, and with the fulcrum of a man unstuck, rolled the FREE*Dom* boulder back into its seditious saucer. It was still there the last time I visited Sy a month ago. Still there, but now completely covered with a fresh coat of white paint. Part of a deal he and the Lawrence College gal worked out with the new Executive Manager, Thea Kalkevic, who replaced the hastily relocated Phyllis Soriano in June. Never found out what happened with Phyllis. None of my business. Which, if you count eulogies, is the second business I'm out of.

$$\mathcal{E}$$

TURNED OUT THE LIEUTENANT'S bars were on loan as well. I have to present them to Sy whenever I return to catch up with the guys in the circle at the Wrenthfield VA. Or, to be more precise, catch them coming out of the circle. There I do my work in the parking lot and at the Dunkin' Donuts a mile and a half down on Agannis Road. EJ or Huss introduce me in the parking lot, then I buy the coffee and donuts, which makes me more of a benefactor than a writer doing research for a book proposal.

Hey, look at who just called himself a writer. If Sy heard that, he might say, "Traub, you're finally filming your life in something other than Hackneycolor." Although, probably not. He already said it when I saw him last month, and he has yet to swing the same brickbat.

I have a more efficient setup at the Bronx VA, where I've been a volunteer since June. There I sit outside the circle, in the kitchen off the meeting room. I set up the chairs, make coffee, clean the coffee maker, put back the chairs, mop the floor. And don't listen or take notes. That's the deal. If a guy wants to retell the story he just told in the circle, he has my number. It's like EJ Breen told me that first call: "Every time I talk about it, a little comes off my back."

The proposal is just about finished. I've been working on it the last four months. When I'm done, I'll turn it in to an editor at a big house, whose father is the actor Fritz Weaver, but whose more stunning connection is that she went to Smith with my ex-wife Jennifer. Smith, not Harvard. Ask not for whom the chowder society beckons.

Whatever notions you have about anger management for vets, you're wrong. And you have plenty of company. A firefighter friend who brought EJ to the Wrenthfield VA told him he had PTSD and EJ said, "Fuck you. That's a bunch of crap, I'm not going to be one of those guys who blames everything on Vietnam."

For most of the vets, rage is a pair of dog tags that never leaves your neck. For some, it is an enemy that attacks in waves, with a tide that can stay low for decades. In that first long phone call, EJ mentioned "having a bout" in the 1980s over all the napalm he dropped on villages, this while flying jets for Eastern. Then, as if that siege was a puddle-jump, he bounded to just a few years ago, when he was teaching math in the public school system.

"I taught for fourteen years after Eastern folded," he said. "I got very close to the Asian students. There was an immediate connection to those kids. When I was in the Philippines, we were helping a guy build an orphanage. Two nuns took care of the kids by day and sent them out at night. The kids were trained to run to the bottom of the mountains. I got pretty close to the kids. One day, I was out at the orphanage. Saw some movement a distance away. One kid, naked, looked like he was carrying a sack of clothes. In that bag was his little baby sister. He was covered in blood. Little sister, not a scratch. We would give them whatever we had. After I got back, the NV wiped out that orphanage. Anything with an American attachment they destroyed.

"I thought that's what I was put on Earth to do. Help kids. But eventually I got involved with some gangbangers at school. There was one kid especially, a real piece of shit. He had tried to kill one of the Asian kids. That kid and I went at it pretty good for about an hour and a half. And he threatened to kill me. The administration transferred me to another school and promised me that kid would be out of the system. But there he is in the hallway. Why the fuck is this cocksucker here? Bullshit, this cocksucker is going to kill somebody. He's got the dead eyes. They said, 'We'll make sure nothing happens.'

"A few months later, same kid and I went at it in the hallway again. This time it lasted an hour. I was ape-shit at the non-support of the staff. That started inside me a reaction. The anger came up and became uncontrollable. I didn't like my reaction or my constant anger. I had to leave."

Shortly afterward, EJ ran into his firefighter friend. They have to get to the circle to be eligible to stop soldiering.

In the circle, no war stories are allowed. No graphic descriptions of traumas. There is no room for Dave Hussey's little Asian girl doctor or EJ's orphanage. "We can only talk about what's going on in our lives now," one of the vets explained. "Today. Why is there so much trouble at home? Why is there trouble at work? Why can't you go to Dunkin' Donuts or Burger King without saying or doing something which you later fucking regret?"

It's all about today and moving forward, which you would think would dovetail nicely into this life about which I've been drum-beating the last year. No. No. No. Fuck no. A man who made the guys in the circle his life's work, an expert, explained it to me. The syndrome was originally called "soldier's heart" during the Civil War. After the war ended, soldiers returned to their hometowns, couldn't readjust to what was now defined as peace, and went West. That's why it became the "Wild West." There were no boundaries. Literally and figuratively. The term was changed in the First World War to "shell shock," then "combat fatigue" during World War II. It wasn't until 1981 that the phrase Post Traumatic Stress Disorder surfaced.

"Think about it," the expert said. "You're a boy in a world you really don't understand. So, you're gonna do what we tell you to do to survive. And most of it is contrary to logic. In an ambush, you're trained to go in the direction of the fire. Listen to that. Run in the direction of the fire. That's contrary to logic. If you make friends, you're punished for that. You'll lose them. If you care for civilians, you're punished for that. Innocent people are slaughtered. How can you come back home and turn the switch off?"

An expert told me this. A shrink.

Is *A Little Comes Off My Back* a good title?

That's all I'll say about the book proposal. I'm not quite ready for anyone to look at it. I don't want to corrupt it with any of my nonsense. Let me just say, if you want it to stop being about you, hang out with these guys. And again, by you, I mean me.

ع

THERE WERE A FEW times since I returned to New York in June when I thought about calling Travis to see how he was getting along. That would have been the intent of the call. The purpose of the call would be to see how he was getting along, and to confront him over why he had taken such great pains to have his wife forward the checks I had written back to him to cash at McLean and bust me as a non-sanctioned visitor. I finally decided against it because my behavior was not the issue. That concept is a recently rejiggered plank in the non-psychological life platform. When my behavior is not the issue, there is no issue. Await further instructions. And the instructions are usually *keep moving forward*, which is the rejiggered version of *get cat food*.

Not only that, but after spending time with guys who struggle daily to get out of Burger King or Dunkin' Donuts with a shove-free and tiradeless bag of food, I realized that even the whiff of provocation is no match for the fetid vapor of the other man's pathology. If I can get out of my own way to summon compassion for those whose rage can be ignited in rodeo time, I can release to the wild whatever hands Travis Waldman had dealt me from the bottom of the deck.

And, like I have to tell you, it was fifteen minutes from the very moment when I came to that conclusion that I ran into Travis.

I was walking down First Avenue after taking a squash lesson at the New York Sports Club on Sixty-second Street. Steamed, showered, and quickly working up a nice fatigue/hunger. Racquet in hand, I was headed for the Madison Restaurant on Fifty-third. And I would eventually get there, although I did not heed my own advice. I did not keep moving forward.

"Well, look who looks all trim and athletic this afternoon."

Travis was eating a late lunch at an outdoor café with an older version of an agonizingly familiar man.

"Hello, Travis."

"Charlie, you're good at this. Ronald and I were just having a discussion."

"Nice to meet you, Ronald." I knew him as Ron, and as a former player in the National Hockey League. "Big fan."

"Thank you."

"Big fan of what?" said Travis. "Certainly not the outfit."

"Travis, you know who this is, don't you? This is—"

"Don't bother," Ron said. "He never saw me play."

"I beg your pardon."

Ron continued, "Hockey."

Travis swatted the air before smoothing down his hair, which I noticed was now parted. "Oh that. Ronald mentioned it when we first met, but I didn't bite."

"Well, it was great to see you, Travis. You're looking well. Nice meeting you, Ron, uh Ronald."

My last few words were drowned out by a chair scraping across the pavement. Travis patted the seat. "Charlie, we need you to settle something."

"Travis, please," said Ron.

"No, you please."

I remained standing. Not sitting was the best I could do. I couldn't say I was hungry and on my way to eat because then Travis would have started ordering. I couldn't say I had to go because I am not glib. I stayed because as I have mentioned, I try to get my needs met by being available to the needs of others. And I stayed because, as I have also mentioned, I am almost completely full of shit. I would have loved to put my hand on Travis' shoulder and half-chuckle, "I'm really not comfortable with this situation. You take care," but I could not because, well, have you met me?

"Okay, I'll start," Travis continued. "Before you showed up, this one was asking me if my wife and I sent him a wedding present when he got married EIGHTEEN MONTHS AGO. I said of course we did. And then this one says, 'Well, we never sent you a thank you card because if there was a gift you didn't include a card. Didn't you think that was odd that you never got a thank you card?' And I said, 'Honey, there were many things odd about that day. Not getting a thank you card did not make the list, thank you very much.' And then this one says, 'Well, do you remember what you gave us?' And Charlie, for the life of me, I have no idea. I guess I can check my Visa bill from EIGHTEEN MONTHS AGO, but I don't think there'll be a notation next to the store charge that reads, 'for Ronald's—air quotes—nuptials.'

"So, be a lamb and settle this, Charlie. I say if you don't bring it up for ninety days, you need to move on. Don't serve it to me with my pear tartlet and double espresso."

Actually, as I think about it now, peering out at Montauk *as the ocean unfurls an endless gray flag*, I recovered well after making the mistake of standing there and listening to Travis provide vamp access. Quite well. We are all two people: who we think we are, and who we are. And therein, whacked up accordingly, lie the things we wish we said and the things we said. If I'm honest, the two rarely intersect. Maybe when I met Paul Newman at a benefit in 1995 and said, "Thanks for tonight, and thanks for everything before tonight." That was good. That one I don't want back.

Add to that what I uttered then, after Travis finished and awaited whatever it was he awaited.

"Don't be afraid," he prompted, "to tell Ronald she's being silly."

"I'm sorry, Travis," I said, "but our time is up." And then I shook his tablemate's hand and said, "Ron, you could do better."

A month later, I listen as Travis leaves this message on my answering machine. I know, I know. I try to be available to the needs of others and that way I get my needs met. But I believe I said that during a time when I was unaware of what my needs were. Which is a period that roughly extends from my birth until my machine clicked on that day. I could have said I didn't hear the message until I got home, but that is not the person I am. Although, now that I reflect, which is what I no longer do, that is what I wish I'd said.

Let me call in from my cell phone and play it for you. It's still on my machine.

> Charlie, Travis Waldman. Hope you're well. I am calling because I received a check from your insurance company a few weeks ago for three hundred and ninety-two dollars, which I believe is seventy percent reimbursement for our four hundred and forty dollar sessions while I was hospitalized. I'm sure, since you already paid me, the check was meant for you, but your carrier must have mistakenly assigned the benefits to me. I was calling to ask for your address to write you a check covering this amount, but now that I think about it, why should I? Or should I say, why the fuck should I?
>
> The fact that you see nothing wrong with humiliating me in front of Ronald at the outdoor café, when it was obvious to even the bum peeing against the side of the building that I am quite vulnerable emotionally when it comes to him, is behavior nothing short of inhuman. Perhaps I put you on the spot with the wedding gift quandary. Perhaps it was an uncomfortable situation. Well, boo fucking hoo. You responded like you were on your way to a meeting with Cardinal Egan and I had asked you to beard for me. Did I ask you to beard for me? No. Why? Because I understand what friendship is. You, sadly, do not. But enough about you. When does it finally get to be about me?

(three seconds of silence...)

Charlie, I need to apologize. I'm going in for surgery on my shoulder next week and they have me on this shit for pain, Tramadol, and I think it doesn't play well with others. Namely, the Seroquel, Nardil, and Wellbutrin I already take for my sparkling personality. So, between that and Dead Dick Syndrome, I'm not exactly Loretta Young these days.

Hey, I think we did some good work. I'd like to know if you're still trying to pull off a life between sessions. I hope the badminton helps. Yes, I noticed the racquet you were carrying. I still notice things.

Okay, my friend, send me your address. Love to you-know-who...

"I'M ON THE PHONE!!! I'M ON THE–JESUS, FUCKING C–"

Aᴍ I ᴛʜᴇ ᴏɴʟʏ one who heard that? Not *"Love to you-know-who..."* Before that. *"Okay, my friend..."*

Yeah. And that was it until the call yesterday from Muriel.

Travis Waldman had died early that morning, a little over two months after his shoulder surgery. He had never left Lenox Hill Hospital, like the thousands of others who gingerly walk out after rotator cuff repair. The ultimate cause was acute respiratory distress syndrome, but the debate rages about what made him linger for the last nine weeks, alternating between coherent thrashing threats and gentle babbling. The hospital claims the complications were hatched by a rare, impossible-to-detect condition, fat embolism syndrome, where bone marrow seeps into the bloodstream during orthopedic surgery and winds up in the lungs. Muriel and her lawyer believe it was the interplay between the anesthesia and Travis' various meds, and responsible physicians would have seen weakened lungs in a pre-op chest X-ray and postponed the surgery. Or at least started administering oxygen earlier than two days after the procedure. Something like that. Muriel didn't want the legal glove-swatting to interfere with booking a speaker, and the only reason she got that specific on the phone was to sweeten the shame pot and get me to cough up a *yes*.

She didn't know who she was dealing with, which may be the only thing I have in common with her late husband. She didn't know—how could she?—that the non-psychological life is without shame. Without. *Get cat food. Keep moving forward. Await further instructions. Stay in the moment.* Jesus, we've been over and over this. There is no need, no need, to stare in the rearview mirror, unless you are switching lanes on the LIE on your way to Montauk. Which is where I am. Smiling at my destination. *5:57* P.M. *October 14, 2007*.

Maybe I should call Julie Markakis, Tony C's girl. Introduce myself. Ask her if she still follows The Boys. Tell her I got her number from EJ Breen, who said she never got married. Ask her if it's better this way.

Excuse me.

"Hello, Muriel. This is Charlie Traub. You still looking for somebody for the day after tomorrow?"

XIII

"THANK YOU, CHARLIE," THE rabbi said. "I am sure, well I am not sure, but I hope each of us will take away our own piece of that, uh, vivid portrait. What is the word they use in the tell-all books? Unflinching. I am reminded of Isaiah, Chapter 53: 'He was despised and we esteemed him not. But surely, he hath borne our griefs and carried our sorrows.'"

The rabbi glanced at the podium, then took off his reading glasses and looked around the room. "I was told by Travis' family we would have one other speaker. Did Bonnie Dressler ever arrive?

"Bonnie?

"Ms. Dressler?

"Okay then, those of you who wish may join me in the Mourner's Kaddish..."

XIV

I think I need to see somebody.

Acknowledgments

Stop me if you've heard this.

Philip Roth walks into a delicatessen. Waiter takes his order, then tells him he's a recently published first-time novelist and gives him a copy of his book, Balls. Roth says, "Great title. I'm surprised I didn't think of it myself." Waiter returns with a plate of nova, eggs, and onions. Waiter (who may now be an ex-waiter for shamelessly self-promoting a customer), writes essay about incident. Other novelist reads essay, buys waiter's book, reads it, calls agent, tells agent to send his latest novel to waiter's publisher. Waiter's publisher buys his novel...

...And then, after blowing the cab driver, the nun says, "Well, I also have a confession. My name's Steve and I'm on my way to a costume party!"

I hope one day to get the chance to shake Philip Roth's hand and hang on for the five seconds it would take me to say, "Thanks for letting me know it was safe to go ahead and try all of this." Until then, I really need to meet Julian Tepper and tell him, "Thanks for having Balls."

But Phil and Julian ain't here, so I'll thank Tyson Cornell of Rare Bird Lit, who did four simple things: Read it; got it; said yes; and never used the phrase "sales track."

Here's the deal with Rare Bird Books. It's not just a name, it's a mission statement. Tyson, his partner Julia Callahan, and their beyond thoughtful managing editor, Alice Marsh-Elmer, are as rare in this business as a publicist who makes follow-up calls.

I finished the original manuscript of Shrink Thyself in May, 2011. Which means my agent, the indefatigable Mary Evans, worked for free on my behalf for almost three years. How do you ever possibly show your profound appreciation for that, other than with nova, eggs, and onions?

My wife, Adrianne Tolsch, is much funnier, much smarter, and much, much more courageous than I will ever be. And six years ago, when she went out to dinner with her ex-therapist, she gave me the idea for this book.

You know what? I sound like an utter fraud. I should stop.

Just a few more.

Barbara Gaines has read every word of the five novels I've written, as I've written them. She is the only person who has done that, and I'm including myself.

Carol Pepper spent two mornings with me, just before heading to chemotherapy, generously sharing about her experience in a psychiatric hospital. I would give anything to be able to thank her in person.

I started out as a sportswriter and I always felt the story of Tony Conigliaro was undertold and underexamined. I never dreamed that Dave Hussey, his wife Judi Van Loon, his buddy EJ Breen, and his former high school classmate Julie Markakis would be so forthcoming and compelling that merely transcribing their interviews would hand me the last piece of this book, and my first piece of nonfiction in 30 years.

In the spirit of accurate reportage, I've had a blog for the last five years. Six people read it. Six. So, thank you Cathy Armstrong, Jim Westfall, Ed Markey, Noel Nitecki, Pat Vickers, and the other guy.

And everyone else: Nancy Agostini, Jonathan Alter, Larry Amoros, Manjit Bains, Mary Barclay, Mike Barrie, David Bauer, Chris Belair, Richard Belzer, Jude Brennan, Julia Cameron, Michael Cantor, Larry David, Houston Day, Laurie Diamond, Susie Essman, Marilyn Gallo, Jill Goodwin, Julie Halston, Don Harrell, David Hirshey, Michele Jasmine, Howard Josepher, David Kelly, Joan Kron, Denis Leary, Dave Letterman, Elinor Lipman, Mike Kennedy, Joan Kron, Dusty Maddox, Merrill Markoe, Paul Masella, Bruce McCall, Kathleen McCarthy, Tim McCarver, Brian McDonald, Jennifer McDonald, Pat McGrath, Richard McKelvey ,Jamie McShane, Jim Mulholland, Gerard Mulligan, Lisa Napoli, John O'Leary, Priscilla Painton, Mark Patrick, Scott Raab, Sylvie Rabineau, Donna Reilly, Gerry Rioux, Matt Roberts, Bob Roche, Tom Ruprecht, Dennis Schoen, Bruce Schoenfeld, Maria Semple, Grant Shaud, Eric Sherman, Mr. Siegel, John Singer, Heather Spillane, Sarah Stemp, Brendon Stiles, Jeff Stilson, Drew Storen, Scott Stossel, Chris Tangney, Ben Walker, Lydia Weaver, Gary Wynn, Steve Young, Alan Zweibel. And my mom, Gitty Scheft. Thanks for the gig.

My time is up. You've been great. Enjoy The Truants.

Bill Scheft
New York City
October 2013